Fun Fact: I Love You

Fun Fact: I Love You

GINA LYNN LARSEN

SHADOW
MOUNTAIN
PUBLISHING

Taps mic, shields eyes from spotlight, looks into the crowd

Ah, there you are. I'd like to dedicate this book to YOU!

If life is throwing you for a loop, just know I've been through a few loops myself. I get it. It's hard and scary. But the ride isn't over yet.

Hang on tight, scream if you must, but keep going.

Unexpected plot twists make for excellent and memorable stories.

Visit us at shadowmountain.com

Library of Congress Cataloging-in-Publication Data
Names: Larsen, Gina Lynn, author.
Title: Fun fact : I love you / Gina Lynn Larsen.
Description: Salt Lake City : Shadow Mountain, [2024] | Audience: Grades 10–12. | Summary: "High school senior Nellie has her future all planned out—except for a disastrous first kiss, a hurtful prank, and the unexpected twist of falling in love with her childhood friend"—Provided by publisher.
Identifiers: LCCN 2023058707 (print) | LCCN 2023058708 (ebook) | ISBN 9781639932450 (hardback) | ISBN 9781649332561 (ebook)
Subjects: CYAC: Secrets—Fiction. | Friendship—Fiction. | Love—Fiction. | High schools—Fiction. | Schools—Fiction. | BISAC: YOUNG ADULT FICTION / Romance / Contemporary | YOUNG ADULT FICTION / Romance / Clean & Wholesome | LCGFT: Romance fiction. | Novels.
Classification: LCC PZ7.1.L359 Fu 2024 (print) | LCC PZ7.1.L359 (ebook) | DDC [Fic]—dc23
LC record available at https://lccn.loc.gov/2023058707
LC ebook record available at https://lccn.loc.gov/2023058708

Printed in the United States of America
Publishers Printing

10   9   8   7   6   5   4   3   2   1

CHAPTER 1

The Vote

Nellie

In ten days, I'll never have to eat lunch here again. Just ten more days.

I plop my backpack on the olive-green cafeteria table, and my Rainbow Dash key chain swings back and forth like she's dying to get out of here too. Truthfully? We're all ready to fly this coop.

I recognize the abandoned bags on the bench—specifically Britta's messenger bag. I glance around, looking for my best friend and her boyfriend. Usually, they'd be here, swapping spit and Oreos, which is straight up disgusting. I spot them over in the south corner.

They're at Sterling's table, of course, along with most of his crew. He the brightest star here—both the class clown and our running back—but in two weeks, even his light will dim. This is the end of the line for cafeteria lunches, lockers, and student IDs. No more dances or drama, but also, no more moments like this— where everyone is huddled close, laughing as if they haven't a care in the world. But that's not true. Finals are looming, but my 4.20 GPA is secure, of that I'm positive.

Instead of joining my friends, I sit and crack open my soda and allow myself to feel nostalgic. I'm going to miss this place.

I know I shouldn't drink my calories, but as I take a huge swig, I remind myself that these last two weeks of school are special. I'm allowing myself one soda a day until graduation. After that, it'll just be a few short months until I'm off to UNLV.

The studying has paid off, I've got my associate's degree, free, thanks to dual-credit classes, and my acceptance letter to UNLV is in the bag. What I want most is within reach: a degree in physics so I become an astrophysicist and my own place. Nothing's going to stop me, and it feels amazing.

I brush my bangs aside and see Britta beelining her way to me, bringing her energy with her.

"About time you showed up. Come vote," she says, smiling.

"Vote for what?" I ask, taking another sip.

"The guys want to know which of them has the best lips."

I nearly choke on my drink as I laugh.

My attention flies to Sterling. He's puckering his lips and showing them off, as if that's necessary. "Seriously?"

"Yeah."

I also locate the other boy who holds my interest. Just like how I can always find the Big Dipper in the night sky, I seek out Jensen, the only boy I've known my whole life. The boy who *was* my best friend long before anyone else. The boy who is always within earshot of Sterling.

Big Dipper, Little Dipper.

"They're holding a contest," Britta continues. "You gotta come vote."

"Uhhh–no."

"Why not?" She leans in close, whispering. "You've liked Sterling since eighth grade."

"Yeah, but I, Nellie Samsin, refuse to participate in their shenanigans." I inject some bravado into my voice.

"Exactly. It's time to carpe diem!"

Her grin is contagious, but I can't give in. If I do, it's over, because while I'm technically part of their solar system, I'm more like a constant, reliable moon.

"If you'll come vote," she says, "I promise not to tell Sterling you like him."

I narrow my eyes. "You wouldn't."

"Oh, yes, I would." This time she's not teasing.

When my phone dings twice in a row, I'm grateful for the distraction, until I see the group message.

"Who is it?" Britta asks.

"My mom."

> Sean, you forgot to close the garage again. Stop doing that. And Nellie, you forgot to get coffee at the grocery store. Please get some TODAY. I can barely function without it.

"You'll survive," I mutter, as I read my dad's response to her.

> I thought I did close it. I'll check it when I get home. And Nellie, we appreciate all you do to help us out. Thanks.

The ache isn't new, but I still push it back. They've been arguing a lot lately. No big blowups—mostly ice. Lots of things being said under their breath. It's a harsh environment these days, and I wish they'd just sort out whatever it is.

Britta doesn't ask for details. If she really cared to know, she'd ask. She always offers her opinion or has a comment, even if I don't want to hear it, so her silence means she's not really listening to me. When I look back, I find her watching Sterling and his friends.

I can usually tell how she feels because she is the most colorful person I know—always changing colors like a mood ring. Her fake sad is charcoal. Her fake happy is orange. But right now, she's blue.

"A contest?" I say, regaining her attention. "For best lips?"

"It's just for fun. Come on." Her voice is laced with longing.

"Fine," I sigh.

She grins, grabs my hand, and leads the way.

Truth is, I want to go, but I feel awkward when it comes to this kind of thing. I wish I was more shining star like her and less lunar rock. But I'm not. I'm well-read, cool and collected, and I'm going to be an astrophysicist. It's my entire future.

However.

When I see Sterling smile, everything inside me shifts until school no longer matters.

He turns and meets my gaze.

"Best lips?" I say, my voice weak.

"Sure," Britta says, as the first layer of freshman fashionistas and sophomore simps peel back for us to pass. They shouldn't treat us like we're queens of this place, but if I'm the moon, Britta's the sun.

Sterling and I stare as if we have history, as if we need to talk. Our silent conversations are the best and worst part of my day, because he has a lot he never says.

He licks his lower lip, and my stomach flip-flops like it's on a roller coaster. Then, he jerks his chin at me, extending a hello of sorts. I'm never sure what he means when he does stuff like that, but it makes my temperature rise, giving Venus a run for her money. Okay, not really. Fun fact: The surface temperature of Venus is 464 degrees Celsius.

I know. I'm a freak.

But it's how my brain works. It's a habit I can't explain, a mechanism I fall back on to feel in control. Facts to keep me anchored to what's real.

There is a long list of reasons why I should not have a crush on Sterling. For starters, he's trouble with a capital *T*, a son of the devil on most days. I can't imagine him ever *asking* a girl on a date. Not that he's shy. Heck, no. It's because that boy doesn't have to ask. Any girl who wants to go out with him *can*. He made a public announcement at the start of the year that he'd go on at least one date with any girl who asked, so long as they were sixteen or older and paid for the date.

Yeah. But he's nice to me; he's not a jerk.

Another reason I shouldn't crush: There is a printed calendar doubling as a sign-up sheet on his locker, and every night up until graduation is booked with a girl's name. Like, first off, how old-school are we? A paper calendar? And two—*what?* Just thinking about it makes me nauseous. And three—why hasn't an admin taken it down?

After Christmas break, Britta wrote my name down on an available date slot. *Resolutions, Nellie!* she said. I managed to scribble it out before anyone saw. She hasn't tried it since, but I keep a close eye on Sterling's locker. Which makes me look like a stalker.

I exhale a shaky breath as I try to focus on his lips, but really, it's not a competition. Of course I'm going to vote for Sterling. His smile outdoes everyone else's. His upper lip is perfectly shaped, but the pout to his lower one—oh man. And when he bites it, out of confusion or when he's studying or when he's teasing, I'm always left flustered.

One fact stands: God gave Sterling the eyes of an angel, but the grin of a devil. It's wicked sexy, and the thought of those lips?

I. Can't. Even.

I lick my lips, suddenly conscious of them. I need lip balm, stat. When someone bumps into me, I'm jolted back to reality.

This is a stunt. A stupid game the guys have concocted for attention, and if I play along, I'm not going to have time to eat, and if I don't eat, I'll get a headache, which is the last thing I need on the heels of my mom demanding coffee and giving Dad a hard time about something that's not his fault.

I turn to leave, but then Jensen hollers over the crowd. "Okay! Everybody listen up!" He hops onto a chair and raises his hands to quiet the crowd, knowing full well that we'll all obey. Maybe it's because I'm feeling sentimental, but there's a piece of me that belongs to him, a puzzle piece that looks like childhood and summer days. Occasionally I miss that era, when grades and expectations were at an all-time low, but frequently, I miss *him*.

Jensen is probably the reason why Sterling and his friends aren't in jail, so we always thank the universe for him.

"All votes for Sterling go here." He holds out his navy-blue hat to serve as the ballot box for Sterling, and then he points to Britta's boyfriend, Marbles, who holds up his ball cap. "Lenox's votes go there."

And that's when I learn Sterling's competing against his

younger brother. I glance at Lenox, and in two more years he might give Sterling a run for his money, but not today.

"Write your name on your ballot," Marbles says. He hands some cards to Jensen, who hops off the chair and starts passing them out.

Everyone smiles at Jensen as he works his way toward us. He defies the laws of high school society—students and teachers alike love him. It's like he enjoys getting perfect grades as if to prove how smart he is, but then if dared, he'll light the trash can on fire and pull the alarm.

Maybe it's stupid.

Maybe it's brave.

I don't know. What I do know is that if he'd run for class president back in September, he would've slaughtered me. Instead, he's one of our yearbook photographers by day and our quarterback at night. And he has a way with the English language that should make him the chief editor of the yearbook instead of me.

"Give me a card too," Britta says when Jensen comes to her. "Marbles won't care."

Then Jensen turns to me. Unlike Sterling, Jensen barely meets my gaze. He doesn't smile, either, but our fingers brush when he hands me a card. Light-years ago, I could read him the way I read Britta now. Instead, there's this quiet intensity that keeps us apart.

After he's out of earshot, I whisper to Britta, "Something's up with Jensen."

"Doubt it."

"I'm serious. He looked . . . worried when he gave me a card."

"No, he didn't," she says. "Don't forget to write your name on your ballot."

"And that's another thing—"

"Nellie. Don't overthink it."

I fall silent as she writes her name on her card, embellishing it with swirls and hearts. While I wait for the pen, I consider her comment about Jensen, but I think she's wrong. I also decide she's being weird. She has a boyfriend. Why is she voting? *Marbles won't care.* I wonder if that's true. Marbles and Britta have been together for almost three months now, but when I glance at him, he's with some sophomore girl, gently pulling on her hair. How juvenile, and confusing, and maybe there's some trouble in paradise that I'm not privy to just yet. And then there's the matter of our names on the—

"Hurry up!" someone calls. "We don't have all day."

I'm pulled from my thoughts, and as I write my name on my card, I get caught up in the hype. It's like the soda. Special. Unique. Carpe diem.

Britta grabs my card, unites it with hers, and drops them in. With our ballots gone, I turn to her. "Why did I need to put my name on it?"

"What?"

"My name on the ballot? That's weird. What are you not telling me?"

All the guys are backing off, taking their seats at the lunch tables, but the girls stick close.

Britta, who has an orange glow to her now, is faking. She's not happy. She forces a smile. "Okay, fine. I'll tell you, but stay cool."

"Stay cool?"

"Look, the winner is going to draw a name out of his stash and that girl gets a kiss."

"A kiss? Are you kidding?" And then it sinks in. "Britta Tayvier! You are dead to me."

"No, I'm not. If I had told you before, you wouldn't have played along. You would've freaked out."

"Not true."

"You're freaking out now," she deadpans.

"Yeah, well . . ." Thanks to Britta, everybody knows I haven't been kissed. No wonder she wanted me to vote.

"Relax. I doubt you'll win," she says.

"I better not."

When it hadn't happened by my sophomore year, I swore off boys and added *no kissing* as an amendment to my five-year plan—the plan that gets me to grad school. Admittedly, it was mostly to make me feel better, because it sucks when the guys notice your BFF without even acknowledging your existence, but now it's part of "The Plan." I hate it when she does stuff like this to me, like she has to spoon-feed me. It's annoying, and rude.

But I put all that aside, because what if I win? My insides melt at the thought of being kissed for the first time.

Do I want to be kissed?

Uh, yes, of course I do, but—

Marbles hops up onto the table, breaking my train of thought. He clears his throat, but then has to holler twice to get everyone's attention. He makes a grand, swooping gesture with his hand, bringing the chosen ballot close to his face like this is the freakin' Hunger Games of Fifty Shades of Grey. Do we have a tribute, someone willing to make out right here, right now?

My hand finds Britta's because this is excruciating. Britta squeezes back, probably wanting to win. *No.* She wants me to win.

And I've gotta give the boys credit. We're going to remember this stunt forever.

"Sterling takes the win!" Marbles yells. Giggles and screams ring out. I exhale a breath. I forgot they needed to name a winner first. Of course Sterling won. That's no surprise.

"And it's Nellie!" Marbles yells.

I jerk—*wait, what? I missed something.*

"Congrats, Nellie!" someone calls, singling me out.

I won? That can't be right.

My heart thumps hard, my mind shuts off, and all I hear is a fever-pitched buzz. I thought slow motion only existed in the movies, but it doesn't. From every corner of the room, people turn their attention to me, mixed expressions on their faces.

I'm underwater. I can't breathe. My feet are anchored to the ground, and numbness saturates my whole body, only to morph into sheer panic as it sinks in.

I won.

Sterling is going to kiss me.

He's going to own my virgin lips. *Holy crap.* He's going to kiss me in front of everyone. I've got to get out of here. But before I can run, we lock eyes. This time, it's different. The vague, wordless conversation we've been having for years finally has a voice.

Sterling's smiling like it's the best day of his life, and my body betrays me, because I smile back. How many times have I envisioned kissing Sterling? Let's not do that math.

The fire in his eyes brings goose bumps to my arms. It's like we're celestial comets destined to collide since the beginning of time. Behind him, I catch a glimpse of Jensen. He's removed himself from the crowd and is leaning against the wall, eclipsed in shadows that rarely touch his starlit smile. I don't have time to figure out why he's no longer playing along, because Sterling is in front of me. Maybe he moves at superspeed, or maybe this is a dream— which clearly is a sign I've read one too many fantasy novels.

Sterling's so close, I see the flecks of green in his dark-brown eyes, and he's wearing the perfect amount of cologne. His height compared to mine is ideal. My peripheral vision goes fuzzy, and suddenly, it's as if we are alone. I want to press my palm to his chest—not to push him away, but to find out if those hard-earned pecs are as solid as I suspect. I can tell he wants to touch me too. Which is insane.

No. This is Sterling. Nothing about it is insane. It's just who he is. He can conjure up a storm just as easily as he can make the world fade away.

"Hey," he whispers.

"Hi," I whisper back.

He hands me a green square—a mint strip.

I know. *I know.* Sterling requires very little when it comes to kissing, just a willing mouth and a hint of freshness, and I should be offended, but I'm not. *I'm willing.*

He looks at me like I'm his entire world, and I feel the galaxies spin around us. So when Sterling's hands slide up my arms, igniting my skin with fire, I don't pull back. This is too surreal, too much like my favorite book, and I have to turn the page.

CHAPTER 2

Monday, Monday

Nellie

There's this funny tingling in my throat, and it spreads to my legs and arms. The corners of Sterling's mouth curve upward as if he can't wipe the smile off his face.

Oh, stars. My first kiss is going to be a smiley one.

There's a reason the flesh of the lips is the thinnest skin on the human body. No wait. It's not the lips. It's the . . . I used to know, but the second Sterling's soft lips touch mine, I forget everything. Hopefully, all that knowledge comes back, or my UNLV scholarship is toast.

Sterling presses his lips to mine again, draws back, and smiles again. It's over already? I can't seem to get a grip on my location, time, or reality, I'm so far gone.

"Nellie?" he whispers. "You wanna kiss me back?"

My only response is to bob my head up and down, barely processing.

This time, Sterling comes in faster, and who knew thin skin was so tough.

My mouth works against his, as I copy what he does. The blood in my head rushes to my gut as the heat of his breath blends with mine. I allow myself to really feel it. It's like the soda—it's special. He pulls my body closer, leaving no gaps between us.

I'm floating as his fingers trail up my arms, leaving a trail of molten lava behind, and when he smiles against me, his lips curving against mine, I'm out of this world. Then he grips the sides of my neck, coming back to me, hungry for more, and I realize I'm the one who's starving.

He deepens our kiss, and with my whole body in alignment with his, I let out a soft moan. The kind that an audience hears.

The crowd has gone mad. They're whooping and yelling, but I can't see them or define the noise because Sterling's fingers are at my hips, and clearly, he knows what he's doing. This isn't his first kiss.

But it is mine.

I'm making a complete fool of myself in front of the entire school. The magic is zapped away, and I run cold.

"What am I doing?" I whisper.

"Kissing me," he whispers back.

I hate that I smile at this.

The room starts spinning, and I tighten my grip on his biceps, and he mistakes it for desire, so he kisses me again, a slow, explor-atory one—one that feels less special and more for show—while turning us in a circle, which only makes me dizzier.

"That's enough! Break it up!" someone yells.

Sterling smiles as if he's finally shared his greatest secret with me, and I'm reeling on the inside.

"Not bad, Nellie. Not bad at all," he says before we turn to face the principal. "Mrs. Sharie, you look impressed."

"Mr. Landon, I'm rarely impressed." She's not even surprised to find him here, but then her gaze lands on me. She almost loses her composure when she speaks. "Nellie?"

"Hello, Mrs. Sharie." I can barely look her in the eye.

Public displays of affection are against school rules. I think she was planning on throwing whoever was kissing into detention, but now she looks unsure.

The bell rang several minutes ago, I realize, and *everyone* is late. There's five beats more of silence until someone snickers, and then Mrs. Sharie snaps, "Everyone, get to class!"

She blinks a few times, still stunned to see me with Sterling, but then she turns her attention to the whole room. This is our chance to move. Sterling doesn't spare me a glance.

My whole body freezes. The buzz of the room shifts to chaos as everyone scatters, afraid of a detention slip. I turn to find Britta, but she's also ditched me. Instead, I see Jensen. He's hiding his mouth under a hand. Is that laughter? Or is he frowning?

He heaves a hard breath and then spins away, pulling on his backpack. What was that about?

And then it hits me. I had my first kiss, and nothing about it was special. Tears well up in my eyes. To prevent the waterworks, I weigh it out like I do everything else.

Pros: My first kiss was with Sterling Landon, and I was a willing participant. Isn't that what I've always wanted?

Cons: My first kiss wasn't anything like how I imagined it would be, because I know it meant nothing to him. Truthfully, it meant nothing to me.

The thought eats at me like acid.

I hustle back to where I left my things. I grab my bag and leave my drink. I can't take it to class. I rush past the stragglers, who apparently don't care about being tardy.

I'm about two feet out of the cafeteria when several things happen all at once.

Jensen's in the hall, his back pressed against some lockers. Why didn't he go to class? We lock eyes at the exact moment someone grabs my elbow from behind. I'm not as surprised as I should be when I spin around to find it's Sterling. Detaching from the wall, Jensen stalks off, and then Britta says my name. She's right behind Sterling.

A toothy grin spreads across her face as she joins us, and she's a mischievous magenta. I should've noticed it before. She's probably glad I've been kissed now and thinks I'm finally listening to her—putting my plan aside as she suggested last week and having a little fun before college.

Suddenly, I want nothing to do with her. I fake a smile.

"Talk to you later," Britta says. She's looking at me, but I get the distinct impression that she means it for Sterling.

I don't want to stand here with Sterling, but I don't want to trail behind Britta either. Thankfully, I've always been able to control my facial cues, which in this moment is probably a good thing. I'd be a good poker player if I were a gambling gal.

"Sterling."

"Nellie." His eyes hold mine for a long second, searching for heaven knows what. I'm glad he doesn't seem to see every emotion I feel waging havoc inside. *I hate you. Kiss me again. Did it mean anything at all to you?* It's like I'm three different people right now.

"What is it, Sterling?"

Someone in the far distance whistles at us. We both fight smiles. Stars, what's wrong with me?

"If you want to finish what we started, I'm game."

Words escape me, because he's serious.

"What do you mean?" Is he trying to ask me out? Words are harder for him, unlike Jensen.

"Listen, you don't have to decide right now," he says, touching my arm and sliding his hand down to mine to toy with my fingers. I should pull away, but I don't. Why don't I? "But you're a natural. I'd be happy to teach you a few things—"

Oh my heck.

I pull back, and my hand whips across his face.

He's shocked, and so am I. I've never hit anyone before, and the sting in my hand is immediate. He rubs his cheek as I walk away.

The paper stuck on his locker catches my eye, and I walk right up to it, tear the calendar off, and wad it into a ball. I carry it with me all the way to class and toss it in a trash can.

My teacher is writing out a mathematical equation on the whiteboard, but she won't say anything to me because she loves me and this is my first tardy in her class ever.

I avoid looking at anyone as I walk to my seat, except I can't help but see Jensen, who sits right behind me.

Like the slap, it strikes me why he was waiting. We always walk from lunch to this class together. *I think my brain is broken.* I huff a breath, hating this day even more. My hand still stings, my nose burns from unshed tears, my heart is racing, and though I pull out my textbook determined to catch up, I find myself not seeing the words and not hearing Mrs. Johannson.

I want to turn around and peek at Jensen, but I can't seem to move. Tears prick at my eyes again, and I can't stop one from rolling over my cheek. I wipe it away with the cuff of my sleeve, then turn to my backpack, desperate to find my composure.

I find some gum and an old note from Britta.

Send me flowers for my birthday!
You're the best, N!

Handwritten notes are a thing of the past, but Britta knows I love them over a text, and this is only one of many from her. Unfortunately, she has a habit of telling me what to do, so, because I'm grumpy, her note really escalates my raw nerves. My phone dings, and I'm not surprised it's a message from Britta.

You're welcome for making you vote!
That was awesome!

Bottling a scream, I pocket my phone.

Mrs. Johannson finishes her instruction, noting that the problems on pages 267 and 268 are to be completed before our next class.

"I know you're itching to be done with school, but you're not there yet," she says with a crooked smile before sitting at her desk to grade papers. "The final is next Tuesday."

Minutes later, the volume of the room has escalated, but Mrs. Johannson doesn't seem to care. When Jensen whispers, "Hey," and touches my shoulder, I jump, my hand spasms, and I draw a pencil line across the page.

I rotate in my desk, keeping my elbow close to my side so I'm not intruding on his space.

"I'm fine," I say even though he hasn't asked me anything.

"Uh, that's good. I can't seem to figure out number twelve."

"You're that far already?" I peer at his paper filled with doodles in the margins. Among his many talents, he also draws; spaceships are his best work. I like that about him.

"Yeah."

"*And* you've had time to draw?" I point at the race car. He shrugs. "Well, I'm only on number two, so let me—"

"No, it's okay."

"I didn't say I couldn't help. I'm just not there yet." I hesitate.

"Okay," he says.

"Do you want to see if we can go work somewhere quieter?" I ask.

"You asking me out, Samsin?" He grimaces immediately, as if it's too soon, but there's the Jensen I know, and it's oddly reassuring. Like the whole world isn't totally upside down.

I wrinkle my nose. "I believe *you* asked *me*. I can't focus in here." That's a stretch. I'm not sure I can focus at all right now.

Jensen closes his book, stands up, and walks over to Mrs. Johannson. I can't hear their conversation, but when she glances at me, she nods, and Jensen gestures for me to join him. I quickly gather my things and follow him out.

Side by side, we walk toward the library. I find the gray industrial carpet fascinating all of a sudden, even though I've walked this hall with him a thousand times. His shoes keep coming in and out of my peripheral, and when I look up, it's to make sure I don't walk into the metal divider between the double doors. When we reach the library, he holds the door open for me, which is normal for him, but he bites his lip.

Man, he's acting weird today. I toss a light elbow into his chest as I pass by. "Jensen, you're killing me, man."

I'm glad he can't see my face as I keep walking. I'm sure I look stupid. I feel it.

"I could say the same, Nells."

A knot forms in my throat. Maybe he didn't mean for me to hear it, but I did. Still, I pretend I didn't catch it. "What did you say?"

The librarian looks up at us, a stern expression on her face.

Jensen's studying me like I'm directly out of his favorite sci-fi novel, but then again, I'm noticing him for what feels like the first time. When did his shoulders get so broad? Have his eyes always been so stormy? Is his hair always so stylishly disheveled?

"Nothing. Nothing important," he says. We both swallow, his Adam's apple moving up and down as he adjusts his backpack. He's five eleven, five inches taller than I am, and he doesn't smell of anything in particular, but then again, I'm not standing nearly as close to him as I was Sterling.

"Yeah, right," I say, adding an eye roll for emphasis.

"Quiet!" the librarian says.

"Sorry, ma'am."

"We're here to do homework," Jensen adds. "We won't be any trouble."

"Yeah, right," she mocks, flashing a knowing smile. We laugh a little, and she keeps her eyes on her computer as she says, "Good to see you, kid."

Weird. I know she wasn't talking to me.

Jensen leads me behind several stacks of books to a table near the window. The sun in the cloudless sky provides a warm seat, and I find myself taking in the Wasatch mountain range of Salt Lake City.

"You and the librarian have a little something going on?" I ask.

"I'm in here a lot."

"No, you're not."

"How would you know?" His voice drops a little, and he looks at the mountains too. He's right. How would I know?

Before I can open my book, Britta texts again, followed by my mom.

I glance at their messages real quick.

You're not going to say anything? Britta says.

No response? Mom's annoyed I haven't replied about getting the coffee yet.

Their comments are interchangeable, and that stings. I silence my phone and put it away.

"I guess I don't," I say to Jensen. He's eyeing me, probably wondering who was texting me. "Sorry."

We crack open our books and get to work. When Jensen's foot accidently touches mine, my heart stops, and we glance up at each other. He pulls his foot away, and I see something in his eyes that hasn't ever been there before. It's confusing, having him look at me like he's equally disappointed and interested.

"Sorry," he says. "So, on number twelve, I got x tangent y, but maybe it's y sine x?"

I hear his question, but I'm consumed by what I just saw. Then again maybe I'm still reeling from that kiss. All I can say for certain is now I see his disguise.

He moves his pencil over the numbers, reviewing his work, but he's *pretending* to need help. His pencil quivers, and he doesn't look up at me.

Jensen, who has never been interested in me, is suddenly nervous.

CHAPTER 3

I'm the One Nellie Goes Home With

Jensen

I tap my pencil on my textbook, wishing I could go back in time and tell Nellie not to vote. My anger has been climbing, but it's not pointed at her. No, it's aimed at Sterling, at Marbles, and at Britta. Marbles didn't draw Nellie's name. He just said her name. They hatched this plan simply to rob Nellie of her first kiss, and I should've seen it coming.

Then Sterling started kissing her, and she kissed him back.

I've wanted to punch my friends before for stupid crap. But today? They're lucky I'm not Bruce Banner. I would've Hulked out on them so fast.

Nellie's staring at me, but I can't lift my gaze, too afraid that my emotions are on display.

Ever since she laid eyes on Sterling in the eighth grade, she put me in the friend zone. And admittedly, I pulled away from her, for lots of reasons.

So now, she doesn't know. She doesn't know how often I come here. She doesn't know I've got plans for this summer or that my little brother, Clay, doesn't live with us anymore. She doesn't know her father, Sean, has not only remained my friend but has also become my writing mentor and the closest thing I've got to a father. She just doesn't know.

Nellie leans in, pointing at problem twelve. "Right here, do the double integral and you'll get x cosine $y\ dx$ minus dt."

"Oh," I say. "You're right. You're too smart for your own good."

"You're smart too."

"Not as smart as you. I'll probably bomb this final."

"No, you won't. If you have to take an online summer class, it'll infringe on your playboy summer."

"You make a good point."

She thinks I'm like Sterling and Marbles. And sometimes I am because I have appearances to keep up too. But I hate that I've got the smartest girl around equally convinced.

Nellie has her own appearances, though. She always has a plan. She's able to look at the big picture. She constantly tracks her progress, and I bet her diary is filled with bullet points, pie charts, and bar graphs. She does get a little soapboxy about her life post-high school, but no one faults her for wanting a PhD. She's our best brainiac, our prettiest nerd, our most faithful stargazer. Least, that's what we call her, mostly because *astrophysicist* is a mouthful.

I used to think I'd go to college. And maybe I will, someday.

We tackle the remaining problems, only breaking the silence to discuss our work. Ten minutes before the bell rings, she begins to gather her things.

"You're leaving," I say, hating how stupid I sound.

"Sorry. I need to do something."

She pauses, and I can see her thinking.

"Text me later," she finally says. "If you need more help, or anything."

"Yeah," I say, because I'm super good at English. I call myself a moron as she walks away, but then I hear those words again. *Text me later.* I should come up with something to say, but only stupid pickup lines run through my mind.

Good thing I've got my library card, because I'm checking you out.

I'm not a great photographer, but I can picture us together.

I put my homework away and pull out my phone. I have 319 emails from fans. They want to meet me, they want me to release my books in paperback—right now, they're only digital—and they want my autograph or a selfie. Some want my phone number. I laugh, even though it kind of freaks me out. I have no idea if the people emailing me are seventeen or seventy. It's a mystery.

I know I should sort through them, but there are only two emails that are actually important. One's from my assistant, Rebecca, and the other is from Sean. They are both asking the same thing:

How long until you're done drafting?

Sean's asking because he wants to make sure to schedule time to read my manuscript, and Rebecca is asking because my deadline for book three is June fifteenth.

I don't reply to Rebecca, but I do message Sean back.

I'm swamped with studying, finals, and all the senior stuff. But I'm getting there.

I'm supposed to be doing all the senior stuff with Sterling, but I'm not sure if I want to hang with him now. Not if he and Nellie are going to hook up.

I can't imagine her doing that, but her crush on Sterling has been the worst-kept secret of our entire high school career. If he makes Nellie his final conquest, I'll be sick. She'd be so happy with his attention, but when he dumps her after graduation, it'll destroy her.

To say nothing about "ruining her plans."

I pull my backpack on and skirt around the librarian's desk. Miss Maggie seems to have a sixth sense, and I worry that she suspects I write. That said, no way does she know I'm "Jen Dimes," author of the fantasy romance series Blood Rock that is somehow sweeping the nation. The thought of anyone besides my mother, Sean, or Rebecca, knowing that I write fiction slays me. Writing isn't how one acquires street cred.

I self-published the first two books, thinking a pen name would keep me safe—which it has—and that an ebook at two bucks a download would pay for a new Xbox.

That's all I wanted. A gaming system.

I never suspected it would boost my bank account comfortably into the six-digit range, which feels totally surreal. After I hit fifty thousand downloads, Sean Samsin suggested I get myself an assistant. Together, he and I found a boutique editing company that could help me manage the unexpected waters I found myself in. Rebecca is worth every penny.

As I make my way to my locker, students—fans—pass me, clueless. I've heard them whisper about my books, and I've had to learn to mask my response. I can't smile every time I hear a junior say how sexy Hagon Vasco is. Hagon is my main male character, and he's the exact opposite of my deadbeat father.

Likewise, I can't laugh when I hear a bunch of girls debating whether or not Sokha, my main female character, deserves Hagon. They love to hate her, they love to dissect her decisions, but above all, the girls love the kissing scenes.

Which I didn't want to write.

It's to Sean's credit that I did.

I believe now that the romantic tension is the sole reason *Blood Rock* has become what it's become.

But without Sean, I'd be nothing. He's the master planner, having helped me chart my course since I was a kid. Not to mention, he and Nellie have been mapping out her ten-year plan. Or is it five? I'm not sure. I don't ask. I can't afford to risk his friendship for one with Nellie. I can't afford to lose him.

I lose count of how many times I say hey to passersby as I drop my stuff off at my locker. I have nothing that suggests I'm a writer, but some of the fan art for *Blood Rock* is to die for. If I could, I'd wallpaper my office with the artwork of MeganLovesHagon257. She's a FanFavorite.com artist, and she spends an obsessive amount of time on my characters. Someday, I want to meet Megan—but only with a bodyguard by my side.

Instead, I have a picture of me catching the winning touchdown of our last football game taped on my locker door. It seems like something a cocky jerk like me would have. It's the only great shot Shalee, the other photographer for the school, has ever caught, I swear.

Okay, maybe I'm a cocky jerk, but I'm a better photographer.

Other than that, I have some stickers on the wall that I'll get fined for after graduation, but so what. The school can bill me. But they'll be sending it to my personal address, since I already have my own apartment lined up.

Marbles comes up, leans against the locker next to me, and nods at people as they pass by.

"Hey, man," he says.

"Yeah, hey."

"What's up with you? You're avoiding us."

"Headache," I lie.

We walk to our next class together, and thankfully, he doesn't press me about my mood. We're too cool to have emotions. After taking our seats, I start sketching while Marbles reads some political news on his phone, neither of us paying much attention to our government teacher.

I try to draw Nellie's eyes, but I can't get them right.

I should've taken art instead of photography.

I have a photo of Nellie that I took at a ball game. She looked right at me, and in that moment, I think she saw me for me. I keep the photo tucked between the pages of a thin book under my mattress. I know how that sounds. But honestly, it's just to keep the photo safe, and hidden from everyone, including my mom.

This leads to me thinking about the secrets we all keep and how everyone around me could be living two lives like me.

I don't like thinking that everyone is a fake, but on some level, aren't we all? By the time class ends, my brain hurts, and I really do have a headache.

As I finish out the day in my weight class, I really push myself. I thank the tech gods for inventing headphones. I'm on my last set of squats when Coach hands me a blue slip from the office.

Please come to my classroom ASAP.
We have a yearbook problem.
—Mr. Kaempher

"We can't have a yearbook problem. We submitted everything last week," I say.

"Better go now," he calls over his shoulder as he walks away.

I hit the showers fast; I'm not going to sit in my own sweat while Kaempher has a panic attack. Ten minutes later, I'm the last to arrive at the emergency meeting. There's only twelve minutes until the last bell rings, but by the sound of things, we're going to be here for a while.

"I don't understand," Shane Brewster says.

"This is their fault, not ours," Nellie says as I take a seat across from her. We share a glance, and there's nothing awkward from before. Just pure annoyance that we have a problem.

"Yeah, can't they just reformat it?" Shane asks.

I'm out of the loop, so I don't know if his question's a good one.

"Harper Press said they *were* going to print," Kaempher says, "but the alignment was off. They've fixed it, but now they're saying our formatting is wrong."

"No," I say. "No way. Nellie doesn't make mistakes."

"That's nice of you, Jensen," she says. "But it's not true."

"We don't have to pay for the mix-up," Mr. K says. "But we will have to fill ten blank pages."

"Just designate them for signatures," I suggest.

"We already have eight pages for that." Mr. K heaves a sigh.

"So we'd have eighteen blank pages."

"The jock can add," Shane mutters, and I shoot him a sharp look.

"Eighteen pages is too many," Nellie says. "Can we delete the extra pages?"

Mr. Kaempher runs a hand over his bald head and paces in front of us. "They say no. I propose we divide the space up. Nellie and Jensen, if you'll fill five pages worth with what's trending, and if Shane and Shalee dig up more photos, then I think we'll be fine. We have to have the files by tomorrow morning."

"Seriously?" Shalee says, piping up for the first time. "I have a date."

"So reschedule," Shane says. For a change, I agree with him.

The bell rings, but the meeting takes ten more minutes. Shane and Shalee head out first, muttering. Nellie approaches Mr. Kaempher with a few clarifying questions, in pure Nellie fashion. Honestly, I'm just grateful that he paired me with her instead of with Shalee.

"I'll wait for you in the hall," I say, showing Nellie my phone. If we're going to work late, I need to make a phone call.

I call my mom to explain what's going on. She brought my fourteen-year-old brother, Clay, home from his care facility for the weekend, and she took today off to spend with him.

Clay's paralyzed—a quadriplegic—because one day, when he was a tiny baby, my father, Kohl Nichols, shook him so hard to make him stop crying it caused permanent damage. That's when Mom got us out of there.

"The occupational therapist is coming over," she says. "Would it be awkward to go to Nellie's? Will Sean be there?" Our home is small, and even smaller when the therapist is there to help move Clay's legs.

Plus Mom has rules: No girls in my bedroom.

"Sean teaches on Mondays and Wednesdays, remember?"

"Oh, yes, that's right. Sorry."

"It's fine. I'm sure Nellie and I can go to her place, or something. I'll be home before midnight."

"Weeknight curfew is still eleven," she counters. She has so few hot buttons, but I manage to push this one all the time even though I've been eighteen for two months now.

Never mind that she trusted me at a very young age to watch Clay after school while she worked dead-end jobs. Or that she let me decide if I wanted to move out or not. Or that, when I made my decision, she helped me pick out an apartment.

But I still have to be home by eleven?

She makes no sense.

"Fine," I say, only because I *am* moving out soon. Though we both know I'd never abandon her. I'm not like Kohl. The only two things that man ever gave us were bruises and a last name. So, eleven it is.

I say goodbye and turn to see Nellie still talking to Mr. K.

So I just watch. She talks with her hands, just like her father.

In first grade, she told our teacher a lengthy story about the scar on her chin.

By the end of the year, Nellie was friends with everyone in our class and invited the whole group to her birthday party. I gave Nellie one of my mom's old Koosh balls and a My Little Pony from the thrift store, and right after that, I met her dad.

Years later, when I ran into Sean Samsin at my first writer's conference, I panicked and ducked into the bathroom, embarrassed. Because what freshman quarterback writes fiction?

I wanted to leave, but my mom had saved for months so I could go to the conference, and I was looking forward to hearing the keynote speaker, Brandon Sanderson. So I stayed.

One conference led to an invitation from Sean. He said we could meet monthly, and we would hold each other accountable to writing, and he'd give me ideas, and help in any way he could. One night, Sean said I needed to add kissing scenes to *Blood Rock* because a YA fantasy mixed with some romance would probably sell like "hotcakes." His word, not mine.

Just before Christmas my sophomore year, I told him I was going to self-publish *Blood Rock* under the pen name "Jen Dimes." We had a good laugh.

"It's perfect," Sean said.

Later that week, Sean emailed me some cover art he'd found and helped me format my ebook and upload it to Amazon.

His gift to me has done far more than either of us ever thought possible.

A year and a half later, I returned the favor and gave him twenty thousand dollars. He tried to turn it down, but I insisted. He finally took it, with a very sincere thank you, and since he had no way of explaining the money to his family, he decided to keep it a secret. I vowed to keep it a secret too. Seemed only fair.

He bought Nellie a car, and then put the rest in savings.

When she turns to me, her brows are knitted together, and she huffs a big breath. "Where do you want to work?" she asks, pulling at the strap of her backpack.

"Clay's therapist is coming over, so either your house or the library."

"Oh." There's a beat of silence, and I sense her pity. She knows about Clay. "My dad's got classes, and my mom's working. So, sure."

"She still cleans at night?" I ask.

"She says she loves it."

"Moms are weird."

"Amen, my brother."

Brother. Something inside of me snaps. We only have a few days left, and I don't care if Sterling's playing her. If this is a game, then I'm in, because if anyone's going to win Nellie, it's going to be me.

Tonight, and for the remainder of the school year, I'm going for it. I've spent years perfecting the craft of getting-the-girl. I've just never chased the one I've actually wanted.

"So," I say as we step outside, "I'll need a ride."

"Yeah, sure," she says.

I have a car, but no one knows. It's parked at my apartment, but I can't explain how I have it to my friends. They know my mom doesn't make much money.

"Actually, could you give me a lift for the rest of the year?"

She glances up at me, and I see the question in her eyes. Why would I need a lift when I always ride with Sterling? From the look on her face, she can't deduce the answer. The years between us have left gaps in our friendship, and there are things she doesn't know.

There's so much I can't tell her without confessing that I'm Jen Dimes.

Nellie's confusion remains, but she gives me the answer I want. "Sure."

CHAPTER 4

Lasagna and Laughs

Nellie

Jensen and I have been crossing paths our entire lives, and yet he's never once been in my car. I toss my bag into the back seat, and Jensen does the same. One of Britta's scrunchies is on the passenger seat, and I toss it to the back. Scrunchies aren't my thing. My hair is long, and I can get it to do anything: curls, waves, braids. You name it. And Britta is jealous that it's so soft. So there's that.

Britta. I still haven't texted her.

Or my mother.

Before we go anywhere, I send a message to my mom:

> I'll get the coffee.

But Britta? I have no words right now.

Jensen slides the seat back. He has long legs and long fingers and long eyelashes. He's muscular and his stomach is flat, and his shirt hugs his biceps. I know that he's been more man than boy for a while, but today, it feels new.

With Jensen in the car, and the yearbook problem, and the way I'm feeling about Britta, and my parents fighting, and Sterling's kiss—I'm spinning. I feel sort of sick. I touch my lips, finding that there is a sensation trapped there, and if I close my eyes—yup. I can still feel the kiss.

How long is that going to last?

"Sorry I talked to Mr. K for so long," I say. "I have concerns about Shane and Shalee getting their part done."

"Valid."

"I know, right? I told him we couldn't take on their portion, so he needs a plan B if they bomb."

I take it slow as we leave the parking lot, crossing over the speed bumps, and merging with the traffic.

"What's he going to do?"

"I have no idea. You hungry? I need to stop at the grocery store for something."

"I could eat."

"Me too. I didn't really get lunch."

My comment results in awkward silence. I bet he's thinking about the kiss; I'm thinking about it.

"My mom made a lasagna yesterday for me to heat up since she's working late," I start. "Or we could just swing through for some fast food—my treat."

I tack on that last bit and hope he doesn't think anything of it.

"Lasagna sounds great," he says. "We could get some French bread while we're at the store."

"Yes. All the French bread."

"Hey, what does a loaf of bread say when breaking up with his girlfriend?" He waits for my reply, but I don't have one. "You deserve butter."

I laugh and switch lanes, heading to Macey's grocery. "That was terrible."

"Sorry."

"Actually, it *was* funny. But if you're going to use Laffy Taffy jokes all night, I might leave you in the produce aisle." I'm careful not to call them dad jokes.

"Fair enough."

I turn the radio on, a '90s XM station that plays songs I can simultaneously enjoy and ignore.

"That whole 'driver picks the music' thing is overrated," he says.

"Fun fact: I first heard that in the TV show *Supernatural*—Driver *does* pick the music; shotgun shuts his cakehole."

Jensen rolls his eyes at me and switches stations. "In the Still of the Night" emerges from the speakers.

"The '50s? Really?"

He concedes and selects another station—opera.

I shake my head, laughing again.

Less than ten seconds later, he picks another station. It's pop country, and he must like it because he settles into his seat.

Minutes later, we're parking at Macey's. I kill the engine, but I don't move. I've been trying so hard to push the kiss away, but it's right here, holding me hostage. It was delicious and scandalous, and I can still hear the crowd and feel Sterling's lips on mine. It's tainted though, knowing he used me. I was the keystone to one of his schemes, and I hate it.

I touch my lips again. How long will I feel like this?

"Nellie? You okay?"

I drop my hand. "Yeah."

"You're thinking about what happened at lunch, aren't you?"

And then I remember—Sterling didn't walk away totally victorious.

"I slapped Sterling," I blurt. "Did you see?"

"What? When?"

I tell him what happened. It's important to me that Jensen knows for some reason.

"He offered to teach you. And you slapped him for it." Statements, not questions.

"Yeah." I refuse to think about how many girls have said yes to Sterling's offer. I hate the thought that follows: *Has Jensen ever offered to do the same?*

"That sounds like him. I'm glad you said no."

I don't want to think about how worthless he made me feel, but the thought rises like a winter moon, cold and bright. I have to push it away, so I tell Jensen about how I threw away Sterling's stupid calendar. I can't believe how much I'm confiding in him.

"I realized that the kiss meant nothing to him. *I* mean nothing to him. He just wanted to be the one to, ya know, kiss me first, and then he made me feel . . . disposable."

"I'm so sorry, Nellie. Are you okay?"

I swallow a knot in my throat, look out the window, and wipe at my eyes. I exhale a shaky breath. "I don't know."

He touches my shoulder. "You're going to be all right. It's been a weird day."

"The weirdest," I confess. "And thanks."

"Yeah."

What I don't say is that he's a major part of the weird.

We get out of my car, and as we walk, I feel lighter. And proud of myself. I needed to talk to someone, and I did. Just not to the person I thought I would.

"Was Britta in on it?" I have to know.

He looks thoughtful. "I honestly don't know, but I can find out if you want."

The thought of him gathering information feels wrong. "Let me think about it." Then I brave my next question. "Were *you* in on it?"

We walk through the double doors, and Macey's smells like donuts and fresh flowers.

"I—I didn't know you were the target."

"I see."

"Come on, let's find the French bread."

With that, we're done talking about it—and I feel a little better.

I follow him through the aisle of books and magazines, toward the bakery in the back. Today, the Harlequin romances catch my eye. My grandma calls them "naughty nickels."

I've never read one. I've never even picked one up to see how much they actually cost, but I'm sure they're not a nickel anymore. Still, the covers suddenly command my attention. Stupid kiss.

I walk faster, my cheeks warm at the thought of how easily Sterling swept me into his arms. How willingly I fell into them. I love books, but right now, I hate this aisle.

It's not until we're staring at loaves of ciabatta and sourdough that I'm breathing normally again. I force myself to think about the yearbook problem, determined to control my brain.

"What if we do a two-page spread on the Blood Rock series?" I ask. "It'd be a great way to fill the empty space. People love to speculate about Jen Dimes."

Jensen nods to the rack of French bread loaves, each one wrapped in foil. "One or two?"

"Just one. What do you think?"

"I thought you said *all* the French bread?" He ignores my idea and grabs two loaves. His unguarded smile causes me to smile back.

"I did say all the French bread, but you know what I meant. Put that back."

"So five loaves, or six?" He scoops up two more and reaches for a fifth.

I'm smiling so wide my cheeks hurt as I try to get him to put the bread back. I look around to see if anyone is watching, but no one is. He finally puts the extras back, but he hangs on to two loaves, raising them high above his head.

"We're taking two," he says.

"Put one back." I shake my head and reach for the extra loaf.

"I will—if you can touch it." He smirks, and for a second, my brain kicks into gear.

I poke him in the stomach, and when he bends, I touch the bag. *Yes!*

"One loaf," I say triumphantly, but the moment I turn my back on him, he smacks me on the butt with the other loaf. I screech and put my hands behind me as I spin around to face him.

"Well, we can't get this one," he says. "You touched it with your butt."

"You did that."

"Prove it," he says as he puts it back and grabs a different loaf.

I'm grinning like a fool as we grab my mother's coffee. We go through the self-checkout and we're back in my car before I know it. Jensen rests the loaf across his lap while I drive.

I am desperate to puzzle him out. Is he flirting? It feels like he's flirting. But that makes no sense. Why would he flirt with me?

"You never answered me," I say as I park in my driveway and turn the engine off. "About *Blood Rock*."

We collect our things and start walking toward my house.

His joyful smile vanishes as he shrugs. "I don't care."

I open the front door. "You don't like my idea. Why?" A different kind of excitement blossoms inside of me. "Because *Blood Rock* is a total phenomenon. Everyone's reading it. Men, women—"

"Please don't say children."

"I can practically name those who haven't read it on one hand."

"Have *you* read it?"

"Obviously." I note how he holds back a grin. "There are fan sites on every social media platform, people are begging for physical books, and a movie is rumored to be in the works. We *have* to mention it. The only reason we've haven't put anything in the yearbook until now is because we thought we weren't going to have enough space. So give me a good reason why we shouldn't include it. I'm all ears."

"You say phenomenon, I say fanatics. You say rumors and I say, yeah, *rumors*."

"You haven't read it," I say, guessing.

"I've heard of it," he says, looking a bit chagrined as he tightens his hold on the bread.

"I've heard of it," I mutter as I drop my backpack to the floor. "I've heard of it, he says."

Jensen does the same, setting his schoolbag on the floor by the leather couch, and then he stares at our family photo, and then at my telescope.

It's collecting dust—which Mom has complained about so many times. But I've been slammed with school the last several months, so I haven't had time to use it. She's threatened to toss it, but Dad says it's okay to stay where it is; it's not hurting anything.

"This thing work?"

"Yes. Of course it works."

"Cool."

"I could show you, sometime. Maybe. If you want." Man, what am I saying? I feel so dumb.

On the coffee table is a large art book about Yellowstone, and next to that is my dad's morning coffee mug. It's empty and it's not on a coaster. I grimace. Mom will freak if she sees that, so I grab it.

She doesn't need more ammo.

Dad's got a pen and scratch pad next to the mug with a list of things he has to do. Jensen picks it up, and I know what he'll read:

Mow the lawn. Grade papers. Clean my office.

"I'm fine to feature the Blood Rock books, but there's more to our culture than that," Jensen says, setting down the notepad. "The couches are new. Well, new to me."

For a second, I'm taken back in time to fifth grade and all the afternoons we played together. Then I shove the memories aside. We're not ten anymore.

"We got them last year. And I know there's more to our culture. This is me you're talking to. But this is a *pop culture* assignment. So . . ."

"Yeah, books aren't popping."

"Okay, so what else? Music, movies, actors, and influencers? The royal family? Or would you prefer sports?"

"That's a good list. You want to write it down?" We both glance at the notepad.

"Nah," I say. "I trust my memory."

"So do I."

When my phone dings again, I see it's another text from Britta. I thought I silenced it, but apparently not. I know she's wondering why I'm giving her the silent treatment.

"Let's eat," I say, shoving my phone back into my pocket.

"Smells good," Jensen says with a low, appreciative growl as we step into the kitchen.

It looks like an episode of *Chopped* meets *Jaws*. Red sauce is splattered all over the stove, counter, and island. Shredded mozzarella cheese has fallen to the floor. Two empty jars of Alfredo sauce sit next to each other, each with a spoon in them. The sink is overflowing with pots, coffee mugs, wooden spoons and silverware, chopping knives, and a colander.

The kitchen table is buried beneath paperwork, bills organized in piles. The broom has fallen to the floor. There's a pile of my dad's clothing in a basket by the door to the laundry room.

My stomach pains, and it's not from hunger.

"Sorry about the mess," I say.

Another glance at the bills, and it's not hard to guess what happened this morning.

Britta tells me her mom deep cleans when she's mad. But not my mom. She cleans on a daily schedule, until something sets her off. Then she lets it all go, as if she has to prove to us how much she does.

There is, however, a pan of lasagna.

"We should do the dishes." Jensen says. "Your parents might appreciate it."

I glance around once more. "Yeah, I'm sure they would."

"First, we eat."

"Agreed."

I turn to grab some plates. Jensen clears a spot on the island and cuts up the bread, while I dish up some lasagna and heat it in the microwave. When everything is ready, we talk in between bites about different subjects for our yearbook pages.

When we're finished, Jensen pushes up his sleeves and starts running hot water in the sink. I begin unloading the dishwasher so we can reload it, and because I don't live in a mansion, we bump into each other. The square footage of the kitchen is shrinking by the minute.

So naturally, I scoop up a few bubbles from the sink and slather them on his arm. But Jensen, having spent all his spare time in the company of pure menace, retaliates instantly. He smacks white bubbles at me, and they splatter all over, and he laughs. So do I.

We're definitely flirting like we've had it in us all these years.

I grab a washcloth and dunk it in the water, but before I can throw it at him, he captures my hand in the water. With his face close to mine and our hands linked, he meets my eyes. There's a smolder there—one he's never directed at me.

"You better stop this," he says, leaning in, his breath warm against my ear. "Or you'll regret it." He tightens his hold as if to remind me that he's stronger. I like that he's stronger than me. I also like the way his shirt clings to him, and whoa, it's as if I've entered uncharted skies. I'm suddenly lost, and all the energy in me vanishes. I can't remember what led to this. All I know is that whatever is happening here is happening too fast. I need air. I need space. I squirm, trying to get free, and he mistakes my actions.

"Don't do it," he says.

When I speak, the words come out sultry. "Let go."

"No way, Samsin."

I spread my fingers, letting the washcloth go, and the back of my hand slides along something sharp—a knife. "Ouch."

He immediately lets go, apologizing for hurting me.

"No, it wasn't you." I raise my hand out of the water, and blood drips off my ring finger, right above the knuckle. Three, four, five drops of blood fall to the water.

He grabs a dish towel, but I stop him.

"Not that. My mom would freak." I squeeze my finger, forcing more blood out. My brain cells are dwindling in his presence, but I think I want it to bleed so that it washes away infection. Or is that with poison?

"I'm really sorry," Jensen says again.

"Seriously, it's not your fault. It's barely a scratch."

"I knew there was a knife," he says, his eyes tight on mine.

"I forgive you. I was having fun and messing with you."

"Yeah, but—" He stops himself and redirects his comment. "You were messing with me?"

CHAPTER 5

Control Freak

Jensen

What does that mean? I apologize once more for good measure and busy myself with the dishes. For a moment there, it was all I could do not to kiss her, and I had to keep reminding myself that *that* would be too much, too fast.

Once we have the kitchen under control and the first aid kit put away, we sit down on the couch. I yawn; she sighs. We're spent, and we haven't even started.

"You want some coffee or something?" she asks.

"Maybe. How long do you think this is going to take?"

"Forever, unless we get started." She chuckles softly, grabs some paper, and draws a large circle. A few minutes later, Nellie has a pie chart, and our five pages mapped out.

Me? I feel like eating pie.

I glance at their family photo. What would Sean think if he saw me sitting here? What would he say if he'd seen us earlier? What would he say about us sitting shoulder to shoulder here on his couch?

"So," Nellie says, "we do a two-page spread on the Blood Rock series, then page three can be sports and celebrities, page four music, fashion, and slang, and lastly, page five will cover television shows, three major news events, and video games."

"If we cut back on that book we could do an 'around the world' sort of thing," I say.

"Got any specific ideas?"

There are probably thousands of guys my age who could

answer her question. Guys headed to Ivy League schools who will leave this world a better place. I, however, am not one of them.

The fact that the girls have all ditched their regular hairstyles for pink-tipped milkmaid braids like Sokha's isn't my fault.

Well, it's not entirely my fault.

Okay, it's my fault, but no one is pointing a finger at me.

"What about that earthquake in Japan?" I say. "Or the floods in Iowa. Scotland had a record-breaking wet season—"

"Scotland's wet season? How do you know that?"

Research. I was researching Scotland's rainfall for book three.

"My mom," I scramble. "She's got a crush on the country."

"And she pays attention to their weather?"

"She'd move there tomorrow."

Nellie runs a hand through her hair. "Okay," she says. "I like the idea of some down-to-earth stuff too. I'm a little embarrassed I didn't think of it."

"That's why Mr. K put us together," I add. "We're a good team."

"That's true."

"Yin and yang, peas and pods. Peanut butter, jelly time."

"You're weird." She locks eyes with me, and I can't tell if she's teasing or not.

"You love me for it," I say, struggling to keep up my arrogant façade.

"I do."

Again—what am I supposed to think about that?

Nellie pulls out her laptop, and I dig up some gum from my bag and share a stick with her. She's focused on creating a document for us, and I study her as she works.

I love that Nellie's hair is long enough for milkmaid braids. Admittedly, I've studied her hair habits for over a year now, calling it research. I'm probably a little too invested in her hair honestly.

"What should we start with?" I ask.

"Well, if I were working on this all by myself, I'd start with the least interesting thing to me."

"So sports."

"You think I think sports is the least interesting of all this?" she says, gesturing to her pie chart.

"I remember a certain essay where you threw some shade on all of high school sports—and football in particular."

"It's not that I hate sports—"

"I know. You like watching me play, don't you?"

"Yes. You're awesome. And it was an argumentative paper. I had to write it in opposition."

"I know. So are we starting with sports or not? Is there something less interesting to you on your list?"

I don't know all of Nellie's little quirks, but I know a couple. She toys with her hair when she's unsure, which is what she's doing now. She pulls it back when she has to take a test, and she puts a soft wave in it when she dresses up—like when Theodore McNell took her to Winterfest.

She's a fan of braids, all kinds. And when she pulls it up into a bun, or a topknot, as I've learned it's called, it's probably because she hasn't washed it.

Like I said, invested.

"Fine, you win," she says. "We start with sports."

I laugh, and she types in the search engine "websites for popular football teams this year."

"You're looking for ESPN.com."

Immediately, article after article pops up. I take notes in my math notebook as she dictates what we can include, and we banter back and forth until she's grumbling.

Then my phone starts pinging. I check my messages and find that Sterling is buzzing me about Friday night. Dude is such a princess.

"It's Monday," I say as I write it.

"What?" Nellie asks, her attention on the computer screen.

"My *other* mother is harping about Friday night."

"It's Monday," Nellie says. Our shoulders brush against each other, and we switch topics—fashion.

"Let me guess," I say after a few minutes. "You hate all the trendy clothes too."

"Not all of them."

For the record, I didn't start out using Nellie as inspiration for Sokha. They do have the same hair color, but where Nellie is soft, Sokha is hard and sharp. The same can be said about Sokha's heart, but not Nellie's. Her heart is big but difficult to win.

Also, Hagon would be torn between Sokha and Nellie, but he'd spend his whole life defending them both because they're the gold and silver of the world, the reason some men get up and go to work . . . or school.

No, I don't put all of Nellie in my books. I just borrow elements of her because I can't capture her on paper any more than I can sketch her eyes.

"Jensen?"

I jerk, not having heard Nellie. Stupid brain can't seem to not wander.

"Sorry. What?"

"Do you like this outfit? I mean, in all reality, what we think doesn't matter. It was the most popular look of the year."

"It's all right."

"Yeah, I'm not loving the shirt," she says.

"Too flowey?"

"That's not a word."

"Sure it is. Flowey. It's the essence of movement caught in regards to fabric. Flowey."

"You're such a word nerd."

"Yeah," I counter, "well, you're a control freak." I instantly regret my words.

She blinks, and then pulls away from me, her expression hardening.

"I'm sorry, Nellie. I am being a jerk today."

"You're not a jerk." She pauses, and I want her to go on. "I *am* a control freak. Just didn't expect you to say it out loud. It's no secret that I like things a certain way. Don't worry about it. I've been called worse."

"By who?"

"Hey, look at this." She steers our attention back to a photograph of a flooded coastline.

I try to summon up anything negative I've heard about Nellie. Stargazerblue is her username for most things, and occasionally, we call her a nerd or a brain. Then it hits me. Britta, queen of the backhanded compliment.

Good thing you're smart.

Half your outfit looks fabulous.

Your Instagram makes you seem so fun.

Thanks for being my DUFF.

"Nellie?"

"What?"

"By who?"

"Not you, if that's what you're worried about." She turns back to the computer.

"Promise?"

"Yes." When she glances at me, she presses her point. "Seriously, Jensen. It's not a big deal."

"I think it is."

"I think we've got enough to move on to the good stuff."

She is undeterred as she moves on with our assignment. I've never met anyone who can stay on task like she can. She forces me to move on to the world of entertainment, and I let her. Movies. Music. *Books.* I can feel her mood shift from bored to excitement, so I fake a yawn. That's when Nellie remembers her previous offer.

"Oh, gosh. I'll get you that coffee."

"Can I get some H2O instead?" She looks at me weird, so I add, "What? I thought I was the word nerd."

She laughs sarcastically, and then sets the laptop aside. I follow her into the kitchen, and it feels good to stretch my legs.

She grabs two glasses and fills them with water.

I glance at the clock. It's almost eight. I can't believe I've been with her for four hours.

I run my hands through my hair, taking a deep breath as Nellie hands me a glass.

I'm parched, I realize. I drink, and drink, and drink. From the corner of my eye, I watch her watch me.

"Thirsty?"

I laugh because that word has more than one meaning these days. And she's no innocent as she says it. The result? Water goes down the wrong pipe. I cough, and then to my humiliation, belch.

Nellie laughs, her eyes dancing as she shakes her head at me.

I pound my chest and release another softer burp.

She takes a dainty sip of her water, all proper-like.

"Oh, sorry," I say, faking an English accent. "I didn't realize it was teatime." I lift my pinkie finger and take a tiny sip of my water.

"We need a break," Nellie says, cautiously setting down her drink.

I couldn't agree more. And some fresh air. Normally, I'd go outside and shoot some hoops.

"What do you suggest?" I ask, in an effort to be a good guest. "Scrabble?"

I let out a short laugh, happy to own up to my vocabulary prowess. "Think you can beat me?"

"Is that a challenge?" She puts a hand on her hip.

"Yes, but maybe another time. What we really need is to get our blood flowing."

"Oh, so what, shoot hoops?"

"Or . . ." I start, thinking about what else we could do to get our blood going, "what about—"

"I've got it. Yoga," she says.

"Uh, what? No. But only because I forgot my yoga pants. Let's go for a walk, like normal people."

CHAPTER 6

Before We Knew

Nellie

I grab a jacket and fish out one of my father's hoodies for Jensen. The temperature is dropping with the setting sun. Clouds cling to the mountains, and while I can't see the peaks, I know there's still snow up there. As we head away from my house, I can't help but smile at the yellow daffodils that line my sidewalk. Mom and I planted them several years ago, back when we did stuff together. The only thing we do these days is argue.

Astrophysics? What kind of career is that? You'll rely on grants your whole life. Don't you want a job that will have a lasting impact, even after you stop doing it? Staring up at the night sky is a hobby.

I don't want to think about her right now, so I push the thought away, and look up at the sky, almost out of spite.

"The flowers are pretty," Jensen says, not knowing my thoughts.

"Thanks."

"Every year, about this time, my mom comments on them. 'Look at Nellie's daffodils,' she says. It's her not-so-subtle hint that I should plant some for her."

"You should. I could help you. We'd need to plant them in the fall, though."

"Sounds like a date."

"It can be." I'm a little surprised by my words, and so is he. But when he doesn't say anything else, I wonder if it's because he's realizing we'll be miles apart by fall.

"Fun fact," I say, unable to take his silence. "Did you know that Utah is one of the top five driest states?"

"It is?"

I am one hundred percent nerd as I talk about how dry Utah is while we climb slowly toward the mountain trails. My soliloquy ends with a passionate review about International Dark Sky Parks. He is politely captivated.

The last time we spent a whole day together was in seventh grade, when his mom had to take Clay to the hospital. Clay had had some seizures, and all I remember was how scared we both were. I thought Clay was going to die.

Jensen did, too, I think.

It's amazing how much our brains develop during those middle school years. Now, we know more. We know better.

We're drawing close to Jensen's house, and I try to remember the last time I came up here. He lives in the cul-de-sac at the end of the road, on the left, and we used to ride our bikes in endless circles here. But because it's a dead end, I haven't driven up here in a long time. This section of the neighborhood was born when the mountain was formed, I swear. My house is newer than his by about forty years.

Which means that the Nicholses have the most beautiful backyard. I love their trees and how ivy climbs up the brick of his house. But the paint on Jensen's home is wearing off, and the railing sags with years of winter wear, and despite all the yard work Jensen and his mother do, their place, along with a dozen others, needs major facelifts and upgrades, and in some cases, extensive repairs.

I never noticed these things as a child.

I swallow an unfamiliar lump in my throat as I recall the emerald-green backsplash of his kitchen, the royal-blue bath mat next to the tub, and the Star Wars bedspread he got for his ninth birthday.

Of course, this was all before I shot up to five foot six.

Before he started shaving.

Before we learned how difficult it was for boys and girls to be *just friends*.

Now, I'm unable to ignore how close we walk to each other, or how we both avoid stepping on the cracks, and how, without saying a word, we begin zigzag walking like we used to. I think about putting my arm around his waist, about him putting his arm over my shoulders, but we don't, and that makes me a little sad.

When the sidewalk ends, we stop walking, but the fact that it happens so naturally makes me smile.

The air at the base of the mountain smells more like pine than parking lot, and even though the sun is setting, I can still feel its warmth.

"Jensen, look."

We turn around, the sunset capturing our full attention. It's casting pinks and oranges along the Oquirrh Mountains in a triumphant display. The gray clouds are silver-lined, and miles and miles away, the Kennecott Copper Mine, which can be seen from just about anywhere in the valley, is even more prominent against the darkening mountainside.

We say nothing for a long time, soaking in the sight. Maybe it's because we know this moment will never happen again. Maybe it's because he's remembering our childhood like I have been. Maybe it's because we're on the edge, teetering between childhood and adulthood. I feel so ready for what comes next. It's scary, but I wouldn't have it any other way.

Maybe this contemplation of mine is a sign that I've read too many coming-of-age novels.

A chill wraps around me, and the need to stay warm becomes more important than the pretty view.

"Come on," I say. I tug gently on his arm, and then drop my hand. We cut through Mrs. Miskin's yard in order to connect to another street, one that keeps us in the neighborhood instead of going up the mountain trail.

"So, an astronomer, right? That's the plan?" Jensen kicks at a stray rock on the sidewalk, eyes fixed on the ground.

"That's the plan. What about you?"

When he says nothing, I start to worry that I've offended him somehow.

"Jensen?" I whisper, no louder than a rustle of leaves, but he still says nothing.

We approach a red Little Free Library and Jensen stops. He looks up at me and says, "I don't have a plan."

I'm thrown for a second. How can he *not* have a plan? I would die. The uncertainty, the vagueness. For Jensen, however, a higher education might be tied directly to his mother's income. But he's certainly smart enough for scholarships—

"Do you ever borrow books from this?" He unlatches the glass door to the miniature house-turned-library.

"I don't. I should."

He runs a finger over the tattered spines of *The Lion, The Witch, and the Wardrobe*, *Twilight*, *Goodnight, Moon*, and *Anne of Green Gables* and five other titles I've never heard of, but when he touches *Ember in the Ashes*, he taps it and then pulls it away from the rest.

The red-and-white spine is thick, and the cover captures my attention. The girl's hair, twice the length of mine, blows to the right while a man kneels at her feet, almost seductively. If it weren't for the sword in his hand, I would think it was a romance.

"Have you read this?" he asks, handing it to me.

"I haven't. You?"

"It's better than your precious Blood Rock books."

I flip it over to read the back, while Jensen closes the library door and starts walking away. I'm unable to finish reading the summary, but I keep the book and jog to catch up. I'll have to bring a book of mine—one that I can let go of—to trade out for this one. Jensen just picked out a book for me! I'll keep it forever.

However, he's walking so stiffly that I wonder if I upset him by asking about college.

"Hey, you okay?" Again, I catch him by the arm.

"I'm fine. Really." His expression is indifferent, but something in his eyes says he's lying. It's not hurt or anger, just a small sort of desperation.

I let go and take a small step back, hoping he'll confide in me at some point.

"I'm excited to read this," I say, hugging the book to my chest.

"I think you'll like it. When you're done, we can talk about it."

We can talk about it. We can plant flowers together. This is starting to feel like a promise of things to come. I flash him a smile and agree to tell him as soon as I'm done with it.

"We should get back," I say.

"Yeah."

As we walk, I decide the subject of graduation is probably less awkward than college.

"Do you feel like last week, and even today, that there's been this tangible shift in the senior class? A sudden camaraderie that hasn't existed until now?"

Jensen scratches the bridge of his nose, a cute gesture I've noticed before and I find even cuter today.

"Yeah. There is definitely a buzz. I think that's one reason why Sterling . . ." Jensen flushes red and looks away.

I burn hot under my jacket and look away.

Not bad, Nellie. That's what Sterling said. Am I really not a good kisser? Threads of embarrassment and indignation curl in my gut. I can't stand the thought that I didn't ace my first kiss, and as my thoughts circle back to Sterling's offer to teach me how to kiss, I am a country divided. The idea is indecent, as disgusting as it is enticing.

"So what's next?" Jensen asks.

My brain glitches, and I'm not sure what he's talking about.

"Do we just need to format the pages?"

Oh, right. The yearbook pages.

"We need to decide if we're going to feature the Blood Rock books first. It's like you want to forget they even exist."

"Oh, I know they exist. Trust me."

The sidewalk narrows, forcing us to walk closer, and my arm brushes the sleeve of his hoodie, and he doesn't try to put space between us. The longer we walk like this, with the soft brushing sound between us, the more I silently compare him to Sterling.

Jensen's creative, which I totally adore, but he's also smart. And he makes me feel smart—or rather *smarter*. I'm not stupid, but Jensen has a way of making me think.

With Sterling around, however, the only thing that lights up is my limbic system, drawing attention to those primal needs that ensure man's survival.

I like Jensen's smile more than Sterling's. Sure it's a mischievous one, because hello, but he doesn't guard it or hide it. It's just there, flickering off and on like a motion-sensor night-light. Instead of blinding others, he has a way of just glowing at all the right times.

And speaking of lights, I didn't leave the house lights on, so the windows look lonely and bleak.

It's nearly nine, and my dad probably won't be home for another hour. Mom cleans from nine until whenever she's done, usually around midnight.

I flip the switches to light up both the exterior and the interior, and we put our jackets away. Jensen goes to the sink and refills his glass. He swallows down more water, and then asks to use the restroom.

The main bathroom in the house is the same one I use as my own, so that means my mom expects it to always be clean. I show him where it is, though I suspect he remembers. I step into my bedroom and change into Nike sweats, pull my hair to one side and braid it into one thick rope, and mentally prep for another hour or two of homework. I have always liked working with Jensen, but this has been more fun than I thought it would be.

And to be clear, Jensen's cute, but he's more than that. He's kind of sexy. Okay. Wow, I'm really *distracted*. I remind my body that Jensen and I are just friends, but it's futile, considering the teasing and the downright flirting. It's like a side of me that has been dormant for years has woken up, and I don't know how to get it to go back into stasis.

We reconvene on the couch, me with my laptop and him with his notebook.

The first thing we research is the Blood Rock series. Dozens of websites pop up. The number one question in everyone's mind is: Will the books ever be tangible, hardback, priceless treasures that we can pluck off the shelf in our hour of need? What about an audio version? A soundtrack! A blockbuster movie! The ebook isn't enough! We need more!

I envision what *Blood Rock* would look like as a book. It'd be like a Bible, I think, with a soft leather cover, engraved with Hagon's family crest. No title required.

Okay, so confession. I'm actually a huge fan, but I don't let anyone know it. I guess it's because I don't want to be like everyone else. So, I tell everyone the diluted truth. Yes, I've read them. (To date, I've read them three times each.) Yes, I am Team Hagon. (He is officially *my* book boyfriend.)

I do not tell them that I stalk MeganLovesHagon257 and her glorious fan art. I do not tell anyone that I've signed the petition for the books to be printed, and I do not, under any circumstances, tell anyone that I want to be kissed by someone who will kiss me the way Hagon kisses Sokha.

Interestingly enough, for someone who's such a hater, Jensen's glued to the computer screen as I scroll. I don't think he blinks, and it makes me wonder if he's lying like I am.

Could we possibly share the same secret?

When I click on a fan fiction site, I glance up at him. His eyes are hooded, his lips are in a straight line, and his whole persona has dimmed.

Never mind. He's not a fan. Haters gonna hate.

I leave the site and search for statistics and facts and original release dates. I find that Jen Dimes's website was updated last week—as I knew it would be. She posts about twice a month—little tidbits, lines that had to be cut, links to her favorite books and movies. She always ends her posts with a gracious thank you to the readers. And the comments, now in the thousands, cover a whole lot of everything.

You're books have literally saved my life. Thanks you for writing, for sharing Sokha and Hagon with us. As soon as you decide too meet fans, I'll be their!

Amandapanda_24 wrote that comment nearly two years ago, and the typos drive me nuts. She was the first person to ever comment on www.JenDimes.com, so her comment remains at the top. She's first in a very long line.

Jensen and I move on from the website and end up looking at the cover art for both *Blood Rock* and *Shadow Stone*.

"They're very professional for a self-published title," Jensen says in a flat tone. It's like he has to force himself to say something nice. I laugh, because the covers are not just professional, they're "artistically engaging," which is a term I learned after spending six hours on a fan site solely dedicated to fan art, which is where I first saw MeganLovesHagon257's work. The cover art and Megan's art look nothing alike, however both have masterfully captured the feel of the stories.

Jensen and I try to calculate the number of downloads of both *Blood Rock* and *Shadow Stone*. This gets tricky because we can't find a website that is freely disclosing those numbers to the public. We find one website that looks promising, but we'd have to purchase a membership to access it. So we decide to rely on a different website that seems fairly accurate.

I keep spewing tidbits for Jensen to jot down, and with each bullet point, his face seems to morph deeper into disgust.

"You really hate these books?" I say. "Covers aside."

"I don't hate the books."

"Your face says otherwise. Have you even read them?"

"I've been busy."

"Are they too girly for you?"

"They're epic fantasy. That's hardly girly."

"Then why haven't you read them?" I turn my whole body to face him, demanding without words that he come clean.

He levels his gaze on mine. Inhales, exhales. "There is enough talk about them that I will never have to read them."

"Oh, so because they're popular, you're not going to read them."

"It's clear *you're* a fan. I'll bet the author would love you."

He clears his throat again, a slight blush on his cheeks, and I have no choice but to laugh.

I shake my head and turn back to the pages to start formatting. It takes forever, but once we have the last two pages done, we polish all five, and I open up my email. As we wait for the pages to load, Jensen touches the screen.

"I like your email," he says.

Stargazerblue@gmail.com has been my email since fifth grade.

"Thanks," I say. Once the pages are done loading, I hit send, and with a big sigh of relief on our part, we slump on the couch.

"It's finished," I say.

"Thanks to you."

"Thanks to us both." I glance at the clock. It's late. Almost eleven. "My dad should've been home by now."

I pull my phone out to check my messages but Britta's the only one who's trying to communicate with me. I read, and ignore, her latest texts.

"He's never late," I say.

"Never? I doubt that."

"Well, it's not like him."

Jensen stands up. "Then call him."

"Are you going?" I ask. Part of me panics at the thought of him leaving.

"My mom will ground me if I don't get home."

I nod as I dial my dad. I expect Jensen to walk out, but he stands and waits, as if he wants to make sure I'm not entirely alone before he leaves.

CHAPTER 7

Call for Help

Jensen

When Sean doesn't answer, Nellie tries his office line but doesn't get an answer there either. Then she tries her mother. I pretend it's no big deal, but Sean's a texting freak. He can out-text Sterling. His phone is usually on vibrate, hooked to his hip, and unless he's teaching, he's usually quick to respond.

When Sean says he'll be there, he is.

When he's running late, he calls.

When he promises to read pages, he does.

"She didn't answer, either." Nellie grips her phone with both hands, confused.

Discreetly, I text Sean myself:

> Long story short, but I'm with Nellie. She's worried because you're not home. What's up?

I can picture his confused expression. He'll wonder why we're together.

He used to ask me about Nellie. How she was doing, what I thought of her new haircut, if she had a boyfriend, but the questions stopped after a while, and I have often wondered why.

I sit back down with her, and we stall, both of us focusing on our phones. I finally text Sterling back about Friday night.

> I'm game for whatever.

Nellie is texting, too, and I find it funny that we both put off our best friends. I peek at what she's writing to Britta, curious.

> I've been busy. I'm actually really upset about what happened. Was it your idea?

Britta's response is immediate; Nellie's phone doesn't even chime because she still has the app open.

> What's there to be mad about?

Nellie shuts her phone down and looks at me. It's been five minutes of radio silence from Sean, so I ask, "Do you want to drive over to the university?"

"Not really. Not by myself."

"I could maybe come. Hang on." I text my mom and explain what's going on. I frown at her response.

> I don't think so.

> But mom.

> But son. Nellie's not a child.

> But she doesn't want to go alone. She's worried.

Mom doesn't respond for a hot minute.

> Fine. But you're cleaning the toilets this week.

> Fine.

"I can go," I say.

"Yeah?"

I shrug as if it's no big deal, but she examines me as if I'm lying. She's reading my facial cues, so I layer on my stoicism.

Nellie Samsin's studious expression is one to behold. She really thinks things through—usually. I can't explain her behavior with Sterling, but the wheels are turning now, and she has me completely captivated.

"Do you think something's wrong?" she asks.

The truth is, I don't know what answer is best, but she needs one, and I have to go with my gut.

"Yes. I think something's wrong."

"Like a flat tire."

"Sure." If he had a flat tire, he'd text back. I can't think of a single good reason why he wouldn't respond, but a million bad ones come to mind.

"Jensen."

"I don't know, Nellie, but what I do know is that if you say he's never late, and you can't get through to him or your mom, then something isn't right."

As soon as I acknowledge this, something deep down in my gut, some dark fog I can't quite describe, moves forward and shades my mind. There's a power behind it that I don't like, and despite my spiking concern, I consider the emotion, so I can use it when I get back to Hagon. I can't help it—I look at situations differently, and I tend to dramatize things in my mind.

"Okay," I say. "Let's drive over to the university. Or, if you've changed your mind, I can go home."

"Don't go."

She says it without thinking, and she closes the gap in our friendship with those two words.

"I won't leave you."

She bobs her head up and down, but I'm not sure what she means by it, until she says, "Let's go."

I grab her jacket and the keys to her car and hand them to her, because it's cold outside and we'll have to walk to get to his office. I remind myself that I shouldn't know that.

"Will you drive?" she asks, surprising me.

It's unlike her to relinquish any control over a situation. I learned that at a young age, and then relearned it when we got to high school. I'm genuinely surprised when she places her hand on top of mine, as if she's entrusting me with more than her car.

Once we're on our way, I notice how uneasy she is. She covers her belly with one arm, and toys with her teeth and lips as we drive. I've never witnessed this nervous habit before, but it can't be new. I just haven't been around her enough to know.

"It's going to be okay," I say. "There's got to be a good reason he's not texting us back. Maybe his phone is dead." There. There's one good reason—except I know he has a charger in his office, one in his computer bag, and one in his car.

"No." Nellie shakes her head. "He has a charger in his car, in his office, and in his computer bag."

I almost laugh. "Well, then that isn't it."

"Could he be grading papers?" I ask. "Isn't this their last week?"

It's almost the end of the semester for college as well, something I know for sure.

"Oh my gosh. You're totally right. He's probably grading papers. I feel so dumb. Turn the car around."

"Don't feel dumb. If he's grading papers, then we'll find him grading papers, and everything will be fine."

We catch green light after green light.

Nellie purses her lips and nods, and a part of me remembers that those lips were kissing Sterling earlier, and suddenly this day feels like it's been going on for way too long.

My legs feel heavy as we get out of the car, and I click the automatic lock button, but when I offer Nellie her keys, she doesn't even try to take them. It's darker and colder than when we went on our walk, and because of all the light pollution around campus, the stars are weak and distant. The moon is hidden behind the clouds, and the campus security lights stand ready to guide us to the front doors.

I spot Sean's Prius, but I pretend I don't know which vehicle is his, and I wait for Nellie to point it out. We walk over and peer inside as if that'll set everything right. There's nothing out of place.

The main doors to the Fine Arts building are locked, and I doubt any of the other entrances are open. Nellie tries calling her father again, but no one answers.

That's when I suggest we call campus security.

We walk back to one of the blue emergency light posts, and I make the call while Nellie taps her foot and pulls on her hair.

"Campus security. This is Annabelle." Her voice has a deep Southern drawl to it.

I explain our problem, and Annabelle is happy to help.

"She's calling his office," I whisper to Nellie. She nods and forces a smile. We didn't get an answer, so it seems unlikely Annabelle will get one. The dark fog inside of me swells, and I want to force it back. I don't like it.

"I'm so sorry," Annabelle says. "He's not answering. I'm sending someone over."

A few minutes later, a security guard shows up, and Annabelle offers up a hospitable goodbye and wishes us well.

"Nellie Samsin? Jensen Nichols?"

"That's us," I say.

"Eric Molifua."

"Thanks for this," Nellie says as we walk. Next to Eric, Nellie is tiny. His Polynesian build is exactly what any football coach would be looking for in a defensive linebacker.

"I'm sure he's fallen asleep on his sofa," Eric says, his deep voice reassuring even to me.

But I doubt that he's sleeping. I've seen his sofa. He's probably wandering the halls, plotting out his own story, and completely unaware of the hour.

Inside, we take the elevator up three flights, and then walk down the hall to Sean's office. I force myself to look around, like I've never been here. There is a plaque with his name on it along with the room number 378.

Eric knocks twice, and then in a clear voice announces himself. "Professor Samsin? Security."

Nothing.

Eric opens the door with a master key. It's not a very large office. Maybe one-third the size of my bedroom. There's a desk, a sofa, and shelves bowing under the weight of books, as any art history professor would have, and a few inexpensive prints from Sean's favorite three periods of artwork. Baroque. Impressionism. Romanticism.

But I see none of that. All I see is Sean.

At first, I think he's fallen asleep at his desk. But the smell of urine hits me, and my whole body shudders. Then, I really see him. His jaw is slack, his eyes are wide open, and his arm, which hangs at his side, has turned purple.

"Dad?"

Nellie steps forward, slipping through my hands before I can hold her back. She moves like she's approaching a wounded animal and puts a hand on his shoulder. My heart thunders in my chest when she cries out. The sound of it fills the small space, causing every hair on my arms to rise.

"Sean?" I hear my voice, but I don't recognize it.

Then things move at lightning speed. Nellie crouches down, trying to see into his dead eyes and her cry turns into a sob. The security guard leans over Sean's body, checking for a pulse with one hand while using his walkie-talkie to call for help with the other. I realize Eric isn't attempting any kind of rescue.

Nellie runs back into my arms, burying her face into my shoulder, and I can only stare, expecting Sean to wake up. I can feel Nellie's hot tears almost instantly, her body shaking violently against me. As I move to lead us out of the room, I hear Eric relaying the scene to whomever is on the other end of his walkie-talkie, and I don't want to hear it.

Within minutes, there's a police officer and EMTs or medics or whatever. I hear someone say, "He's gone."

And my body is wracked with confusion while it also accepts

the truth because I saw him with my own eyes. Sean's dead. The two words repeat in my mind until they blur into one, but he can't be. We were texting earlier today. This isn't possible.

One of the officers asks us our names, and I manage a response because Nellie is sobbing in my arms. Nothing feels real, not even her holding on to me. I'm completely numb.

Someone introduces themselves as the county coroner, but I don't see his face or understand why he's here.

We're asked to wait down the hall in the foyer, and an officer encourages us to sit down on a leather bench while putting blankets around our shoulders. He offers us a box of tissues, and we both take several.

"Did someone call his wife?" I say, but no one responds.

"I don't understand," Nellie says in between sobs. She is curled up in a ball, her head on my thigh.

I hide my face behind one hand, while the other rests on Nellie's shoulder, and I close my eyes. I should call my mom, but I can't seem to get my hands to stop shaking.

Nellie's grip on my leg tightens, and I want to help her, but I'm losing it too. I just lost one of my closest friends, the first man to ever champion me. And no one knows what Sean means to me, besides my mom, and they never will unless . . . unless I reveal who I am. And I can't. It's not the right time. It wouldn't even sound real.

After a brief moment, I find my voice. "Did someone call Mrs. Samsin?"

A nearby officer comes over and puts a hand on my shoulder. "She's already on her way. So is your mom."

And that's it. That's all the help I can give them. I don't even question how it's possible that they know who I am or how they got ahold of my mom. I just know she's coming.

While we wait, Nellie holds on to me as tightly as I hold on to her.

CHAPTER 8

Back to Normal

Nellie

I ride home with my mom, who takes my hand and holds it as she drives. How is she able to drive when I can't even see straight?

It's somewhere around two thirty in the morning when we zombie our way into the house. Immediately, my mom collapses on the couch and makes a phone call. Who is she calling in the middle of the night?

I'm halfway to my room when she says my name. I spin around.

"You don't have to go to school tomorrow."

"I have a final." This comes out without thought.

"It will wait." She uses her Mom Voice, and I don't want to argue. Then she says, "Hello, Bonnie. I'm sorry to wake you—" And that's when she finally starts crying. Her sob breaks me into a million pieces, and I rush to my room, not wanting to hear her tell my grandma what's happened.

I lay on my bed, numb and unable to sleep, but when my mom's feet cast a shadow below my door, I pretend I'm out.

The light from the hallway spills across my face, but I don't open my eyes.

She stands there for a whole minute as if she's debating whether to wake me, but she says nothing. Then without saying good night, she shuts the door.

"Love you too," I whisper, and my walls come crashing down.

Somewhere around five, I wake up and run to the bathroom,

certain I'm going to be sick, but I just lay on the cold tile, nauseous and sweating. I can hear some low voices. I think. I can't quite tell if it's real or if I'm hearing the television.

When I crawl back to bed, my fingers and toes are freezing, my head is hot mush, and though I never pray, I beg God for sleep. When my alarm sounds at 7:45, I hit the cancel button and roll over, telling myself that ten more minutes will set the world right. Those ten minutes are exactly what I need, too, because in the stasis of sleep is the abyss of nothing.

When I do wake up, I check the time. It's 11:18.

"No!" I throw back the covers and rush into the bathroom. Currently, I'm missing an AP final. I never reviewed my notes last night. Too busy with the yearbook. Too caught up in Jensen.

And then it hits me all over again.

My eyes burn and my nose stings as I reach for the tissues. In my mind's eye, I can see my dad. It drains me of all my energy.

When I spot Mom's note on the bathroom counter, I freeze. I pick up the paper but have to read it twice before it makes sense.

I'm at Larkin funeral home. If you want to join me, just call. I've informed the school. I'll handle everything since you've got enough on your plate. Even though I don't know what I'm doing.

I don't want to go to the funeral home. But I also can't stay in this house alone for another minute. My mouth is dry, my head is spinning, and I wade through some murky thoughts that threaten to pull me under. I don't want to wallow in that darkness, so I search for what brings me happiness, and find . . .

The last bit of warmth and happiness I felt is associated with someone, not something, and I feel shallow for thinking of Jensen right now.

Something's definitely wrong with me.

I get dressed, brush my teeth, and pull on a baseball cap. I smear some concealer on to hide the dark circles under my eyes. The shadows are a physical manifestation of the pain in my heart. They'll probably never go away.

Tying on my sneakers, I have the desire to run for the first time in years, and that's how I know my brain isn't functioning right. But, still, I have to take that final. I grab my bag and go to the key rack to get my keys. But they're not there.

I always keep my keys in the same spot. I begin hunting for them, and after a few minutes, I slam a fist on the kitchen table.

"Where are they?" I go to the living room and part the drapes. My car isn't here. It's . . . I suddenly remember.

It probably still on campus. Forcing the memory of last night away, I shoot Jensen a quick text.

> Sorry to bother you, but I need my car. Where is it?

He texts me right back.

> It's at my house.

He sends me five more messages with instructions on how to get into his house and get the keys. I don't understand why he's not at home. I send him one more text.

> You went to school today?

> Yeah. I have a pounding headache, though.

I feel bad for him. Actually, I feel a lot of things in regards to him, but I can't deal with that right now. Instead, I focus on what I need to do. Maybe I can take the final during lunch.

The back door of the Nichols home is unlocked, just like Jensen said it would be, and right inside there is a bowl on a credenza with my keys in it. There's another shiny key chain that catches my attention. It has the word Porsche written on it as clear as day. Why would Jensen or his mom have a key to a Porsche? My brows bunch together as I pick it up and run my thumb over the smooth metal. I lack the bandwidth to figure it out, so I drop it back into the bowl with a clank and leave.

When I climb into my car, I decide to text my mom.

I try hard not to let her last message bother me, but the thing is—it's not just that one. It's the one before it and the one before that, and about a hundred more like it. All of them digging at me, and I hate, hate, hate that my dad's messages of love are interspersed between them. And then like some kind of ninja jerk, grief hits again.

I scroll back through my phone.

> And Nellie, we appreciate all you do
> to help us out. Thanks.

That's the last thing he ever said to me.

Tears are rolling down my face again, but I start locking the messages, so they can't accidentally be deleted. Later, I'll print them out and save them. Because phones don't last forever. Friends don't last forever.

Apparently fathers don't either.

I wipe away the tears, and then start a new text message, this time just to my mom. I tell her I'm headed to school.

Then, as my grief slinks away like a horrible coward, I text Jensen again.

> Do you know if Shane and
> Shalee got their pages done for
> the yearbook?

If I have to choose between death and deadlines, I pick the latter.

His response comes through as I pull out of his driveway.

> No idea.

I know it's not my responsibility to follow up on the year-book, but autopilot.

Which is how I drive to school.

The senior parking lot is full, but I don't have to search for a parking space. It's tradition that seniors can rent a spot; however, as class president, I automatically get one. Those who rent a spot are allowed to paint inside the yellow lines, and most everyone does. Dad bought me the paint so Britta and I could paint ours the same day, last summer. Mine is a galaxy that's now fading. I don't like the symbolism of that thought.

I prickle when I absorb another thought. Dad won't be around to buy me paint anymore or give me gas money. He won't drive me to UNLV or carry my boxes into my apartment. He won't see me graduate. I take deep breaths, but it doesn't help.

I close my eyes and lean into my steering wheel and imagine him sitting beside me. And when I do, I can feel his hand on my shoulder.

I can hear him telling me to focus and move forward, talk to Britta and sort things out, and not to worry about him. Stick to the plan. Get good grades. *You've got this.*

I hold on to those words of encouragement as I walk toward the main office, my backpack square between my shoulder blades.

A gust of chilly wind follows me inside, and I glance back at the skies. Endless gray, with no defined clouds. Super.

"Nellie! What are you doing here?" The receptionist rises to her feet, her chair rolling back.

"Hi, Mrs. Archer. I don't have an excuse note, but can you check me in?"

"Oh, honey, you don't need a note. You don't need to be here—I thought—I thought you were—"

"I have a final."

"All of your teachers are aware . . ." She can't bring herself to finish. "No one is expecting you to be in class today."

"I expect *me* to be here, ma'am."

"But, Nellie . . ."

I rarely show my mother's side of me. I call it the Angela Glacier. The coldness resides deep down in my gut. I try to keep it from moving, but glaciers are always moving even when they appear to be stationary, and often a slab of ice breaks off. In the wild, it's called calving. In my world, Mom calls it a meltdown.

And thanks to the gray skies, I remain frozen.

"Just check me in."

Mrs. Archer lowers herself back into her seat and pulls out a blue slip.

I watch her write my name and the time, and when she offers it to me, the hesitation is rolling off her in waves.

"Thank you," I manage without meeting her eyes. If I look into them, I'll see the heartache I'm trying to ignore.

I head straight to Mr. Rose's classroom. The bell rings, and students spill into the hallways, excited for lunch, but I have no intention of eating. I don't think I could, anyway. Mr. Rose is putting away some papers when I step through the doorway.

"Mr. Rose?"

"Nellie? What are you doing here?" He rises to his feet, and his eyes—just like I thought. It's hard to ignore the pity, but I tell myself not to acknowledge it.

"Yeah, hi." I hold out the slip. "Would it be possible for me to take the final right now?"

He hesitates.

"I know you need to take lunch, so I can sit in the library. Miss Maggie won't mind."

He blinks, and the pity is gone. I think he remembers who I am. He clears his throat as he moves some papers around, producing a blank test packet.

"That won't be necessary. You can sit in here. I just need to make a phone call and then I'll come back."

He proceeds to give me instructions and then hands me the final. Except, he doesn't let go.

"Nellie, I'm so sorry."

"Don't be." I tug on the paper. He relinquishes the packet,

and I take a seat, front row and center. I replay my words as he walks out.

Don't be.

Don't be sorry for me? Is that what I meant?

What a terrible thing to say. I mean, I don't want him to be sorry for me, but why didn't I say "Thanks" or "I appreciate your concern" or something? When he returns, I should apologize.

I bury my face in my hands and breathe until I find the mental space where I store my AP physics information. Calculus based, this is my jam.

When the lunch bell rings, I'm on the last three questions. I quickly write out the answers and turn in the packet.

"Mr. Rose," I say, pausing at the door. My lip quivers. "I just . . . You're one of my favorite teachers. Thanks for everything you've done for me."

"Of course," he says, dumbfounded.

I weave through the students who are coming in. I feel better having said that, like I'm back on track. No one looks at me the way Mrs. Archer or Mr. Rose did, but as I get to Mrs. Johannson's class, a lump forms in my gut.

When I step into the room, several eyes land on me. I spot Jensen immediately. He's got a ball cap on, too, and I smile, until I wonder if I look as masculine as he does. I inhale and go to my seat.

"Hey," I say.

"Nellie?"

"I'm so tired of everyone saying my name like it's a question. Yes, it's me, Nellie."

"Sorry. It's just that—"

"—you weren't expecting to see me here today. I know. You and everybody else."

Immediately, I feel bad. I'm being a jerk.

"I'm sorry," I say over my shoulder.

"You're okay."

He forgives me too easily, but it's not like I'm going to turn around and tell him not to.

I pull out yesterday's assignment. Even though my world is falling apart, numbers are steady. I welcome their secrets because I can puzzle them out. I can organize them, knowing they're not going to prank me or pull the rug out from under me. They don't pity me.

Twenty minutes later, everyone's working, but I've gone catatonic. I'm studying Mrs. J's handwriting. It's better than mine. Mine's nearly vertical, showing no hint of fluidity or curve, as if every letter and number must, and will, stand on its own.

Graphology. The study of handwriting. Maybe in another life, that's what I'll do.

Jensen's fingertips find my shoulder blade, but I don't flinch. It's as if I knew he'd touch me at some point. I close my eyes and inwardly sigh, because his touch is a balm. He doesn't pull away either, as if he's trying to soothe me rather than summon my attention. For a long moment, I fantasize about his touch. Britta wouldn't wonder or fantasize though. She'd go exploring. Just like Sterling. Ugh.

I don't want to think about them, but when I clear my head, it's only to relive last night. The bite and burn of it all hurts so profoundly that I exhale audibly. I draw the classroom's attention. My cream-colored desk blurs before me, and when a painful cry escapes me, I jump to my feet and run.

I need air.

I sense someone following me, but I don't stop until I step outside.

I hear the door open, I hear him pull on the rug so the door doesn't lock behind us. I sit on the curb and bury my face in my knees.

Sterling threw me off course, but that was just the beginning. Without my dad, I'm lost. There's no getting back on track. My plan is falling apart, and I can't piece it back together.

I gasp for air. My face tingles, and when Jensen puts an arm around me, it feels like he's built out of heavy materials and his job is to shield me. From what, I don't know, because it's too late. I'm already broken.

"Take a deep breath, Nellie. You're hyperventilating."

"I can't." My voice is wheezy.

"Yes, you can."

I try. I try so hard. He coaches me, and we breathe together. After a few minutes, the tingling in my face fades. Then, very softly as if speaking to a child, he says, "Do you want to get out of here?"

I don't answer immediately.

He has to coax an answer out of me by asking again, and then taking my hand and asking once more.

Finally, I find my voice. "Yes."

"Good. I texted Britta. She's coming."

And all the anger in me toward her vanishes. She's coming. She's coming to hold me, and I need her. I don't know why he called her, but maybe it's because he can't handle another round of me bawling my eyes out.

I have no sense of time, but at some point, Britta arrives, holding a box of tissues. I take it, and she hugs me, and then the nonstop chatting begins.

She's so sorry, and I'm so strong to have come to school. And I probably aced Mr. Rose's final because I'm smart even when I'm sad and hurting, and then she hugs me again.

She's shades of white, which tells me that right now, her ego is tucked away. She's going to take care of me, and the sting begins to fade.

"What do you want to do?" she asks. "Have you eaten any-thing?"

"I doubt it," Jensen whispers.

I startle. I forgot he was still here. That's how out of it I am.

I think they keep talking, but my brain shuts off as I clutch her arm and rest my head on her shoulder.

"Okay, come on." When she guides me to her pickup, I mechanically obey.

She's there as I climb in, but Jensen doesn't follow. I'm oddly disappointed.

As Britta drives, she tells me about her government final, and she's still her animated self. I try to listen, but I'm thinking about her and Marbles, and only them, because it distracts me from everything else. They're not unkind to each other, but they're also not in the frosting phase anymore—the sugar-sweet stage of a relationship—so they snap at each other. Britta and Marbles don't make sense. Sometimes you have the stereotypical relationships, and other times, there's that one couple that makes you go "Hmm."

I don't ask Britta about him or their relationship status. Not because I don't care—I do—but I never ask because she always tells. But today, there's no update.

We end up at her favorite diner, and she asks to be seated in the back room.

"Is it just the two of you?" the hostess asks.

"No. There'll be eight."

"Who's coming?" I ask, but my question is ignored as a waitress says she'll push a table up to an empty booth.

"Scoot all the way in," Britta says to me.

I'm against the window, and she takes the other side and orders for me. Fries and a soda. Then, a laugh coming from the front of the restaurant pulls my attention. Sterling charms the waitress with a compliment, Marbles on his heels.

Britta is quick to slide out of the booth and greet them—well, to greet Marbles.

Marbles and Sterling are followed by Shanna Ferrer, Tomas Balderas, and Jeigh Meredith—which is weird because they're not that good of friends. Then I realize they're all TAs and were probably just bumming around. Sterling is a TA for a weight-lifting class. As if he'd assist any other class.

And behind them all is Jensen. His gaze meets mine, and I suddenly panic about who will sit next to me. It needs to be him.

"Found you," Marbles says as he sits down with Britta. He takes the window seat, so he's directly across from me. His feet touch mine, and I draw back. "Hiya, Nellie."

I force a response. "Hey."

My hands are clammy as I watch the rest of the gang find a seat. Jensen tries to snake around Sterling and Shanna, but Jeigh steps in front of them both and slides in next to me. The others file in, but Jensen ends up sitting last.

We're as far apart as we can possibly be while sitting at the same table.

We stare at each other for a moment, and then, as if we're afraid of being caught, glance away. But in that split second, I saw in his eyes what I feel in my whole body.

Jensen joins a conversation with Shanna about some college thing. I can't help but notice Shanna's homemade Blood Rock shirt. It's one of the better ones I've seen. Almost looks professional. Just last night, Jensen and I were talking about those books. Now, that feels like it was a light-year away.

I stare at my silverware. Food is ordered and delivered, and no one talks to me. They pass around the ketchup and salt, and Marbles's feet constantly bump mine, and he apologizes every time.

"Sorry about my long legs," he says.

It's the only thing anyone says directly to me.

But like a winter sunrise, I start to feel the warmth only Britta can spark. Why I ever thought it would just be the two of us is ridiculous. Eating out with friends is normal to her, and on any other day, it would be normal to me too. Slowly, the feeling of being surrounded by other human beings dulls the sharp images that are quickly becoming my demons.

My phone dings, and I find a message from Jensen.

You okay?

I'm quick to reply.

> Not so much.

Me either.

I'm smart, but I'm not always quick. He hasn't said much this whole time, probably because Shanna is still going on about college.

For the first time it occurs to me what last night must've been like for him. I hate that he was a witness. It must have been horrifying. At one point, my dad was like a father to him. Jensen even called him "Dad" when we were little, and no one ever corrected him.

I can't handle the thoughts that follow, so I try to listen to Jeigh's story, but the questions I'm trying to dam off overflow my weak barriers.

Does anyone know that Jensen was there?

What is Jensen telling others?

What does Jensen think now?

How come our friendship has suddenly changed?

Has my father's passing cemented our relationship in some way?

After yesterday and last night, any walls we unknowingly built between us over the years are totally pointless. We stare at each other, off and on, as if we can't focus on anything but each other.

Then I feel Britta's gaze on me. I'm quick to redirect my attention, because of course she'd be the one to notice the silent conversation Jensen and I are having. Fun fact: Body language speaks volumes. Fifty-five percent of communication is nonverbal. Why am I like this?

I avoid looking at her, and when the bill is due, no one asks me for any money.

Everyone parts ways, and Jensen and I share one last glance, and in that moment, I feel the pull to go to him. He is the Earth, and I am the Moon. Gravity holds us apart, but the tides are shifting. We know nothing is going to happen right now, and then with a nod at me, he's gone.

When my phone dings, it's him.

> We can talk later.

I warm from head to toe and tuck my phone away, hoping I look indifferent.

"So," Britta starts. "What's up with you and Jensen?

"Nothing."

"Okay, but you're lying."

I don't say anything, and she fills the silence between us by repeating everything that was said at lunch as if I wasn't there. Truthfully, I wasn't.

"That was weird, having them with us," she says, referring to Shanna, Jeigh, and Tomas. "But fun too."

Britta drives me back to school, walks with me to get my stuff, and then puts me in my car and tells me to go home and sleep, and that if I need anything, I can just text her. She'll be right there. Then, on second thought, she offers to come with me, suggesting that maybe I shouldn't be alone. And to be honest, she's probably right, but she's draining me.

"I'm fine," I say, needing some space. "Really."

"But we have a lot to talk about—that kiss, and Jensen, and your dad."

No one should be talking about their first kiss, how they're crushing on a different boy, and the passing of a parent at the same time. They're topics that shouldn't ever share a breath, but Britta's a shade of lavender. She's curious, and she wants details.

I'm infuriated that she'd even so casually want me to talk about any of it. It's insensitive. Uncaring. Unthinking.

"Are you kidding me?" All the anger I felt before at being tricked into a kiss rushes at me. "You were a part of that plan— to get me to vote—weren't you? You knew they'd pick me. You knew they'd say Sterling's name, Britta!"

"I thought you'd—"

"Be happy?"

"Yeah."

I glare, and it takes her a second to process that I'm upset. She starts to say something, but I cut her off.

"Don't. Just don't. I can't."

I slam my car door shut, but I can hear her yell.

"Wait, you're mad at me?" She's incredulous, as if my anger should be directed at Sterling. And it is, but she had a part in it too. If not, she would've adamantly professed otherwise.

I want to yell back, but I just drive. After a few blocks, I compartmentalize Britta. I'll deal with her later. New questions push at me, and "distracted driving" takes on a new meaning.

What's the plan for Dad's funeral?

How are we going to afford the house?

What are we going to do, now that he's gone?

Do I need a black dress?

When I pull onto my street, there's a black Camry parked in my driveway. I stop, confused. No one in our family drives a Camry. I go through the front door instead of the garage, and I regret it immediately.

On the love seat, my mom sits with a man I've never seen before. I don't catch any of his features because all I see is her pulling her hand out of his. And then we lock eyes. I see instant guilt in hers.

Mom rises to her feet; so does the guy. I bolt to my bedroom, but I hear her call my name.

I can't. I can't take one more thing.

I sit on my bed, backpack weighing me down, and try to breathe. I hear her talking to him, and then footsteps coming my way.

Hang on, she probably said. *Let me talk to her. Let me explain to my daughter that we're just friends.*

I don't want to talk to her. Were those tears last night even real? I'll bet she doesn't cry again. But even if she's steel on the outside, somewhere on the inside she has to be soft, right? Could she really spend the day planning her husband's funeral, only to come home and hold another man's hand? The fire that burned through me earlier rages hot.

I open my bedroom door before my mom can even knock.

"Don't," I say. My shoulder hits hers as I push past, and she doesn't say anything.

I stop dead in my tracks when I get into the living room, but I can't look the guy in the eye. I don't want to see what's there. Instead, I note the details. His black hair is chin-length. It would probably look great in a man-bun. His broad shoulders and muscles stand out because his shirt is too tight, and I hate him. He's the kind of sexy that my loving, devoted father wasn't. Mr. Home-Wrecker wears a sorry expression, but who is he to feel bad for me?

"Get out," I growl. "Get out, and don't come back."

I don't wait to see if he'll leave. I walk on, going straight to my car. I didn't shed my backpack, so I sling it across the seat before I get in. I don't even check for oncoming traffic when I pull away from the curb.

And I don't care that it's against the law to be on my phone. I call Jensen anyway. When he answers, I say, "Can I come over?"

CHAPTER 9

Is It a Game or a Test?

Nellie

"Yeah, no problem. I'll even put pants on."

"Whatever. You have pants on." His humor dispels my anger. He's magic like that.

"You don't know that."

I laugh, because I can picture him coming home and falling onto his couch in his boxers and a T-shirt and reaching for a game controller.

He adopts the voice of the Count from *Sesame Street* and says, "You're laughing. My work here is done!" and then cackles, "Ah, ah, ah," and I die. I haven't heard that voice in years. He seems to stitch me back together just before I fall apart.

We hang up, and my phone starts dinging with messages from my mom.

> Nellie, where are you?

> You can't just take off. You need to come home.

> If I have to call the cops, I will.

I want her to say, "Let me explain," but that message never comes. I'm not sure it ever will.

"I'll be fine, Mom," I say out loud. I'll be eighteen in a few short weeks, so I guess I'm ready to test her. Go ahead, call the cops.

I start to feel guilty, but my anger is stronger. Too many feelings are pressing me flat, but with a few deep breaths, I force myself to think.

What's the plan, Nellie?

Text her back and smooth things over. Then, avoid home. Spend time with Jensen. It's a decent plan.

As soon as I park in Jensen's driveway, I write out my message to her.

> I'll be home soon. For what it's worth, I have my backpack, a charger, and eleven dollars cash. But right now, I need to breathe. And I can't do that at home.

I usually get what I want by being mature and rational. I'm not sure I'm either of those things right now, but whatever.

I hit send.

Jensen opens the front door and waits for me. At first, it feels like I'm walking in thick mud, but by the time I'm standing before him, I feel lighter.

"My mom's not here," he says, his tone conspiratorial. It should probably give me pause, but it doesn't. It makes me smile.

"So what are we going to do?" I ask, dropping my backpack on the floor. I look around, remembering his house, and a flood of comfort comes over me. I feel safe here. I can breathe again.

"The world is our oyster," he says.

"What about Clay?"

"He doesn't live here anymore." Jensen sighs, and looks away from me. "He's at a care facility."

"I didn't know that."

"Yeah. It's been good for all of us. Don't get me wrong. We miss him." Jensen offers me a sad smile as if he's revealed himself too much.

"I am glad he's getting the care he needs, and in a way that lifts a burden off your mom."

"Me too."

"Speaking of her, she will be home eventually, right?"

"In like, an hour."

We're only a few inches apart. My heart thumps hard in my chest. "So, we need a world domination plan, and we have sixty minutes to execute it."

"Totally doable."

And then he grabs my shoulder and pulls me into a hug, and all the tension lodged between my shoulders dissipates. The warmth of his embrace pulls every cold tendril of fear and anxiety from me, and he lights the darkest corners of my soul. The most luxurious fabric in the world can't compare to his T-shirt, and I sink into him a little more, and it's interesting how a cut, hard body can be so soft. It's strange to experience desire right now, but I don't fight it. It's too hard to try to control everything, and so I run one hand over his shoulder and down to the small of his back.

His hug, his shirt, the smell of him—all of it. It's absolute perfection. I turn my face into him, and my lips inadvertently touch his neck. He hums against me. Oh my gosh—did I just kiss him? I didn't mean to.

"Sorry," I say, pulling back. "I'm sorry. I didn't—"

"It's okay. Don't freak out. Just . . . let it slide, okay?" he says, and I nod.

"You wanna sit down?" he asks.

"Yeah, sure."

We sit on the couch, and I'm awkward now. I wasn't awkward when we had homework, but this is different. I don't know what to say. He's fall-day-cool as he pulls me closer to him. He's all the colors of autumn, and right now, I just want to be his favorite jacket.

He pulls up some of his favorite online videos, and even though my body relaxes, my brain does not because I can't stop thinking about what just happened.

Did that even count as a kiss? If he liked it, why didn't he make a move?

I'm afraid of the answers, so I bury the questions deep inside of me. I don't have the energy to take this kind of test. It's an exam I'll most likely fail, too, because how do you know what the score is?

And is he even taking the same test?

Still, he seems to want me close, and heaven knows I want him close, and there's no reason to fight it, I suppose. I don't have a wedding ring on my finger.

And just like that, my own possible happiness is chased away by the bitter thought of my mom holding hands with that man.

Jensen and I don't say anything as we watch video after video, and when his phone's battery starts to wane, we turn it off. But we don't move.

I trace the faint scar on his knuckle and ask him how he got it, and as he recounts the story, I close my heavy eyes.

The sound of Jensen's voice is captivating. There's something about the way he blends his words together. He lulls me into a hypnotic state, and when he ends his story, he's tracing the lines of my palm. When he looks up at me, I meet his gaze, and for a split second, I know the answer to one question.

Yes. He wants to kiss me.

He clears his throat and pushes himself to his feet.

So there's an unknown factor. Great. But before the cold wave of complete rejection crushes me, he extends both his hands toward me.

I weigh my options only briefly. Not taking them means I'm rejecting him, and I don't want that. The only way to solve this equation is to do the math—old-school if necessary. One step at a time, solving for each variable as we go.

So I take his warm, strong hands. The hands that sketch rocket ships and catch footballs and trace lines on mine.

As if he's calculating every move, he slowly puts one hand on my shoulder, his thumb stroking my collarbone. At this, my hand does its own thing and takes hold of his hip, and I hook my pinkie through a belt loop. And we just stand there, connected like there's a huge plus sign between us.

He leans in, resting his cheek against my forehead.

"What are we doing?" he murmurs, his words humming through my whole body. I'm surprised by his question. I feel like he should know.

"I've taken AP chemistry, and there's nothing in the books about this."

He doesn't laugh. Instead, his hand travels up my neck, and he gently tightens his grip, and that's when I think: *He's going to kiss me.*

But then he leans back, just a bit. "You're right, Samsin. This isn't in any *chemistry* book. Come on," he says, taking me to the kitchen.

I'm trying to decipher what he means and why he didn't kiss me and what's happening, but before I come to a definitive conclusion, he's got me, hands linked like we're compound elements.

The Band-Aid on my finger is a subtle reminder of last night, and déjà vu sweeps through me, but I'm not afraid of it.

He produces a bag of Doritos. Nothing kills a potential kiss like a bag of cheese-flavored chips. I swear he wanted to kiss me. Is it possible he chickened out?

Just then, the back door swings open. It's his mom, Sumerli. Her name reflects her personality. She's wearing a blue infinity scarf, a jean jacket, and black leather boots. Her silky brown hair is braided to the side, and her makeup is perfection. Even Britta would agree.

When Sumerli sees me, she rushes to my side and pulls me into a hug. I smile and eventually I return her embrace. She holds on for dear life, and I begin to feel the weight of it. She knows pain, and as she tightens her hold, I struggle not to lose control. This is the kind of hug my mom should have given me last night. Or today after school.

Jensen meets my gaze, and mouths "Sorry," and with that one word, the world shifts and I find my footing. We smile at each other as his mother continues to hold me, and somewhere in the back of my brain, I know there's health benefits to physical touch, but the facts are elusive. The energy I felt before returns as Sumerli sighs and squeezes me, and I remember something. I remember how I feel about this woman.

I freaking love her, so I squeeze her back before we part.

"Now," she says, locking eyes with me, "you need to eat."

"I don't, not really."

"Well, I do. Which means you have to."

I laugh at this as she takes us back in time, to a time of grilled cheese sandwiches, popsicles, microwave popcorn, and oven-baked corn dogs. Those were the days, I suppose.

Sumerli fixes us French dip sandwiches, which seem more grown-up. And she doesn't ask any probing questions about why I'm there or how I'm feeling. She pours herself a drink of water, but then, as if we are still little, she fills two tall glasses with chocolate milk. Maybe not the perfect drink and sandwich combo ever, but today, it works. Then we all sit down to eat. Jensen seems embarrassed, which is cute. I add that to the growing list of things I like about him.

After Jensen finishes his first sandwich, he announces, "We skipped school today."

"Who is *we*, and what did you do?" Sumerli asks, barely looking up from her plate. She's completely unfazed, her expression neutral, as if this is typical for Jensen.

This kind of announcement would not be cool with my mom. Her face would redden, and she'd give me a stern look. I'd explain but she'd remain silent, and when I was done, she'd remind herself that I was, like, still alive and stuff.

"Just a bunch of us—the guys, Britta Tayvier, some of her friends. We took Nellie out to lunch. It helped, I think. Nellie?"

"Oh, sure. Pin this on me!" I say.

Sumerli laughs, a sparkly, bubbly sound that makes me laugh. I didn't realize it was so distinct. "Did it help, Nellie? Or is Jensen telling me a whopper?"

Jensen coughs on his drink. "Hey, Mom? Grandma called and she wants her verbiage back."

"Of course she called. She's a terrible texter, and she told me that you're a nerd for using a word like *verbiage*."

They banter and tease each other, and a ping of jealousy runs through me. I circle back around to Sumerli's question, thinking about how Jensen was there for me when I lost it in class, how he summoned Britta—which I understand why—and how I wanted to sit next to him at lunch.

"Yes," I say when they're done laughing. "Lunch helped."

"Then, good for you," Sumerli says. "Jensen, did you pay for Nellie?"

"Not this time."

"Jensen."

"It's okay, Mrs. Nichols." I hate to think she's worried about money. I'm glad she doesn't jump online to transfer funds around to cover a seven-dollar expense. "Britta paid. It was her idea, anyway."

"She didn't, actually," Jensen adds. "Sterling covered it."

"All of it?" I can't imagine Sterling doing that.

"Yeah. You're surprised?" Jensen says.

"Very."

"Sterling's good at putting up a front," Sumerli says, "but he's also very generous."

I'm about to say as much, thinking how *generous* he was with me, but Jensen changes the subject, and it's probably a good thing. I suppose it's better than getting into an argument about Sterling and his generosity.

"Nellie's valedictorian," he says to his mom. Then he turns to me. "They told you, what, last week?"

"Yeah."

"Doctor Nellie Samsin, astrophysicist."

When Jensen says it, my whole body overheats.

"Can you even spell that word, Jensen?" Sumerli teases. Then she turns her smile to me. "What does an astrophysicist do, exactly?"

I wish my mom would ask me that question. But no, she sees it as a waste of time, to study the heavens. *What good does it do us, when we're only here for eighty-ish years?*

"Research. Lots and lots of research," I say. "It's the universe, the cosmos, the study of dark matter and the fundamental physical laws."

I can tell I'm losing her, but she's trying to follow me, so I give her the other side of it.

"I could also teach—chemistry, physics, all the math."

"That's incredible," Sumerli says. "And it sounds like a lot of work."

"It's a lot of school," Jensen says.

"I like school," I say.

"And you're good at it," he says.

"Thanks. It's taken lots of work to get to this point, but being valedictorian was always a part of the plan."

A plan originally initiated by my dad. The weight of this bears down on me, but I don't think they notice.

The plan was that he'd be here, that he'd cheer me on, and that he'd move me into my apartment for college, and my mom would tag along.

Suddenly, I go still and stare at my plate, and just when I think I'm going to buckle beneath the weight of my own comment, I feel Jensen's hand on my thigh. He squeezes softly, and it draws my gaze upward.

"You've probably had your speech written since third grade," Jensen says and then he takes a big drink of his milk.

"No." I laugh softly and so does Sumerli, but then I have to admit the truth. "But I—I did write a draft my sophomore year."

Jensen laughs so hard, I think he's going to snort chocolate milk. Instead, he mentions that, as class president, I'll be responsible for all the class reunions. When he proudly tells his mom about my scholarship to UNLV, I try not to blush, but I can't help it. But it's Sumerli's incandescent smile that knocks me off balance. Mom never smiles at me like that.

And my dad will never smile at me again.

"Excuse me," I say, jumping to my feet. My voice quivers, and my fingers tremble.

"Sure," Jensen says, as I step out of the kitchen.

I remember this house, and I know where the bathroom is. I know that Jensen's room is on the right, and his bedroom door is open, but my vision is blurring by the second, and I need a tissue, now.

I lock myself in the bathroom, close the toilet lid, and sit down. I force myself to breathe slowly and deeply. I blot at my mascara, knowing that holding my tears at bay won't keep my eyes from turning red and puffy. I hate that I have to blow my nose. After a few minutes, I run some cold water over my hands, and then turn my wrists into the stream.

It's a trick I learned in health class. The colder the better, and in thirty-second increments, the cold water will significantly lower the temperature of the blood in my arms, which will help my whole body cool down. I focus on my breathing, and when my hands are ice-cold, I dry them and press them to my cheeks. I'm starting to feel better.

I'm nervous that Sumerli will call my mom. I'm afraid that I'll hear a knock on the door, and my mother's voice on the other side. That's not something I can handle.

My stomach tightens, but before I melt into another puddle, I dig out my phone and stare at the insta-call icon for Britta. Britta will come save me, I know she will, but her coping mechanisms might be worse than facing my mom. I close my phone, not wanting to deal with her high energy right now.

I'm a wreck, and I'm not sure what I'm going to do, but when I unlock the door and crack it open, I realize I've been in hiding for too long. I can't hear Sumerli and Jensen talking, which isn't good. All I hear is the soft clinking of dishes being loaded into the dishwasher. The sun is starting to set, and the hallway is dim. The glow from the kitchen is all my tired eyes can handle.

I move quietly and peer around the corner.

Jensen is alone, doing the dishes. His shoulders sag, and he leans on the counter. His hair, which is usually perfect, sticks out all over the place, like he's run both hands through it with wet fingers. He looks out the window for a long moment, and I lean against the wall, watching him. With his back to me, I notice his lean body even more than I did before. He's really beautiful, and he always has been.

Before he catches me staring, I announce myself.

"Hey," I say, grabbing our empty glasses from the table and bringing them to the sink.

I can't help but notice how he wipes at his face with the back of his hand. My senses kick in instantly, and I wonder if he's sad for me, or sad for himself. He loved my dad. My dad loved him, and even though there's been years of separation, that doesn't erase all the good that once was.

"Hey back," he manages.

"I'm sorry—I'm sorry I ran off like that."

"There's no need to explain." I notice how red-rimmed his eyes are.

"I don't want to go home, but maybe I need to?"

I'm honest with him. I don't want to leave, but I also don't want him to feel trapped.

"You don't have to go."

"Are you sure? Where's your mom?"

"Yeah. We're good. Every night after dinner, she goes to see Clay."

"And you didn't go?"

"Not this time."

Guilt trickles down my back. I am sick that he stayed here for me. I'm about to say so, but he opens his mouth first.

"I—did you finish your calculus assignment? I'm not done. I could use some help if you're up to it."

I purse my lips, knowing this is a lie. He doesn't need my help. But maybe he doesn't want to be alone either. So I offer him a closed-lip smile, and we go back to the couch to work, and somewhere around midnight, he insists on driving me home, in my car.

I sigh with relief when I see that the Camry is gone.

"Thanks," I manage, and what I mean is thanks for everything—for last night, for today, for dinner, for cheering me up and for holding me when I was falling apart, but I don't say all that. I just hope he knows.

"You're welcome. And thanks for the help. I might actually pass calculus, thanks to you."

He slides a hand over, and I take it. We sit there for a long time, staring at our laced fingers. I draw strength from him, like an emotional vampire. Always taking, never giving. But then again, not everyone sees vampires as awful. Maybe, just maybe, Jensen is drawing strength from me, the way I pull it from him.

What are we doing? His words play over and over in my mind. I have no idea what to make of us. When it's time for me to go, I keep my voice low. I don't want this moment to end, but it has to.

"Why don't you just take my car home and pick me up in the morning?" He looks like he's about to say no, but I beat him to it. "Seriously. It makes sense."

"Okay."

I wanted him to kiss me earlier, but now, all I feel is the need to be seen, and it's like he knows this. As if everything we're feeling and thinking can be conveyed without words, his brown eyes anchor me to reality, which is both painful and needed in order to keep me from floating adrift into a universe of dark matter and dark stars, lost in a black hole of nothingness.

I wonder what he sees, what he feels, when he looks at me.

It takes most of my energy to let go of his hand, and after I shut the car door, he rolls down the passenger window.

"I'll see you in the morning, Nellie Samsin."

And then, he's gone.

My mom is out cold. She doesn't even flinch when I crack

her door open to tell her I'm home. I wouldn't be surprised if she drank herself to sleep. I'm exhausted, but sleep seems impossible. I stand there for a long minute, staring at her. The hard lines that frame her are still there when she sleeps, like her scowl and the crinkle in her nose have become permanent.

When I turn to leave, I notice she's already started packing up my dad's things. I leave with a heavy sigh, pretending I didn't see the flannel, the dress shirts, the ties, or jeans.

There's a piece of paper on the kitchen counter that draws my attention as I grab a drink of water.

From what I can tell, my mom is ordering death certificates, but my attention drops to one word at the bottom of the page. Aneurysm. Mom's written it out and underlined it.

I set the note down and take a step back as the word grows.

Aneurysm. A brain aneurysm.

At first, I barely react, but then like a light bulb popping, something inside of me snaps. I take a photo of the paper and send it to Jensen without explanation. He won't need one.

I sure don't.

I crawl into bed and stare at the ceiling, haunted by thoughts of the circulatory system. I hate that I took a college anatomy and physiology class so I know what an aneurysm is without Googling. I hate that I know that a blood vessel in my father's brain was weak, and that it ballooned and ruptured. I hate that I know aneurysms are rare, and that most of us aren't walking time bombs, but then I think of how heart disease is the leading cause of death, and that if he'd had a stroke, he probably would've survived.

But he was rare, so naturally he died in a rare way. And my soul takes a beating, leaving divots and dings as I lie perfectly still, until there's a hole in my heart.

I can't sleep, and when I finally shift my weight, I notice a gift bag on my desk. It's pink with zebra-striped tissue paper.

I turn on my lamp and reach for it. There's a note inside.

N—

I know you didn't mean to get mad at me earlier
today. These are some of my favorite things to
have when I'm upset. I always feel amazing when my
makeup is on point, when I have my favorite treat,
and when I feel pretty. I know you need help with
these things, so here you go.

Britta

Her gifts include a pink tube of waterproof mascara, a jumbo
bag of dark chocolate, and pink lace. It's underwear from Victoria's
Secret. I try to convince myself that she knew we wouldn't get to
the laundry this week. Hot tears roll over my cheeks, but I don't
want to cry. I'm so tired of crying.

I tuck the note and items back into the bag and set it on the
ground. I try to compartmentalize all the feelings that come at
me, but mostly I suffocate as my lungs refuse to work.

CHAPTER 10

One More Drawing

Jensen

By the time I get home from dropping Nellie off, my mom has texted me twice. However, her messages aren't urgent—they're informative.

Clay's had another grand mal seizure, so she's staying longer than she'd anticipated. I'm supposed to *get Nellie home, and get to bed, young man,* but her message is followed by a bunch of hearts and smiley faces.

I'm raw with emotions I do *not* want to name, so I play an hour's worth of video games before I finally crash. I wish I could've kept Nellie here all night, and yet, that's a bit extreme.

But in my still lucid but mostly asleep state, I conjure up a plan for next time. Just having her near makes all the difference, because the minute she's gone, the ghouls come crawling back.

I ignore the first one, not wanting to think about Sean. The second creature is one I know intimately. The shadows that haunt me are constant, whispering that I'm an imposter, a liar, a fake. I'm not a real author. I'm just some kid who wrote a story and got people to pay for it. And then there's the twin terror that follows—someone, somewhere, is going to come and take it all away.

And that someone has a name.

I push back, refusing to give Kohl Nichols, my biological father, any space. I'm able to slay this demon. I've had lots of practice. He's not a part of my life at all, but he regenerates every time.

Somehow I know I'm asleep, and yet, I can't wake up to clear my head. Which is why I startle when a hand touches my shoulder.

"Jensen," Mom says. "You're sweating."

I sit up as if I've been awake all night to find myself in the living room, drenched in my own sweat.

"Sorry."

"It's okay," she says. "Are you sick?"

"No. I think it was just a bad dream."

"Do you want some Ambien or Tylenol PM?"

Maybe nightmares are a part of grief—and because I'm unable to disconnect from my writing side, some part of me makes a mental note. When I need to convey Hagon's grief next, I can use this.

I hate my brain.

"Sure."

She goes to get the pills, and then watches like a diligent nurse until I've taken them. She follows me to my room as I crawl into my own bed. She ruffles my hair and kisses my forehead.

"Love you, kiddo," she whispers.

When morning comes, I ache everywhere. I'd rather puke my guts out than feel like this. Things improve slightly when I smell bacon.

I holler, "Morning," in the direction of the kitchen, Mom calls back, and then I step into the shower, hoping the hot water will fix everything.

My mom and I have grown comfortable in our routines, and she's given me space to do my thing. I'm debating crawling back into bed and staying there all day, knowing she won't care. But then I think about Nellie, and seeing her, and driving her to school, and it's all the motivation I need. I'm dressed when Nellie messages me and asks if I'm ready.

Affirmative.

Then I text Sterling and tell him I don't need a ride for the rest of the year, since I didn't say anything to him yesterday, too numb to think.

He actually asks why, but I don't respond. Mom tells me to stay out of trouble, and the look in her eyes says she's not kidding. She pauses at the door, then turns to me.

"I think you need to write. Maybe not on your manuscript, but you should write down what you want to remember about him. Love you, kiddo. I'll see you later."

I nod, but the thought of writing anything is about as remote as Scotland's hills. It's too far away and too cold.

Minutes later, I pick up Nellie.

"Hey," she says as she slips into the seat next to me.

"Hey back."

"So, the funeral is Saturday."

Her tone is almost indifferent, but for me, the statement is a knife to my gut.

I don't want to see Sean lying in a coffin, eyes closed, skin falsely pink from the mortician's makeup. The thought makes my stomach turn, and as horrible as it is, I question whether or not I've described death accurately in my books. If not, it's too late. Sokha's brother's demise cannot be rewritten.

I am a fraud.

Before my thoughts take me down a path that I can't navigate, I clear my throat, and look away in order to ask a hard question. "You want to talk about it?"

"Not really. But, Jensen? Will you take me?"

"To the funeral?"

"And the viewing."

"You're not going with—you're not going with your mom?"

"I'd rather not."

We ride in silence for a few minutes, her glossy lips in a line. I start bouncing my knee at red lights, hoping she'll tell me more.

Eventually, she says, "Yesterday, when I got home, my mom was on the couch."

"Okay?"

"And some guy was with her."

"Okay."

"He was holding her hand."

"Oh," I say, and then process. No, I rationalize. Maybe this guy was just trying to comfort her. It doesn't necessarily mean anything. "Is that it?"

"Jensen!"

"No, I'm just saying, was that it? Hand-holding? Maybe he was trying to console her."

I want this story to have an easy and reasonable explanation.

"There was a vibe. Definitely not just friends. And then we got into a fight this morning about what I'm going to wear to the funeral. She bought this ugly black dress for me. And then there's Britta. You don't even want to know . . . I'm just so . . ."

I can't focus, and she's a mess. What are we doing—going to school? We should do something else. Something not-school.

"I'm pretty sure I'm going to flunk my finals," she says.

"Nah, your brain would never let you."

"You overestimate me."

"No, I don't."

"What do you think happens if I don't show up to take my finals?" she asks.

"They pass you anyway. Teacher's pet and all that."

She gives me a light chuckle, but it doesn't stick, and the melancholy returns immediately.

"What do you think happens if *you* don't show up?" she asks.

"I'm no Nellie Samsin." I've got good grades, but I can't let go completely—not quite yet. I have to hold on with everything I've got. I'm in a on-again, off-again Hollywood relationship with my writing right now, and there's no telling when it will come to an abrupt stop.

I'm officially in a toxic relationship.

Meanwhile, I've got finals, graduation, my mom and Clay, and my reputation. Plus, there's the impending promise I made to my assistant—the big reveal of who I really am. Which I'm fine with, once I put all this other stuff behind me.

"I'll be fine. Where do you want to go?" I finally say, because she's asking me to skip school in not so many words. I answer her previous question too. "And I'll take you to your father's funeral."

"What about the All-Nighter?"

That one's easy to answer. "Definitely taking you to that."

The All-Night Lock-In is being held at the Waterford Event Center. It's to celebrate, they say. In reality, it's to prevent us from drinking. We have to check in by ten, or we're locked out. Once in, we can leave, but there's no readmittance. I'm sure Sterling's got plans for me that night, but I don't care. I'd rather be with Nellie, spending the night rotating from the craps tables to the fortune teller to the henna tattoo artist and eating until we're sick.

At a red light, I quickly group email my teachers who are holding finals today.

I don't know what to say, other than the truth. *I'm with Nellie Samsin, who's really struggling right now. What arrangements can be made for me to take my finals later?*

Since Nellie never said where to go, I pull into the parking lot of the mall. Mr. Simmons, my AP history teacher, replies first. He's understanding, but firm. I have to be in school tomorrow to make up his final or he'll be forced to give me a zero. So instead of having two finals tomorrow, I'll have three.

What if Nellie wants me to skip school tomorrow too?

I push the concern away, since I'm counting eggs before chickens, when I see something weird. We're walking into the mall when I spot a mom with two preteens in tow. She has double French braids, tips dyed pink like Sokha's. Not the young girls. *The mom.* It's so weird. I turn my attention to the shiny new Tacoma pickup on display. I make Nellie stop and enter the drawing.

"I won't win," she says, as she fills out the form. She even rolls her eyes at me.

"Maybe not, but you won the last drawing you entered."

She actually laughs out loud, and I'm so glad, because her

laugh makes me smile, and it's just enough light to keep out the darkening shadows. She pushes me, and I catch her by the arm and pull her closer. After stuffing the ballot into the overfilled box, we walk away, hands linked.

She leans in and puts her head on my shoulder, which for Nellie Samsin is quite bold. I wonder why she does it. Is it because she's vulnerable and lost without her dad? Maybe it's because I was there when we found Sean. Or does she actually like me?

My spine tightens, and my whole body goes rigid. If it's not the latter, I'm being used.

"I feel like I've won the lottery when I'm with you, Jensen."

"You're delirious."

"That might be true," she whispers.

We duck into a store full of oddities and pop culture items, T-shirts, and fandom gear. She gravitates toward items that seem more like Britta than Nellie—*Supernatural*, Superman, and super-heroes. She pulls a Hello Kitty purse from its hanger and drapes it over my shoulder.

"I love it," I say.

I find a pair of fuzzy handcuffs and hold them up, and Nellie chuckles hard and then turns away, blushing. *Good.*

When we finally leave, I hear the clerk sigh with relief and then swear under his breath since we didn't buy anything.

I pull Nellie into Barnes and Noble, and we spend way too much time discussing books. I say nothing about the authors I've met at conferences. I don't tell her that the book she holds in her hands has a weak plot.

I manage to keep thoughts of my own work from piercing through the thin veil that's holding my real life at bay. I have a weird relationship with bookstores. I hate them, and I love them.

When we work our way to a department store, I know it's to find a black dress. She turns serious as she hunts, and I expect she'll ask me my opinion. I'm a bundle of knots at the idea of commenting yay or nay on a dress meant to commemorate some-one's life. She pulls two off the rack and drapes them over her arm. We walk over to the dressing rooms, and I'm pleased to find a bench for me to sit on.

"Be right back?" she says.

"I'll wait right here."

She comes out in the first dress, and it's as standard as funeral attire goes. Calf-length, ruffled, high neck collar, with cap sleeves. It's nice, simple and solemn, even, and maybe it's more to Nellie's taste than the one her mother picked out. She asks me nothing, but holds up a finger and disappears.

When she comes out in the second one, my face gives me away. The plunging neckline is the first thing I see. The only thing, really. It's got a straight-cut skirt that hits her mid-thigh. Long sleeves. A black belt that accentuates her waist.

"You like this one," Nellie says.

"You look amazing."

"My mother will hate it."

"Britta will love it," I say, knowing it couldn't be more true.

"Let's not talk about her."

Again, I have questions, but I swallow them. If she doesn't want to talk about Britta, that's fine with me. "Okay."

"Okay, let me change."

Nellie slips back into the changing stall, and my attention wanders to the men's section. I've got some nice slacks and a white shirt, but I want to look as good as I can standing next to her.

She hangs the first dress on the rejection rack, and I lead us over to the men's section.

"I need a suit, and I need it by Friday," I say to the sales clerk. "I have a funeral on Saturday."

"I can't have one ready by Saturday," the woman says, "unless you pay extra for next-day alterations. The soonest I could have a suit ready otherwise isn't until next week."

"Price doesn't concern me."

The woman proceeds to take my measurements, and I watch as Nellie studies me with curiosity.

Price doesn't concern you? she mouths.

I just wink.

We comb through the suits until I find the right one, and I pair it with a black shirt and a striped black-on-black tie. I drop everything on the counter, including Nellie's dress, and pay for all of it.

Nellie's eyes are huge. I can tell she's biting back her questions.

When we leave, we're physically prepared for a funeral—though neither of us is really ready—and I brace myself for her inquiry.

"Jensen," she says, as soon as we're away from the clerk.

"What?"

"You wanna explain to me—like, how? I mean, I thought . . ." She's gone pale, perhaps feeling awkward or embarrassed.

"You're wondering how I can afford that, since I'm poor."

"Well, no. I mean, yeah, but I'm sorry. I'm just so confused."

"I am poor. But Sterling is rich, and he lost a bet. So his money is mine. Not a lot, but it was worth the gamble." The lie rolls off my tongue, and it must be credible enough, because she accepts it.

"So Sterling just bought my dress."

"No. I bought it. Does it matter where the money comes from? It's mine. It's in my account."

"No, not unless it's like drug money or something."

"It's not. I promise. It's just blood money." *Blood Rock money.*

She laughs, and I feel rather devious, and I like it. I don't love lying to her, but for now, I must.

From that moment until Saturday morning, Nellie and I spend all our spare time together. She picks me up the next morning, and we both spend the day taking finals and catching up on the work we missed. We avoid the masses by hanging out in her car before school and at lunch, and as soon as the bell rings, we skirt out of there. We don't talk to or text our friends. We've noticed their stares, but we don't have it in us to care.

Instead, I focus on making her laugh, because it eases the ache that's taken up residency inside of me. We hold hands and hug, and she plays with my hair, and we waste my phone battery watching videos and listening to music. Not a bad way to spend our time. And when we part ways, it takes everything I have not to kiss her.

I want to. Man, I want to, and making out with Nellie might be a great way to cope with Sean's death. I've nearly kissed her a dozen times, especially after she basically kissed my neck the other day. Since then, there have been several missed opportunities. I'm sure I'm sending mixed messages, but everything we're dealing with is confusing. Still. I'm holding out because I want this to last beyond graduation. I want our first kiss to be perfect. Perfect timing, perfect setting, because she's perfect. Perfect to me.

So when it's time to say goodbye on Friday night, I hold on to her for an extra minute. True to character, Nellie spouts off some facts about how therapeutic a twenty-second hug is and how the vagus nerve system delivers the messages to the organs in the body, including the heart. Apparently, the pituitary gland releases more oxytocin, which helps reduce stress.

But all I can think about is the message she's sending my body with hers.

"You should appreciate the health benefits of my hug," she says, completely oblivious.

I laugh softly, and then hug her tighter. Oh, I appreciate them. Truth is, I can't breathe when she's gone.

CHAPTER 11

A New Plan

Nellie

Saturday mornings I usually sleep in, but I'm not sure I'll ever sleep well again. I'm numb as I shower and indifferent when I hear my mother calling my name. "Move faster" is all she says. But I can't.

I find it interesting that she hasn't dictated any other expectations or demands over the last couple days. Actually, she hasn't said a word about me being constantly gone. A part of me wonders if she's given up on me. We aren't speaking to each other. We're just stating facts and times and making announcements.

"I'm riding with Jensen," for example.

Mom looks up at me, her hair perfectly curled, her black dress indicating that she's a widow, now. But all I really see is that she's not wearing her wedding ring.

"You've been spending a lot of time with Jensen," she says, and then she walks away.

I want to yell, *Where's your ring?* as she slips out of view, but I don't. Instead, I set my blow-dryer down and listen to the back door open and close, and then the garage door, and then the silence drowns me. I stand there, alone, and despite the brittle texture of my friendship with Britta right now, I am thankful for the waterproof mascara.

And the creators of Visine eye drops.

My mom's a mess, and I'm not much better. We're simply coexisting like a cat and dog forced to live under the same roof.

But I've found another home where I'm loved. They feed me.

They pet me. I get the sense they'd let me sleep there every night if I wished it. And I wish it.

I love how much time Jensen and I have spent together, and since Britta has habitually abandoned me in the past to spend time with her boy-of-the-month, I feel completely justified. If she really cared about me, she wouldn't have sabotaged my first kiss. She wouldn't have tried to cheer me up with underwear.

I don't know what's gotten into her lately, but it's like she doesn't know me at all.

I turn the blow-dryer back on and work the heat through my hair. For a change, my locks behave. I'm a rock star as I work it into a style I rarely wear. I give it a soft curl and leave the ends razor sharp, using a pomade to hold them in place. I'm curves and edges, today. And since no one will know, I slip into the underwear Britta gave me, because she was right about one thing. Looking good helps me feel good. And because the laundry didn't get done.

Then, I pull on my dress. Mom hasn't seen it. And once she does, it'll be too late for her to send me home to change. My thoughts turn to Jensen's ability to pay for it. So strange. What bet did he make with Sterling?

The long necklace I chose to wear is cold against my skin, and after I step into my shiny, nude heels, I have nothing left to do. I stand in front of the mirror.

I'm ready, though that's hardly the truth.

When Jensen arrives, he looks incredible. He's ebony on a moonless night, and for a split second, I'm insanely jealous of every girl he's ever taken to a dance. A twinge of regret settles on my shoulders, but I can't linger on that. Side by side, we look ready for a photo shoot.

We stare at each other like it's a competition to see who will smirk or smile first. And this time, I win.

His lip twitches a couple times before he relents, and I'm breathless when he shakes his head at me, a coy smile on his lips.

"You look so pretty."

"Thanks. You're not so bad either."

"In this old thing?" The weight of where we're headed presses on us. "Are you ready?"

I hesitate, because no. I'm not ready. No one is ever ready for this, but I nod anyway. He escorts me to the car.

He's borrowed his mom's Traverse. It's spotlessly clean and smells like leather.

It's a really nice car, I realize, having never been in it.

I thought I'd want silence, but he's got a song playing that reminds me of my dad, and it makes me smile.

"I know this song," I say, though I haven't heard it in ages.

"'You're the Inspiration' by Chicago," he says.

"Yeah, that's right."

"I made a playlist of all the songs I could remember your dad playing for us. This one sort of stuck with me."

"You did?"

"I'll send it to you, if you want."

"I would like that very much." I recognize the next song too. "He really was a huge fan of power ballads," I say.

"Accurate."

I think back to when Dad would sing to my mom, and how she'd sway in his embrace, and they'd laugh while dancing in the living room. I distinctly remember jumping on the couch, and my mom not yelling at me.

It's a beautiful memory, one that comes back full force with the music.

"This is amazing," I say as I turn up the music. It's the best thing anyone's done to honor my dad all week.

When we arrive at the funeral home, Jensen mutes the mix, rolls down the window, and tells the usher who we are. The man instructs us to pull in behind the two cars that are parked behind the hearse. Though he calls it a coach, and all I can think about is how a coach is a form of transportation for royalty. There should be horses and a driver if it's a coach.

Of course, we'll be at the front of the procession, so we can follow the casket to the cemetery.

We go through the front doors, and Jensen leads the way. I look at my feet as he guides me past a line of people. Every face is an acquaintance, a friend, a colleague—someone who cared about my dad—and I wish I had it in me to meet their sad expressions and forlorn looks, but I can't. I don't want to see the look in their eyes or hear them whisper things like, "Look how grown-up Nellie is" or "She's so young."

There's laughter in the distance, and I'm offended to think someone finds something funny right now, here, of all places. I want to deck them for disturbing the peace. Other than that, there's some instrumental music playing and a low-grade hum of voices, and tissues at every turn. I realize the line of people is a greeting line that leads into the chapel. The whole place smells of lilies and roses and decay.

When we get closer, I spot my mom standing at the foot of the casket. She sees me, and my dress, and her expression tightens. People give us space as we approach.

I never came to see him—when they were preparing his body. I didn't want to, and Mom didn't make me. She handled all the arrangements and never asked for my opinion on what casket to get or what songs to play or what he should wear. I'm not sure I would've had the answers, if she had.

She picked out a nice one though. I guess. It's stainless steel and sapphire blue, the color of my soul these days, and I can't stop looking at it. I'm too afraid to look at him, to be honest. He's wearing a light-gray suit with a red tie, but that's as far as I let my eyes travel.

My fear takes hold, and I freeze. I can't—I can't look at his face. I can't have the last image of him be this, but I also can't have the last image be what I saw that night. Everything is awful, and I want to run away, but I can't. I won't. Because Jensen hasn't let go of me, and as his hand finds the small of my back, he whispers into my ear.

"It's okay, Nellie."

He is my backbone, and when I let go of him, it's because I know he'll be there for me when I return.

I walk to my father's side, all eyes on me, but I don't see the crowd. I don't see my mother blot at a tear or glance at her sister. All I see is my father, and he looks like he's sleeping. I spare a glance at Jensen, and wordlessly, he encourages me to keep going.

I hesitantly reach for my father's hand, knowing he'll be cold, but he's my dad—and I'm here to say goodbye. My love for him rises like water boiling. It turns and forms small bubbles at first until bubble by bubble, it rises to the surface, until it's too much, and spills over the sides. The shape of him dissolves as tears fill my eyes.

I withdraw my hand, visibly quivering, and then Jensen's there. He puts his arm around me, supportive and strong. I take and take from Jensen, until I have strength to say goodbye. I whisper, but the room has gone quiet, and everyone can hear me.

"You're the best dad. You were nice to everyone, and I wish I could talk to you again. I miss you so much, and I'm not sure how to keep going on without you. I love you, Daddy."

When I step back, I raise my chin a little.

I take several steps before I realize Jensen hasn't followed me. When I turn around, I see him standing next to the casket; he's whispering something.

Whatever Jensen has to say is between him and my dad, and I don't need to know.

I wish I could go back in time and get a photo of the three of us, of my dad reading to us both or pushing us on the swing set. Anything, honestly.

When Jensen knocks on the casket's edge one time, the whole room goes from paused to play. Everything kicks back into gear, and I finally notice faces and the funeral staff passing out cups of water.

"Should we sit down?" Jensen says, his voice lacking its usual beauty and inflection.

"Yeah," I say, searching the room for an empty seat. Before we get far, my mom is there, blocking our path.

A small part of my brain says this is when Jensen's going to turn and run because my mom is intimidating.

Before he can do anything, I say, "I'll be right back. Will you be okay?" I'm a complete coward, but I don't want to hear anything she might have to say to me right now.

"Of course. I'll wait right here."

He's good at that—waiting for me—and I need to make sure to thank him.

I head straight to the bathroom, but I'm stopped left and right by my dad's colleagues and friends.

Eventually, I make it to the bathroom, and by the time I get back to Jensen, I feel terrible for abandoning him. That feeling intensifies when I find him sitting in a corner, all alone, and it looks like he's been crying. I am the worst.

When he sees me, he quickly stuffs the tissue he's holding into his pocket and smiles.

"I'm so sorry," I say. "It was like the freaking paparazzi back there."

"It's okay. The paparazzi loves you."

"I doubt that. They mostly pity me, I think."

He doesn't say anything as I sit next to him, but he looks really down.

"Are you okay?" I ask.

He looks at me like I should know.

I just nod, even though I'm not quite sure where he's at with his grief.

Knowing that he's sad lights a different fire inside of me, and for the first time this week, I find myself wanting to take care of him the way he's taken care of me. I let that idea course through me, and I welcome the distraction. I start brainstorming ideas and piecing together things that I can do for him because this is more than a distraction—it's a brand-new, totally doable *plan*.

CHAPTER 12

Boy-Space-Friend

Jensen

I hate that I'm so emotional, but I can't help it, so I stop trying to hide my pain from Nellie. I don't explain, and I can tell she's not quite sure why I'm so upset, but that's okay. Saying goodbye to Sean was awful. I felt like I had to hold back. There were too many people watching.

When Nellie left me to face her mom, that was actually okay. I had wanted to talk to Mrs. Samsin, and I didn't realize I'd get my chance right then and there, but I took it. I'm still surprised I managed to get the words out.

"Mrs. Samsin? I'm sorry for your loss."

"Thank you."

"I know this isn't the right time, but I remember that Sean used to love writing."

"He did."

"Did he ever publish his books?" I know he hasn't, but I have to pretend that I don't.

"He didn't."

"Oh, okay." I have to tread lightly here. "My aunt is an editor at Ogma Publishing. I could take a look at his work and see if any of his books would be something my aunt would like. I'd like to do it for him."

"That's really nice of you, Jensen."

"So can I borrow his laptop?" This is my chance to do

something for Sean. The idea came to me last night while I was building the playlist, as I was mourning in my own way.

"Sure. It's in the kitchen, under the papers on the table. Just get it back to me when you're done."

"Okay. Thanks. And Mrs. Samsin? Can we *not* tell Nellie about this? I don't want to get her hopes up."

"She talks to you more than she does me."

"Angela," someone said then, ending our conversation. Mrs. Samsin turned and stepped into the embrace of another woman, and I was forgotten.

Now, as Nellie rubs my back, I shudder with sadness. I hope putting his stories out there is a step in the right direction. I look at him again and grab another tissue. Discreetly, I tuck it into my hands and then bury my face.

"It's okay," Nellie says.

My shoulders round, my head starts pounding, and the world around me blurs. I don't know why I thought I'd be strong enough to handle this without crying in public. I want to leave, but I won't. I won't walk away from my friend as we collectively say goodbye to the one person who has stood behind us both.

So I let all the pain and fear in, but only for thirty seconds. Then, I find my grit and mentally rise from the ground. I wipe my eyes one more time and force a smile. That's all the darkness gets. From here on out, I'll be like Hagon. Unwavering and fierce.

Nellie's soothing strokes on my back ease the tightness in my chest. When I sit upright, I take her hand in mine. I was worried that with her family around she might pull away, but she's a compass fixed on due north, fixed on me.

A half hour later, the funeral director comes in and closes the casket. He asks if we'd like to say a prayer before the service starts. Angela says yes and turns to a man I don't know.

Nellie leans into me and whispers, "That's our bishop."

"You go to church?"

"We used to."

He offers a prayer, asking God to grant us peace. I sit there, wondering if God even hears.

When the bishop's finished, a large arrangement of roses is placed on top of the casket, and six strong men surround Sean. It kills me not to be one of the pallbearers. Now I'm wishing that everyone knew the truth, so I could help lift Sean up. We fall into line, and Nellie's grip on my hand tightens with every step as we trail behind the casket and Angela.

When we get into the chapel, Nellie doesn't sit on the front row, next to her mom. Instead, she takes the second row, and I follow. Angela is quickly flanked by family who cast Nellie odd looks, but Nellie doesn't see.

After a few minutes, Nellie whispers to me who's who. That's when I learn we're pinned between one of her aunts and some second cousin twice removed and their husbands. The couples look to be about thirty or forty years old, and neither have kids in tow.

I fake another smile at them, but their response is less friendly. In fact, they look at me with disdain, and then at Nellie with disapproval, and then at her dress with disgust. I tell myself they're also grieving, but the aunt's expression is so calculated, I can almost guess her thoughts.

I cast my attention to the pulpit as an escape.

"Nellie," the cousin whispers. "Who's your friend?"

"I'm Jensen," I say, since I have ears and a voice and I can answer for myself.

On my left, the aunt perks up. "Did you know Sean?"

"Quite well, actually. I live around the corner."

"And you're dating our Nellie?" the aunt says, as if Nellie is a thing to be owned.

The bishop rises to his feet and steps up to the pulpit.

"Shh," Nellie says, keeping her gaze directly forward. "No one's dating here."

"That dress says otherwise," the aunt mutters at the same time the bishop welcomes everyone.

Simultaneously, I'm questioning what Nellie just said. *No one's dating here?*

My immediate reaction is to be ticked, but before I let that feeling seep into my bones, I reconsider. Maybe she just said that to keep her aunt in check. Maybe she said it because we haven't defined what *this* is.

Maybe we should.

Her aunt makes a good point—that dress does say otherwise. So does our behavior. We don't act like "just friends." Days ago, that was a big question. *What are we doing?* I'd asked, but neither of us had an answer. I feel like our relationship is complex—that the simple relationship status words don't accurately define us. I thought Nellie was feeling the same. She has to know there isn't anyone else, but does she really believe that we're *not* dating?

I feel guilty thinking about this in a church instead of thinking of Sean, and with that, all thoughts of Nellie fall to the wayside as the first musical number begins. I don't know who picked the song, but Sean's friends from the university music department are really talented.

From there, it's a blur. I get the feeling someone is staring at me, and I glance over my shoulder and spot Sterling and Lenox and Britta and a few other friends. Behind them, my mom sits stoic. I knew she'd be here. They all see me, and we meet eyes and their silent communication consists of two words. My mom adds a wink of encouragement.

I'm sorry. Not words that Sterling says often. Marbles either.

I nod in response and turn back to the front.

My whole body feels heavy while simultaneously, it feels like I'm not even here. I tell myself I can handle five more minutes. And after those five, I commit to another five. Minute by minute, we endure a long goodbye, until it's time for the final musical number. A piano solo by Nellie's grandpa—a song he wrote back when he was in high school, someone whispers.

Nellie hands me a fresh tissue, and then someone prays. This time, my thoughts echo the speaker.

We are instructed to follow the casket and get into our cars, but before we leave the room, I want to make sure Nellie sees her friends.

Our friends.

"Look," I whisper as we walk.

Her eyes land on Britta and the rest of the gang. Britta's applying lip gloss; the guys nod in our direction. There's genuine empathy in their expressions. Britta raises a hand but doesn't wave it. Nellie copies her, then turns and walks out. For a whole second, I wish I could leave with them. I wish I could say "That sucks" and move on.

Instead, I follow Nellie out, knowing our friends won't follow. They're not coming to the cemetery, and I don't blame them.

I click the unlock button to my mom's car so Nellie can get in. I should've brought my car, but this wasn't the place to show her my Porsche. Instead, we sit in the Traverse, waiting for the hearse to lead the way.

The funeral director comes around and reminds us to turn on our headlights, though I've already done that. Perhaps he thinks we don't know how it works. Nellie stares blankly ahead.

Angela must have run to the bathroom or something, because she's just now approaching the car. Nellie's uncle holds the door open for her. She pauses to look at us, her face void of emotion. I know she's become distant over the years, and I noticed when Sean stopped talking about her. I wave with two fingers, and to my surprise, she acknowledges my existence with a curt nod. After a few more minutes, we pull out of the parking lot.

"Your aunt—the one I sat next to?" I say.

"Yeah?"

"Did you hear what she said?"

"About us dating?"

"The whole congregation heard that. No, what she said about your dress."

"I didn't. What did she say?"

"Nothing important. She's not a fan. I was just wondering."

"She hates it? I hope she hates it."

"I don't hate it," I say. "Not one bit."

"I know you don't," Nellie says. "I could tell the minute you looked at me."

"Yeah, I don't have a good poker face."

"I'll keep that in mind for the senior All-Nighter."

"Ha! Speaking of poker—do you know how to play craps? Because if not, we should learn before next week."

"I have no idea."

"Me either."

I think about card games and Nellie's dress instead of dwelling on what comes next. I keep telling myself the hardest part is over. It has to be. Watching the funeral director close the lid and lock the casket was awful. Listening to the speakers talk about Sean's life was funny and sad and painful. When they talked about him as a teacher, I kept thinking "I'm his favorite student."

I *was* his favorite student.

When we park alongside the gravel road in the cemetery, Nellie just sits there, showing no signs of moving.

"Jensen?"

"Yeah?"

"Thanks for coming with me. I couldn't have done this without you."

"You're welcome."

"You . . . you loved him."

"Yeah. He really was the best."

We walk, arms linked together until we get to the canopy. She looks at the few chairs meant for immediate family, and then at me.

"Go," I say.

She leans in close, and my breath catches as she puts a soft kiss on my cheek. The one on my neck—I think that was an accident. But this one is on purpose. Her lips are soft like the rose petals on the casket, her fingertips touching my ear and cheek. A lot of people take note of it, but it's over before it begins.

"Thank you, Jensen."

"Anytime, Nellie," I whisper as she walks away from me and sits down next to her mom. I take a spot in the back and listen. Another prayer, more words on Sean's behalf, and I can't take anymore.

I walk away, a fisted hand to my mouth. I put distance between me and Sean's grave and his family and search the clouded sky, considering what happens after this life. I believe in God, and He's been good to me for the most part, but He still lets things fall apart.

He didn't save Sean, and He could have.

He didn't spare Clay, either, and He could have.

He didn't kill Kohl, and He should have.

Why didn't He give Kohl an aneurysm before Clay was born?

"You really screwed that one up," I say to the skies.

But that's about the worst of it, I realize. I got a crappy dad who broke my brother.

Grandparents are supposed to pass on, and mine have. No one in my family has had to battle cancer, or lost their jobs, or suffered a house fire, or a car crash, or any other calamity. My mom is awesome. I've got a future.

The fire building in my belly flickers out like a cheap firework, leaving only a few red sparks that slowly fade to black.

I stop walking and kneel behind a large oak tree. I'm screaming in my head, because I want to be mad at God for taking Sean, but a sliver of light cuts through the clouds, casting warmth over the whole cemetery, over me, and while there's no choir of angels, I do hear a familiar tune, a line on repeat, in a voice I'll never forget.

What do you see? What do you feel? Sean would say. *Write that.*

I imagine Sean telling me to get up and take a closer look at the "hell" I'm in.

That's not fair, I think, wanting him to cut me slack. *I've never had to write without you backing me up.*

But there's no answer from Sean, no whisperings from beyond the grave, and when I glance back at his family all circled around each other, hugging, and the men putting their hands on each other's shoulders, as if to say, *We'll make it through,* my heart ruptures again. Because no one is saying that to me.

Still, I manage to stand up.

Nellie spots me, and the hope in her eyes draws me back to her. She slips into my arms, giving me a big hug, and the feeling that she's missed me floods my veins.

"Let's get out of here," she whispers, and this time, there's no mistaking the kiss she puts on my neck or the way her hands travel over my shoulders. Nellie wants a distraction, a way to feel good, and usually I'd be all for it. Granted, I'm not as proficient as Sterling, but I can't claim sainthood either. But this isn't her—and I worry I'm becoming a drug and she's the addict.

Then again, it could easily be the other way around.

"Not yet." I push Nellie back from me and meet her gaze. "I think you better make a few rounds. Talk to your family and stuff, before we ditch. Plus, isn't there food?"

Several sets of hooded eyes are on us.

"I don't want to talk to anyone."

"I get that, but the last thing you need is for your family to be upset at you."

"I don't care what they think."

"I do. Because I want them to like me." Before I think my next question through, it's out. "Did you really mean what you said earlier, about us not dating?"

"What do you mean?"

"I mean, do you think this"—I wave a finger back and forth between us—"is *nothing*? When I asked you, you didn't have an answer."

"You asked me what we were doing. That's not the same thing."

"You knew what I meant." I glance around, sensing more and more eyes on us. Maybe I'm just super self-conscious right now. I can't tell. That's the end of that conversation because several of her family members join us.

"Nellie," one woman says. "Are you going to introduce us to your boyfriend?"

I'm all for diffusing a tense situation with humor so I say,

"Yeah, see, I'm more like a boy-space-friend. That space between words really matters."

The woman chuckles, but the aunt, the one who commented on Nellie's dress, doesn't find it funny.

Just like that, Nellie flips a switch, the one that empowers her to be the chief yearbook editor, the one that makes her the class president. "Jensen, this is my aunt Sarah, and Jenny, my second cousin once removed, and their husbands—Luca and Stetson."

The men offer me their hands, and I shake them both, flexing. My sixth-hour weight-lifting class keeps me in shape.

"Nice to meet you all," I say.

"So, Jensen, what are you going to do after graduation?" Jenny asks, and as I resort to my standard answer, we're joined by Angela and a few others.

"I'm moving into my own place and working for a while before I consider college." Not how I was going to tell Nellie about my apartment, but I want Angela to know.

"What?" Nellie asks. "You're moving? Where to?"

"Yes, where to, Jensen?" Angela asks. She probably hopes it's out of state.

"Not far. I've rented an apartment at Coventry." It's not upper-class or anything, but it's nice. I smile at Nellie in a way that I hope says "don't worry."

"Roommates?" Luca asks.

"Maybe. None yet."

There's some nodding of heads, some weak smiles. Why is it that every time an adult finds out I'm going to work instead of going to college, the disappointment runs thick? The answer is simple. Attending college is what all upstanding teenagers do after graduation.

They don't rent apartments and work.

They don't give up an education to make money right away.

"Are you two coming to lunch?" Aunt Sarah asks.

"Nellie, are you hungry?" Nellie's mom grabs her by the

elbow, gently pulling her aside. The rest of the group fans out, but not before I overhear Sarah.

"I give it a week," she says, her gaze darting to Nellie and her mom.

"She's grieving," Luca says. "She won't move that fast."

"She moved on months ago."

I'm trying to figure out what Sarah thinks will only take a week. I'm positive they're talking about Angela.

They walk off, taking their gossip with them, and I'm left standing between headstones.

I can't make out what Angela is saying to Nellie, but I can guess. Angela's body language says it all. I don't want them to fight, especially not here. Not today.

Nellie and I lock eyes for a brief second, and I see the panic in her eyes before she turns back to her mother. A hundred things are probably running through her mind. One thought runs through mine though. What if Angela makes her go with them, leaving me to fend for myself?

At that thought, a trickle of panic runs through me too. I don't want to go home alone.

I walk over toward them and cut into their private conversation. "Hey, I can give Nellie a ride to the luncheon."

"Oh, that's nice of you, Jensen, but—"

"No problem. I promised Nellie I'd be here for her."

Me, not Britta. Not Sterling. Not anyone else. Me. And I am not going to let Angela interfere with that.

Angela hesitates.

"Mom, I came with Jensen, and he bought this new suit and gave up his entire day to be here and everything. We'll come eat."

Nellie spins and walks off, and like a tornado collecting everything in its path takes me with her. I keep up with her quickening pace, not sure what's going on.

"Hey, you okay?"

"I'm fine. Just . . . mad. Tired. Spinning. I can't believe you're moving."

CHAPTER 13

These Are Hard Questions

Nellie

I'm being rude. I'm being forward. I'm being mouthy. What's wrong with me?

Instead of discussing his big move or defining our relationship, we drive to the luncheon in silence. It doesn't feel like we're fighting, but the vibe between us is thinning out.

And once we're at the luncheon we're put under microscopes and examined every two minutes. An aunt here, a long-lost uncle there, a half a dozen of my dad's friends from the university.

We're walking down a hallway when a couple I don't know looks at me and Jensen.

"Hi, Nellie. Beautiful dress."

"I'll have to look into it," I reply, so out of my own mind it takes me a second to process. "Sorry, I mean . . . thanks." She's the only person to say anything about my dress, and it was a compliment. That was nice of her.

But it isn't until my dad's friend, Brent, mentions a summer internship that would be perfect for me that I finally snap out of it. He just offered me a position at Goldman, Goldman, and Flax, the law firm he owns.

"That's so kind of you," I say. He nods and walks away, but I'm not sure if I am supposed to call him or if he was serious or if he hired me on the spot.

The questions and comments keep coming as I fill my plate, even though I'm not hungry.

When is graduation?

Are you valedictorian, then?

He talked about you all the time.

Are you still going into physics?

I try to respond to everyone, but sometimes I don't. Mom threatened to ground me if I didn't come. And she meant it. So I'm forced to endure all these questions.

Have you thought about teaching, like your dad?

Are you attending the U in the fall?

No. Sorry to disappoint you and the rest of the valley.

Why not?

Because. Must I really explain? I just buried my father and I'm holding a plate of roast beef and funeral potatoes and Jell-O.

A bubble of anger swells inside me, and my hands begin to shake, but Jensen's there, intervening with a complimentary one-liner about the U, and leading me away from those who keep cross-examining me.

He'd make a good bomb defuser.

My great-aunt corners us, though, and I'm tempted to smoosh my plate into her purple blouse and jeweled necklace and run away, which is juvenile. This is pure evidence I'm crazy. Someone could easily convict me of insanity right now.

So, are you two serious?

Naturally, we step on this land mine as we're fleeing a hot zone.

Her question causes me to freeze. As much as I don't want to answer even one more question, I do want to figure out what we are. I look to Jensen.

He presses his lips together and turns to my great-aunt.

This ought to be good.

Jensen lifts his chin a little, and then says, "Nellie never makes a decision without thinking it all the way through, without considering how it's going to impact her future. You know? She's a serious girl. Now, if you'll excuse us."

As we walk away, I say, "Marry me."

"Don't tempt me, woman."

I want to revisit what kind of relationship we're in, and I

regret not sharing previously how I really felt, but this isn't the best place. The timing is all off.

I think of the book he selected for me to read and our plans to plant daffodils, but how are we supposed to stay together when we'll be miles apart?

With every bite I take, my energy vanishes. Jensen seems to mirror this. We eat in silence. I'm exhausted. My eyes are heavy, my body is worn, and I want to go home. I want to crawl into my bed and not talk to anyone.

"We came, we saw, we conquered," I say, pushing my plate away.

"Can you say that in Latin?"

"Probably, if I think about it hard enough. Will you take me home?"

"Of course. Do you need to get a permission slip first?"

"Yeah, probably. Give me a sec."

I walk over to the table where my mom is sitting and kneel by her side.

"Mom, I'm not feeling good. Please, can I go home?"

She purses her lips, glances at the people at her table, but then she really looks at me, and for a second, I see the woman who danced around the living room to Boyz II Men. And I think she sees me. She finally nods.

"But, Nellie, you better actually *go home.*"

I nod back, understanding.

When I look at Jensen, I give him a thumbs-up. He meets me by the back door, and the only thing I say to him is, "Venimus, vidimus, vicimus."

Then we're like bandits on a heist as we climb into our getaway car.

Britta messages me, asking how I'm doing, and I send her a short text back.

> I'm fine. Thanks for coming today.

She ask if I want to hang out or something, and I text back one little word.

No.

There's a surge of energy between me and Jensen because we're finally free, but it's short-lived. The car basically rocks me to sleep.

"You can just drop me off," I say.

"You sure?" Jensen glances at me. "You want to be alone?"

"I don't know." I debate this. I really don't feel good. I need some serious downtime and to freshen up. However, it's barely after two, so I could be home alone for a long time. "Do you want to stay with me?"

"Do *you* want me to stay?"

I shift my weight around, crossing my arms over my stomach. "These are hard questions, and I don't know."

My brain hurts. I don't know what I want. I want him to want to stay. I don't want to be alone, but I want my bed.

"What if . . ." I grasp for an answer. "What if we park your car at your house, and you walk me home? Can we start there?"

"Sure."

So that's what we do.

When we get to my house, he comes inside with me.

Without a word, I say *follow me* with my eyes, and when he comes into my room, my heart pounds a little harder. He takes off his suit coat and sets it on my bed. His attention lands on a stack of CDs—the ones that used to be my dad's. Bands from the '80s, '90s, and 2000s. I suddenly feel silly for liking NSYNC.

Jensen's go-to response to my brokenness is usually a hug, but the air around us crackles with expectation, and I inhale a nervous breath. I am so desperate for healing, I revisit what his touch does to me, and he must think something similar, because after a long minute, he steps into my space. His attention falls to my mouth, my neck, and then down to my toes. He surprises me when he touches the base of my throat and traces my collarbone.

I let out a soft gasp at his touch, but it doesn't stop him. I don't want him to stop. I've been waiting for his kiss for way too long.

He draws circles over my deltoid, but that's the end of my anatomy knowledge. Every drop of intelligence leaves me, which gives my mind a break from holding on to everything.

He's got more experience than I do, but my instincts kick in. My hand comes up to his neck, and I pull softly. I feel completely vulnerable but ready. Desperate for more than a hug. When he presses a kiss to the top of my shoulder, I lift my chin. His breath travels over my skin, and I am on fire. His lips are a hot breeze on a blazing summer day as they move from my shoulder to my ear, and I welcome the burn.

Everything I know will mean nothing if I don't know his kiss now. He lifts his eyes to meet mine. He's stares at my mouth, and I'm staring at his.

I'm buzzing as his fingers dig into the back of my neck. Electricity whips through my whole body when his mouth touches mine. I'm alive and awake as he and I reshape our friendship.

This kiss says everything we haven't said over the last week.

This kiss becomes the one thing I need to examine and learn and memorize, and the more he gives, the more I give back as if we're passing notes and cramming for a test. I'm surprised I notice the details, though. I feel his hand on my back, in my hair, and at my sides. I never lose sense of where his fingertips trail.

And his breath becomes as ragged as mine. When he stops kissing me, it's only so we can catch our breath, but that doesn't stop him from dragging his lips over to my ear. I grip his head, sinking my fingers into his hair and gently pull. Begging without words for him to kiss me again.

The whole universe spins with us at the center. Gravity gives up, and we float into a starlit moment where everything is perfect. And deep down, I know this means something. I mean something to him, and it's nothing like my moment with Sterling. Thoughts of that boy come and go and vanish. I'll never think of him again.

Jensen maintains a steady speed, and this time, I don't feel clueless. I feel like we've wasted time. All those years we were apart, we could've been together. But then again, we wouldn't be who we are now.

This is what my first kiss should've been like. This is how it happens in novels—and oh my gosh! Jensen kisses like Hagon! I'm sure I don't kiss like Sokha, but Oh! My! Gosh!

I feel like I'm actually higher than the earth's atmosphere. I never want to come down. We do not stop kissing, not until it's time for us to either take the next corner at a reckless speed or tap the brakes. I'm a little disappointed when it's the latter, but this isn't a race.

"Nellie," he says. "I have no words when I'm around you, I swear."

"Well, I can't tell." I exhale and make a decision. It's time to slow down. "Do you mind giving me a minute? I'd like to change."

"Yeah. Sure thing." He steps into the hallway, closing the door behind him.

I've never removed a dress so fast in all my life. I drop it on the floor and pull on a black T-shirt and my favorite rose-gold yoga pants, and for a moment, I take his suit coat and hold it. It's not like having his hoodie, but it still smells like him. When I open my bedroom door, he's leaning against the wall.

We end up sitting on my floor, listening to the playlist he made. I pull all my pillows off my bed, and we get comfortable as he thumbs through my things and my books, and we just talk. We're sealed off from the rest of the world, and it's amazing. If only real life was this accommodating.

We don't kiss quite like that again, but that doesn't stop him from resting a hand on my stomach or my calf or my back, depending on how we rotate. That kiss has definitely changed us.

After a while, Jensen looks at me, and I can tell something is different.

"Could we have saved him, if we'd gone to look for him earlier?" His fingers toy with the fringe on one of my pillows. He visibly swallows, and I go completely still.

"No, Jensen. You can't think that."

"But—"

"It was a brain aneurysm. No one could've seen that coming."

We go completely silent, but I reach over and take his hand, then fall back into my pillow and close my eyes.

"I know," he whispers. "I hate that it was your dad. I wish it had been mine."

I know very little about Kohl Nichols, but what I do know explains why Jensen would say such a thing.

"Why is this so hard?" I whisper.

"I don't know. Life is full of hard questions. We get hit with hard things, and God watches to see what we'll do."

"That doesn't seem fair."

Jensen starts playing with my hair, and we talk about God and life and death, and I make him laugh because that's part of my new plan.

When it's time for him to go, I want him to kiss me and stay instead.

I don't want to be alone, but his mom is requesting that he come home. And I don't want her to be upset with me, or mad at him.

He insists that I just stay right where I'm at and listen to a song of his choosing.

"Just rest," he says. He presses a kiss to my lips and then a firmer one to my forehead.

"Text me when you get home."

"Sure thing."

He picks a song for me, makes me put headphones on, and right before he steps out of my room, he bites his lip and jerks his head at me, and then he's gone.

I sink into my pillow, press play, and listen. "The Glory of Love." It's a song I've heard before but never really paid that much attention to. I quickly search the lyrics and read along as I listen to each line, wondering if there is hidden meaning in them.

I kind of hope there is. I click on information about the song, which leads me down a rabbit hole about Peter Cetera.

When Jensen texts me that he's home, I reply with a smiley face.

> Also, fun fact, did you know Peter Cetera was the lead singer for the band Chicago?

Jensen texts back quickly.

> Be honest. You Googled that. Also Chicago is a city.

> It's also a band.

I laugh, and then without meaning to, I fall asleep, listening to a string of their greatest hits, and dream of floating musical notes and Jensen singing, until two in the morning when I wake with a jolt. I'm sore from lying on the floor, but mostly I feel an urgency. A sense that something's missing. I go in search of that feeling, only to find that Mom isn't in her bed. Her shoes aren't by the back door, and when I head toward the living room, expecting to find her on the couch, she's not there either.

Instead, there's a car parked in the driveway, the headlights off. At first, it freaks me out, and I duck behind the door. But then I realize I know that car. It's a black Camry, and there are two people in it.

They're in their respective seats, but they're not just holding hands.

I'm really going to be sick this time. The events of the day and the fact that my mom is with another man right now is too much. I dash back to my bedroom and pull on a hoodie.

I have to get out of here.

But that's a dumb idea, another juvenile solution to an adult problem.

Besides, where would I go? Instantly, I know. But I force myself to be objective. *Just go back to bed.*

But I'm wide awake. I stand in my room, weighing out my
options. At some point, she'll come in. Alone. Right? She'll get a
drink of water and go to bed. But when? How long has she been
out there anyway?

She could stay out there until dawn.

She could invite him in.

There are other possible outcomes, but these are the only
three I care to consider. And then I come to a conclusion. I can't
sleep through any of those scenarios.

I can't stay here and get the rest I so desperately need. That's
the truth, a fact, something tangible I can work with.

I write a note.

> I know you wanted me to stay home, but Britta
> invited me to her house for movies and a sleepover.

I leave it on the kitchen counter, sneak out the back, and cross
through the Millars' backyard.

I'm a star burning out, about to collapse under my own
weight, and if that happens, then I'll be a black hole, with nothing
to offer anyone.

I stick to the shadows and work my way uphill, toward Jensen's.

I tap on his bedroom window, whispering his name.

When he parts the blinds and peers out at me, there isn't a
hint of shock in his eyes.

"Can I come in?" I say.

He nods and indicates that I should go to the back door.

When he pulls the door open, I rush into his arms, needing
his embrace for both warmth and comfort.

A group of intelligent brain cells band together enough to
holler at me—*His mom's here! It's two a.m.! This is a bad plan, Nellie!*

But I don't care about plans. I divide the cells and scatter
them by giving Jensen an extra squeeze. I don't need a plan.

And those words shouldn't be what tip the scale, but they do.

My best-laid plans have been obliterated, and my future is a big fat unknown.

A cry rips through me, and I hear Jensen say something, but everything inside of me is dying and I can't compute words. My face is tingling, my hands have frozen into fists, and my legs won't move.

Jensen practically carries me to the couch, but it's Sumerli who slips into the space that I need filled. I cling to her, and she strokes my arms and back and hair. Moments later, Jensen hands me a fleece blanket and his mom a box of tissues. After she presses a tissue into my hands, she sets the box aside.

I bury my face and spill my heart—telling her everything I know about my parents icy fighting the last several months and the man in the car she's with right now. I hear myself, but I can't stop my mouth.

Jensen hears it all too.

Once I have practically vomited my life saga onto their living room floor, I fall silent.

"Jensen, go back to bed," she says. "Nellie, I'll stay right here. Just try to sleep."

For the next several hours, I cling to Sumerli like hydrogen to oxygen. I don't want to think about my mom, so I think about my dad. I can still feel his hands on my shoulders, hear his voice, recall his laugh. But if I think about his razor, for example, I know it won't be on the counter in the morning. If I want his advice, he won't be there to give it to me. He'll never yell at me again, or call me his little pumpkin. He'll never congratulate me. He'll never walk me down the aisle.

Dad will live on in my memory, but he doesn't *live on*. And my mother will. This truth comes at me like a destroying army. There is no going around it or stopping it. I have to go through it.

And as I do, Sumerli binds me back together one small touch at a time. She's the one who holds me and comforts me and keeps the tissues coming.

CHAPTER 14

Adrenaline Junkie

Jensen

My whole body aches as I walk away from my mom and Nellie. What Nellie doesn't know is that I was already wide awake. Right before I left her house, I snagged Sean's computer.

And I made the mistake of cracking it open and reading some of his writing.

I wasn't anticipating being interrupted at this hour, so now the computer hides under my bed because I don't want Nellie to see it.

Instinctively, I called out to my mom for help. I summoned her from her bed with an urgent, "Mom, Nellie's here." And I'm glad I did. I feel terrible for Nellie. Sick, really.

Now, as I shut my bedroom door and collapse into bed, my mind won't even take me to Nellie. What a mess.

I'm paper-thin, and the pain I've been storing cuts me like shards of glass, but instead of leaving jagged edges, it's as if Hagon has cut me with his moonblood blade. The cut is precise and clean. I wish I could heal like Sokha in the imaginary world of Hern.

I thought I let all the hurt in earlier today, but reading through Sean's stuff has opened a new wound. His real voice has been silenced, and Sean deserves better. He deserves more.

What's left are pages and pages of his words, and I'm overwhelmed at the idea of doing something with them. In the haze between being awake and falling asleep, my mind leaves Sean behind and faces my own father.

He's mostly a ghost. I can barely recall anything about him, other than the abuse. The day he shook Clay was the last time I ever saw him.

That was the day mom collected what little we had and ran. We ran from Nebraska to Texas to Colorado to Utah.

I have no idea if he ever looked for us.

Which is probably for the best, but it also hurts.

Then, just before I fall entirely asleep, I realize my father could be dead and I wouldn't even know it.

When I wake up with a jolt in the morning, my mind is clear, but I'm covered in sweat again. I'm in and out of the shower in ten minutes, and once I'm dressed, I peek into the living room.

My mom isn't there, but Nellie is curled into a ball, sleeping on the couch. I check my mom's room and find her sleeping. Good. It's nearly eleven, and we all needed the rest. I slip into the kitchen to make breakfast.

When Nellie wakes up, she just lies there on the couch, her expression blank. I take her a tall glass of water. She probably needs it after all that crying. A few minutes later, my mom comes in and sits down on the couch.

"Morning, Nellie," she says and puts an arm around her.

Nellie leans into her, breathing deeply.

"Hey," Nellie says, giving my mom a shy smile.

I bring Mom a glass of water as well. She flashes me an appreciative smile.

"Morning, you two," I say, my voice cracking. Awesome. I feel my cheeks turn red.

"What are your plans today?" Mom asks, her question directed to me.

I shrug. "Not much. Is there anything you need me to do?"

"It would be great if you mowed the lawn."

"I can do that."

"Okay." Mom pats Nellie on the knee and stands up. "I'm going to get ready for the day. Then I'm headed to see Clay."

"Want me to come?" I say.

Mom glances at Nellie, and then back to me, and without words, she indicates I should follow her into her room. For a hot second, I worry that I'm in trouble. She closes the door, giving us privacy.

"Nellie doesn't want to go home, but she can't stay here," Mom says.

"Why not?"

"Her mom called."

"What? When?"

"Around three. That was a fun conversation." Mom looks out the window to our backyard, her expression grim. "Look, I would never turn Nellie away if she were suddenly homeless or something, but she's not. And she's not eighteen, so . . ."

"I get it."

"I feel bad for her. I really do."

"I know. Me too."

There's a beat of understanding, and I know my mom fought for Nellie. I'd kill to know what she actually said to Angela, but I don't think now is the time to ask.

Mom rubs her eyes. "Finish the dishes, too, would you?"

"Sure."

Mom disappears into her bathroom, and I return to Nellie. We say nothing to each other for a long time, but words aren't required.

To my surprise, I find myself compelled to write. I want to capture the ache of last night with the lull of this morning because it's a wicked lovely thing. Nellie came to me. She came here in her darkest moment, and I'm pretty sure this is exactly how Hagon feels about Sokha when they have their moments. Granted, my mother was the one to hold Nellie through her pain, not me, but I think it was for the best. I don't feel angry or jealous. I'm glad my mom is the kind of woman to open her home and her heart to someone I care about.

"You okay?" I finally whisper.

"I will be."

"What do you want to do today?"

"I need to get my life together," Nellie says like she's confiding some dark secret.

"I don't know anyone who has it more together than you." I chuckle softly.

"You say that, but—"

"Give me one example."

"I haven't done laundry in over a week."

"Oh, no, not that."

She elbows me, and I flinch in mock pain.

The thought of a Sunday drive crosses my mind, and I think I'm ready to share a bit more of my real life with Nellie.

She came to me; I can trust her with my secrets.

"Wanna go for a drive?" I ask.

"Where to?"

"I don't know. That's the thing about Sunday drives. You just go where the road leads you. No questions."

"No questions?"

"Come on. Let's get away." I am blatantly disobeying my mom right now. I really have spent too much time in Sterling's presence.

"I don't know. My mom—" She cuts herself off, and the silence that follows presses us flat until Nellie inhales. "You know what? I don't care."

And clearly, I'm rubbing off on Nellie. "Okay. You want to change into something fresh?"

"And brush my teeth." She covers her mouth with one hand.

"You could wear something of mine, if you want. And I'm sure I've got a new toothbrush around here somewhere."

"Nothing of yours will fit me."

"Sure it will. One word: drawstring."

"That's two."

I shake my head. "It's a compound word."

She laughs through tight lips, but I see the spark, the one that brings her back to life. I grab my favorite Nike shirt and my gray joggers. Nellie waits on the couch, thumbing through her phone, and I hear my mom finishing up.

I return to the living room, armed with the clothing. "Will these do?"

Nellie holds the pants up to her waist, and while they're too long, they'll work. "These actually look really comfortable. I love this shirt."

"You remember the shirt?"

"Of course I do."

"Cool," I say, but inside I'm pumped. "Okay, next stop, the bathroom."

I know she's been here a million times, but she's never really needed to clean up at my house, so I dig around under my sink for a new toothbrush and pull a towel from the closet.

"Here," I say.

She takes the items from me, and I point out that she can use all my stuff, even my deodorant, if she wants.

"Thanks, Jensen."

"And," I say hesitantly, "do you think you could do me a favor?"

"Sure. What?"

"I need a day where I don't have to explain myself or anything."

"What? Why?"

"I want to show you something, but I don't want to play twenty questions."

Nellie cocks her head, her long hair slipping over a shoulder. She looks tired and worn, but she's still beautiful.

"I . . . don't . . . need answers," she says, practically choking on her words. I can't help that I laugh at her.

"It pains you not to know something, be honest. Because you, Nellie Samsin, solve complicated quandaries in your sleep."

"I do not."

"Just give me today," I say. "Promise you won't press me."

She shakes her head, before finally conceding. "I promise I'll try my best."

"That's straight-up weak sauce, Samsin."

With a quirk of her lips, she shuts the door in my face.

While she's busy, I tell my mom my plans. She's okay with it, as long as I get Nellie home *soon*. Apparently Angela said Nellie had to be home in time for Sunday dinner. As if they have Sunday dinner. But whatever.

"Tell Clay I'll come see him soon," I say.

"I will. I'll talk to you later."

She pulls me into a hug, and I squeeze her extra hard. "Thanks for last night. For helping Nellie."

"Of course."

Fifteen minutes later, my shirt fits Nellie like it was made for her, and the sweats are baggy in just the right way. She smells like Irish Spring soap, and her hair is pulled up into a topknot, loose strands framing her face.

"Looking good, Samsin."

"I smell like you."

"I smell amazing."

She scoffs and rolls her eyes and then looks at me expectantly.

I pick up the keys to the Porsche and take a deep breath. *Here goes nothing.* Moments later, our Uber arrives. I can practically hear the questions Nellie is holding back.

The driver knows where to take us thanks to his app, and Nellie and I ride in relative silence as Nellie checks her phone.

"Britta?" I ask.

"Yes. And my mom. Britta and Marbles are going to some motocross thing."

"And your mom?"

"Knows I'm with you and is threatening to cut me off."

"For real?"

"Basically."

"Yikes. Should I take you home instead?"

"Nah," she says.

"I'm sure it'll all work out," I say.

"I don't know."

"I do."

At this point, we pull up to Coventry's main building, and I instruct the driver where to go from there. My place is around the back, two stories up, looking out over the valley. Once we're at the right building, I add a tip and pay, and the Uber drives off.

I can tell Nellie's questions are building. We take the stairs, and as I pull out my keys, she finally bursts.

"Is this your apartment? The one you're moving into?"

"I knew you couldn't play this game. Yes, this is my place."

"You're really moving out?"

I almost point out that she's asking me another question, but I don't. I'll just answer her questions with questions.

"Aren't you? You'll be headed to UNLV, right?"

"That was the plan."

"It's not the plan now?"

"I think I need a new plan." Her shoulders slump as we stand at the door with me holding my keys.

"Hey, look at me."

She lifts her eyes and bites her lip.

"I'm sorry your world is upside down. You'll figure it out. You'll find your way. If anyone can navigate these waters, it's you."

"I don't know."

"I do. And I can prove it." This really piques her curiosity. I take a moment before I say, "I wasn't part of the plan, was I?"

She shakes her head. "No."

"Am I a part of the plan now?"

She smiles, and the more she thinks about it, the more I realize I'm right.

"Okay," I say. "Close your eyes. This is it. Casa de la Jensen."

Casa de la Jen Dimes, if I were being honest.

Nellie complies, and I push the door open with my back—and shoot. My nerves take flight, and my stomach wraps itself into knots because I have physical copies of *Blood Rock* and *Shadow*

Stone sitting out. I'd ordered single copies of them from a print-on-demand company. I'll have to hide them without her seeing. My heart is racing, as I try to play it cool.

"You're the first person to see it, besides my mom."

Don't see the books. Don't see the books. They blink at me like red sirens, but that's only because I know they're there. Before she can look at anything too closely, I ask her to grab us something to drink from the fridge, and I casually walk over to my desk.

"There's soda, water, and juice—get something. Grab me a water, yeah? Then I'll give you a tour."

"Okay," she says. When she turns her back, I grab the books and stuff them into the drawer.

Sweat builds at my temples, and I run a hand through my hair to wipe it away.

"This is a nice place," Nellie says, looking at what's behind the cabinets.

I should be safe. Just so long as she doesn't try to open any desk drawers.

But considering how she's rummaging through the kitchen, I might have to steer her away from my desk.

"Matching dishes and silverware and pots and pans. Nice," she says.

"Thanks. A furnished apartment made sense to me, and my mom."

"Furnished apartments cost more, right? So you'll find a couple roommates? To make it more affordable?" She words her questions carefully, as if she's afraid she might offend me.

"Maybe."

I can tell she's annoyed that I'm not explaining more, but what can I do? I say nothing as she walks around, touching things and soaking it in.

When she walks over to my desk, which is positioned by the window, I hold my breath. She doesn't open any drawers, though. She just stares out at valley.

That desk is my new office. Last night I felt lost, but today, I think I'll split my time eighty-twenty. I've got to get pages done for my assistant, Rebecca, and I want to talk to her about Sean and his work. She knows about him, but I haven't told her that he's passed away. I haven't been in the right mindset to go there.

"Do you like it?" I ask, needing to fill the silence.

"Yes, very much. It's very upper-crust."

"It is not."

"I'm so confused."

"I hope you can handle that feeling. It's a normal one for those of us with simple minds."

"Ha ha, you're funny."

"Well, now you know where I'll be this summer."

She bobs her head at me and then scans the room again. "What are you doing this summer that you can afford this?"

"I can't answer that."

"Oh my gosh, it's not something illegal, is it?"

"No," I blurt. "I would never."

She cocks her head at me, and I know that look.

"Just because I'm friends with Sterling doesn't mean I'm a total idiot."

"One could argue." She laughs and I do too.

That's when Nellie goes over to my bookshelves. I've met every author on that bookshelf. It's a goal of mine to collect signed copies. The other bookshelf holds books by authors I haven't met.

"These are some great titles," she says.

"Thanks."

She's wide-eyed and complimentary, but because it's only eight hundred square feet, the tour doesn't take long.

"Ready to go for a drive?" I say, opening the door to leave.

"Sure, but, Jensen, why did you bring me here?"

"You are terrible at this game."

"I know." Nellie's expression falters, and I feel bad.

"Honestly, I just wanted you to see it. That way, if you ever need me, you'll know where to find me."

She looks away, embarrassed maybe?

"Hey," I say, catching her chin and lifting it so I can see into her eyes. "I'm glad you came to my house. I'm glad you picked me."

"It wasn't a hard decision."

"You sure? I mean Sterling's a great catch."

"No, he's not. He's catch and release."

"Tell me how you really feel."

"I did, yesterday, when we kissed."

I laugh hard, because she doesn't do edgy. She laughs, too, and I grab her by the hand, and this time our fingers lace together as our lips connect. I keep this kiss short and sassy, making sure it's the kind that says, "You're awesome."

We head toward the garage, where my car patiently waits for us.

I order my nerves to leave their post. I don't need them on high alert right now. The garage is a tight squeeze for most cars, but not for my black beauty. She's the color of metallic basalt, which means she sparkles in the sunlight. She's a little older, but I love her. She was a great find, and I bought her from the man who'd restored her.

The moment Nellie spots the car, her expression explodes into one of delight.

"Whoa," she says, running her fingers over the trunk. I doubt she knows much about cars, other than this is a sports car and sports cars are expensive.

I pull the keys from my pocket and dangle them.

"Wanna go for a ride?"

CHAPTER 15

The Car

Nellie

Of course I do.

"Yes. Let's go for a drive," I say.

It's not like I've been raised on the track at NASCAR, but I know a sports car when I see one. There are a few kids at Ataraxia High who drive fancy vehicles, but this Porsche is next level. And I've never ridden in one.

My dad was never a knowledgeable car guy. Art, yes. Books, yes. Motors, not so much, and I choke on the uncomfortable ache. That feeling is going to constantly blindside me now, and I'm not sure I'll ever get used to it.

So far, my plan has been to stick to Jensen's side, but with graduation in a few days, I don't know that we can make it last.

Which sucks, because it's working for the most part.

My phone pings. It's Britta, but I ignore her message. She's with Marbles all day today, and she keeps sending me selfies of the two of them.

> Look at this bike! Marbles said it's worth over $100K. Doesn't that seem ridiculous? I think it's ridiculous.

Jensen's a gentleman as he opens the door for me, and when I pause at his side, a rush of longing sweeps through me. A deep longing, a sort of melancholy, that fills me from head to toe, and before it takes root, it's gone. But it leaves an undeniable impression.

And I know there's a word to describe it, but it's lost to me. It's beautiful, and not English . . . What is it?

I push the boundaries of my memory, searching for it. This word—it describes what you feel when someone or something's whereabouts are unknown. Like a lost lover or family member. It's right there, on the tip of my tongue. It reminds me of . . . sad. Sad, sad, sad . . . *Saudade*.

There it is. I unearth it, my shovel nothing more than sheer determination to remember, and I did.

When I'm around Jensen, the power of saudade triples.

I feel better, knowing I was able to remember the word without resorting to the internet. I might feel broken, but my brain isn't.

The smell of spearmint gum and leather enfolds me, as if all these years, Jensen was fast cars and black leather and a force to be reckoned with.

How is this possible? I'm missing a certain variable that would explain all of this, and Jensen wasn't wrong about me—I'm going to go mad if I don't get some answers.

I almost ask, "So, where to?" but then catch the question by the tail and pull it back inside me. I'm sure he has a plan.

I'm not the only one who plans.

When he reaches behind my seat, twisting to get a better view to back out of the garage, I have to look out my window to hide the heat rising up my neck. His nearness gets my blood pumping. He's always been cute, but behind the wheel of this car? Holy smokes.

I note he didn't need to adjust the seat, the rearview mirror, or the steering wheel.

So, yeah. My deductive powers aren't totally shot. He has a car but doesn't drive it to school. *But why?* Ugh!

It's not until we leave the city behind us, headed toward Morgan, that he presses the pedal down hard and my back slams into the seat. The raw horsepower leaves me breathless.

"Did you take driver's ed in Daytona?"

He laughs and shakes his head at me. "No."

That's all he says as we cruise along for twenty minutes. The mountains are starting to bloom green and gold to life after a winter that was more Arctic than affectionate. The sunshine is glorious, and Jensen's got the temperature set to seventy-two, and I'm ridiculously comfortable.

Totes comfortable, as Britta would say.

I've been able to keep her at a mental and physical distance, but after involving her in my poorly-thought-out note last night, she's on my mind again. Apparently my mom called her mom, and when my lie was exposed, it wasn't hard for my mom to do some math of her own and call Sumerli.

"Talk to me," Jensen says as he takes another curve.

"Talk to you?"

"Anything. Tell me a story."

There's a look in his eye and an intense rigidness to his body, and so I start with a memory—one about Britta and me in sixth grade—and realize that this is what I can do for him. If all he needs is for me to do the talking, surely I can handle that. I've got years of listening to Britta in the bag.

The memory isn't an important one, but it's funny and he laughs, and I keep going. However, after four stories, I want to know what's on his mind. Maybe I can find out without asking.

"I can tell something's bothering you." I reach over and put a hand on his thigh. He drops his right hand on top of mine.

"I'm just mad. No, *mad* is the wrong word."

I can appreciate how hard it is to find the right word. "What's the right word?"

"Finding the right word sometimes is like plucking a star from the sky."

I startle. I can't believe he just said that. "My dad—he used to say that."

"I know."

I'm baffled, because how could he possibly know that?

Jensen glances at me and smiles. "You're cute when you're confused."

"Jensen—Please tell me how you know that." Not a question. A statement.

"Do you remember the last time we hung out, I mean before all this?"

That's easy. "Yes. Halloween, seventh grade."

"Yeah."

That was the first time Britta invited boys to the party, and five of them came. Sterling, Jensen, Eli, Ridge, and Mateo. Only Sterling and Jensen remain of that bunch—two moved and one switched schools.

"You and Britta didn't take your eyes off Sterling, even back then."

There's a worn bitterness in his tone.

"We were at your house, waiting for our parents to come pick us up. You and Britta were laughing about something," he continues. "And your dad came over and stood by me. Sterling and Eli were throwing a football back and forth, and Ridge and Mateo were going through their candy. Anyway, he said something I'll never forget."

I turn my whole body toward him. This is a fragment of my father that doesn't belong to me.

Jensen holds the steering wheel with one hand and runs another through his hair.

"He looked at me like I was the most important person in his life, and it made me wish . . . I wished that he was my father. I think it was the first time I registered the huge hole in my life. I wanted him to leave your mom and marry mine."

My jaw drops, but I'm quick to close it as Jensen goes on.

"I was thirteen, so I hope you'll forgive me for that."

I bite my lip, because it's not something I'm going to hold over him. "Of course."

"He put a hand on my shoulder and said, 'I don't know what she sees in him.'"

Me and Sterling. We were thirteen. I'm embarrassed to think my dad knew I had a crush on Sterling.

"Then he said, 'Someday,'" Jensen continues, his tone imitating my father's, "'you'll find the words to tell her how you feel, and when you do, it'll be like plucking a star from the sky.'"

It's just like my father to say something so ambiguous to a kid. And it's just like Jensen to remember it. Any other combination and it wouldn't have stuck.

"I thought he was weird," Jensen tacks on.

"He was."

Our combined laugh, soft and short, has become our song, and I'm cool if it's on repeat.

"I thought he was talking to himself," Jensen continues, "but he wasn't. At that time in my life, he was vital to me. I replayed those words in my mind a lot. To be honest, I wrote them down."

"You did not."

Jensen cracks a sad smile, so I don't tease him about keeping a diary, but I do save this nugget for another time.

"I'm glad you have that memory," I say, lowering my voice. I take his hand back in mine, and I don't let go.

We slow down, and then take a dirt road that looks to lead absolutely nowhere, and I revisit thirteen-year-old Jensen's wish for my father to be his. It's both bitter and sweet.

We hit a particularly rocky patch, and I'm pulled from my thoughts. "I don't think you're the serial murder type, but should I be concerned?"

I flash him a smile, but his response is a wordless look that induces a fever. I almost glance away as my cheeks flare red. He rakes his eyes over my body, and his smile is devious. I see the rogue, the rascal, the devil that he's refined over the years.

But now I know it's a mask, and I bust out laughing, and just like that, the hunter is gone and all I see is a lone wolf.

He lets go of my hand and takes the wheel, a laugh on his lips, and I sink back into my seat. Jensen slows down, but we're stirring up dust, and I wonder if he's worried about scratching his car.

We pass a couple of cabin homes, complete with white, vinyl

fences and horses. But as we keep going, the cabins begin to diminish, the elevation begins to change, the trees thicken, and I start to think we're in the wrong car for this.

I guess if we run out of gas, we're not that far from humanity. We'll be fine. There are signs of life, and horses to ride home if there's a zombie apocalypse.

And this is a sign that I've read *The Hatchet* and *World War Z*.

We drive for another twenty minutes until the road ends in a gravel parking lot for two, maybe three cars. Jensen parks and turns the engine off, then grabs a blanket from the trunk. He spreads it on the hood to protect us from the heat of the engine, and protecting the paint job, I suppose.

"We won't dent the hood?" I ask as he helps me climb up.

"No. She can handle it."

For a millisecond, I wonder how many other girls he's brought here, but I force the thought away.

I distract myself by naming the clouds. And for the most part, it works.

"Most of these are cumulus clouds," I say. "You can tell, because they have a flat base but are puffy like a cotton ball."

"Nellie," Jensen says.

"Yeah?"

"There's something I need to tell you."

CHAPTER 16

I Almost Tell Nellie

Jensen

The words are on my tongue—*I'm Jen Dimes*. I want to tell her. It would make everything easier. However, it's not like I rehearsed a speech on the way up. It's more like water behind a dam, demanding to be released.

And I know why too.

I cracked the flood gate by taking Nellie to my apartment, by showing her my car. If I pull the release now, however, I fear we'll have a flood. I can hear Nellie's skeptical laugh; she uses it around Britta all the time. And I worry she'll realize Sokha is based on her. That fear is enough to clamp the gate shut. Now I have to come up with something else to tell her.

"What is it?" Nellie asks when I don't go on.

"I bet Sterling. The money for the suit and your dress? Came because of the best lips contest."

"What?"

"But honest, I didn't think you'd be involved. It was just supposed to be a way for him to kiss someone in front of everyone, and I didn't think that whoever ended up being chosen would actually do it."

"Why?" Her face flushes.

"Because we're dumb? But it wasn't until after you put your name in the ballot hat that I realized what Sterling and Britta had really planned."

She takes a big breath and looks away. I feel like a jerk.

"I'm so sorry," I say.

"It's okay. I mean, you didn't know."

"Honest. I didn't know—not all of it, anyway."

She has to feel betrayed, but she catches me completely off guard when she says, "It doesn't matter now."

"Why not?"

"Because my first kiss doesn't matter. It was the second one that counts."

"Oh?" She won't look at me, but so what. It's what she says that matters.

"Look, my first kiss was never gonna be magic. But you . . . you delivered." She turns a shade of red I've never seen on her before. I'm equally impressed at her boldness and proud of myself—I didn't realize she felt that way, about me kissing her, anyway.

She turns toward me, confidence replacing the shyness, and I rotate toward her. Lying on the hood of my car isn't as comfortable as you'd think, but I barely notice.

"Someday, when I'm old and reminiscing about my first kiss, I'll remember Sterling, sure. But I'll always think of you. You're the one that counts."

"You mean that?"

"Yeah."

"So what you're saying is that you want more *Fast and Furious* than *Little Mermaid*?"

"Wow. Those movies are old. And dumb."

"Hey, now. Nobody knocks Paul Walker, God rest his soul."

"Fine. You can have Paul Walker as long as I get Katherine Freese."

"Okay, I'll bite. Who's Katherine Freese? A model or something?"

Nellie blurts out a laugh. "No."

"Then tell me. Who is she?"

"You'll laugh."

"I'm laughing now," I say rolling onto my back. I cross my arms and my legs. "Come on."

"She's an astrophysicist."

"Of course she is, and you know that because . . ."

"Because I did my senior research paper on her. I covered her life, her education, and her accomplishments, of course, but I focused most of my paper on her research of dark matter and dark stars."

Nellie beams as she looks up at the sky. I try to picture what dark stars are, but all I can scrounge up are black holes. I like the idea of a dark star. That seems like something I could work into Hagon's world. I'd like to see what a dark star looks like to MeganLovesHagon257.

"Who was your paper about?" Nellie asks.

Every year, a senior picks someone off a list provided by the English teachers. No one can have the same person, so once you make your pick, that name is removed from the list. Next year, the list will be completely new, too, to prevent students from copying someone else's paper.

I was late in choosing someone, so I got stuck with—

"Leonard Bernstein. It was painful. Too bad Leonard Cohen wasn't on the list."

"The famous orchestra conductor versus the man who wrote 'Hallelujah.' Yeah, I can see that."

"Of course you know who Bernstein is."

"Sorry?" She doesn't sound apologetic, though.

"Don't be. It's one of the reasons I like you so much." I wait to see what her reaction is. At first, it's shy and distant, as she glances at the clouds. Then she looks at me, round eyes and quirked lips.

"I like you too," she says. She holds my gaze, and I'm the one who can't handle it. I swallow a lump in my throat and look up at the sky. I force myself to say something.

"So, dark stars, huh?"

"Yeah," she says, and then recounts a few facts. "Dark stars emit very little light and may have existed before conventional stars were born."

Stars are born?

Between admitting that we like each other and this galactic fact, I think she just broke my brain.

I try to understand, but contemplating the universe is not easy for me. If Nellie were cosmic matter, she would be Andromeda. Another galaxy, full of light and color and mystery. I'd be a space station.

"How you remember that kind of stuff is beyond me. You're a freak," I say, nudging her shoulder.

"Better a freak than a wild card."

"Ain't that the truth."

We sit there for a few more minutes, and then I push off the car and reach for her. She takes my hand and slides off the hood.

"We should probably get going."

"You're right," she whispers, staring into my eyes as if she can't quite see me. As if I am a dark star. Again, I'm afraid she'll discover me before I'm ready to shine, so I try to dim whatever light I've got.

But then I realize she's not looking into my soul. She's looking at me, at my mouth. I flash a smile and step back.

"No way am I kissing you now, Samsin," I say, pulling her toward the passenger side.

"What?"

"How can I? I mean, you're wanting speed, and I'm a fan of the *Little Mermaid*."

"So you're never going to kiss me again?"

"No. I'm just going to wait for the right moment."

"Well, you just ruined what I thought was a perfect moment." She looks kinda ticked as she starts to get into the car. So I grab her by the elbow, thinking of the kissing that happens in action movies, and pull her back to me. I'm not going to take advantage of her, and I won't respond to pouting, that's for sure. Pouting is a classic Britta move.

Instead, I whisper into her ear.

"I've liked you for as long as I can remember. And I want to kiss you. But here's the thing. Summer's coming, and I don't want this to be a fling."

She's startled, maybe because I grabbed her, maybe because I'm speaking a raw truth that even I didn't know was in me.

"I don't want that either."

"And I know you're hurting. It's a deep wound that's going to leave a scar. But trust me, I've let girls use me to feel better, and I've done the same to them. It never lasts."

She nods.

"I don't want to be that guy, not with you."

"You're not that guy."

I kiss her cheek, and she wraps her arms around me and hugs me. We stay like that for a minute until she pulls back and says, "Okay."

Once we settle back into my car, we fall into mindless talk about the songs on my XM radio and scroll through various stations until I notice how tired she looks.

"You want to sleep? You can. Really. It's okay."

She reclines the seat, and within minutes, she's out. Without her, the drive holds no spark, and the radio fails to provide a good distraction. Nellie doesn't seem to relax either. She twitches as if she's stuck in a REM cycle.

Once we pull into our neighborhood, I start to plan my moves. I want to kiss her good night, for sure. A classic, front-porch kiss. As soon as we turn on to our street, Nellie wakes up and flashes me a smile.

"Sorry I crashed," she says, rubbing her eyes and sitting up.

"Nah. I'm glad you got some rest."

As soon as I pull into her drive, though, we spot her mom, staring at us from the living room window, her lips in a hard line, ice in her eyes. The timing seems uncanny.

She sees the Porsche, she sees Nellie, and when her gaze lands on me, the chill in my bones is definite. Everything in me tells me to throw the car in reverse and take off, but Nellie's hand on my arm stays me. She gives a little squeeze, her attention on her mom.

"Thank you, Jensen. I'll see you Monday."

And then she's gone.

It's barely past six, but Angela peels herself away from the window. I am careful not to spin out or squeal the tires, because maybe she didn't see me. Maybe the Porsche threw her off. Maybe?

Doubt it.

I dash home to grab my laptop and Sean's, but from there, I'm in a haze as I drive back to my apartment. At a red light, I text my mom and tell her I'm going to do some writing. She replies with smile emojis and clapping hands, and that's it.

When I get to my apartment, I set down Sean's laptop and take mine to the desk. I can't tackle his stuff right now. No, the words in my mind are burning, and the only way to put this kind of fire out is to turn blank, white pages into lines of dialogue and description. Sokha and Hagon will have to deal with me now.

I let the world around me go and step into the world I've made up. In here, I'm the god of this place—and I can do whatever I want. The world of Hern takes me far away from reality because I can pour what I'm thinking and feeling into Sokha and Hagon instead of dealing with it myself.

A fleeting thought comes and goes—this is probably cheaper than therapy.

I don't care if the timing is off or if the scene will need to be completely scrapped later. Sokha and Hagon have been apart for so long. They've known bloodshed and war, and I want to take them away from it all. I want to make them forget. I want to forget.

They've killed, they've hunted, and they've stolen. Sokha bleeds left and right, but she heals quickly. Hagon's training has come at a price, and he swears at the moon and curses hell, and even though he's burdened with protecting the Blood Rock, he thinks of others first.

And they kiss. Of course they kiss.

They've kissed in rotting barns when they've hidden from the ghouls of Neferler, and Sokha stole a kiss in the craggy cave of Mount Velour before Hagon jumped across the Crevice of Souls. They kissed along the River Swheren before parting ways at the end of *Shadow Stone*.

But they've never taken their clothes off—unless you count the time Hagon pulled back Sokha's shirt to examine her already-healing wounds because he didn't know she was magic.

Or the time Hagon undressed so he could bathe. Sokha turned her gaze away.

The buildup is there.

It's been six weeks since their last kiss, and I don't care if giving them over completely to instinct is right or wrong or poorly timed. I write each sentence with more intensity than I've ever written anything. I rely on what I've seen in movies, on television, and on my own experiences. I've never gone all the way, but I have a pretty good idea of what I need to make the scene work.

I try to always be true to my characters and honest with myself about them, but now, I take control, because it's the only place where I can make things go according to my plan.

And let's be real. Hagon and Sokha aren't going to complain.

CHAPTER 17

Nellie Likes Jensen! Nellie Likes Jensen!

Nellie

My stomach is in knots as I approach my front door. I've probably got an ulcer. Too bad a couple of antacids won't fix my problems.

As soon as I enter, I notice the two glasses of wine on the coffee table, but I don't look directly at them. Instead, my attention goes straight to my mom's face. I see a crimson heat swirling with black clouds, and my defenses go up, because I've faced this kind of storm before.

"Hey," I say. *Remain calm.*

"Where have you been?"

"With Jensen."

"You were supposed to be home hours ago."

"Sumerli said you said before dinner."

Beads of sweat form along my hairline. I feel like she's going to ground me, and if she does, fine. I'll move out. Technically, I could. I'm old enough. The day after graduation, I could do it. I have my own checking account, and I could get a job. I was going to move out anyway, right? The only real question is where would I go?

Jensen's.

His name pops into my mind as the answer for everything now.

Mom says nothing and just pins me with her stare.

There are three stages to the life cycle of a typical thunderstorm: cumulus, mature, and dissipating. I hear Mr. Miskin's voice all of a sudden. But my mom isn't typical. Most times, I have no idea where we're at in the storm's cycle.

"It's late," she says as thoughts of my sophomore science class fade away.

"It's only six."

"I know what time it is." She turns her back on me, picks up the glasses, and finishes off the last of her drink. I silently acknowledge the second glass, and my stomach tightens and my palms go sweaty.

I have questions, but I'm too scared of the truth. When she turns back to me, she looks at me in surprise. "Don't you have homework or something?"

Jensen and I got the yearbook straightened out, and everything's been sent to the printers, and finals have been taken. I don't even have to go to school this week, to be honest. All that's left is graduation rehearsal and the senior barbecue and the buzz of wrapping up.

Say what she wants to hear.

"Yeah, I've got some studying to do," I lie.

Mom heads toward the kitchen. Over her shoulder, she says, "Well, then, you better get to it."

Thunderstorm Angela moves from stage one to stage three effortlessly. Fun fact: most storms cool temperatures by ten to fifteen degrees, but she's more like a summer storm with impressive theatrical skills because she can take a balmy ninety-seven degrees down to a chilly winter day in less than an hour.

"You're doing okay?" she adds.

She doesn't really want the answer. If she did, she'd have sat me down and rubbed my back and talked to me. She should've asked me days ago if I was okay. She should've hugged me and held me through my tears. I'm realizing now that moment is never coming.

"Yeah. Being with friends helps." *Not a lie.*

"Hard to come home, right?" Her voice almost suggests she feels pain.

I wait, hoping she'll say more. A long moment passes, and I give up.

"I'll be in my room."

With every step, I wonder if she remembers the last thing she and Dad talked about. Maybe she can recall their last conversation verbatim. Does she think about the small things? Like how Dad always mowed the lawns on Wednesdays and Sundays, and how he'd wake up late but still make it to work on time? Does she realize he'll never read in his brown recliner again?

I keep wondering as I lay in my bed, not about the stranger who was here drinking wine with my mom, but about the man who was always here. I wonder if he had regrets. I wonder what he was like when he was my age. I wonder what he would've said if I'd told him about Sterling, about Britta betraying me the way she did. I'm conscious of the single, hot tear that spills over my cheek as I stare at the ceiling when I wonder if he felt any pain when the aneurysm ruptured.

I hear the television, and if Mom goes to bed, I don't know it. Sunday night comes and takes me with it.

When Mom knocks on my door in the morning and calls after me to get up, I can barely open my eyes.

"You're going to be late if you don't get up," she hollers. "I've gotta go. I have a meeting this morning about your father's life insurance policy."

I hear the back door close, the garage door open and close, and the purr of her car fade away, and I fall back into oblivion.

A faint thumping sound wakes me hours later. I squint to read my alarm clock, and I don't even freak when I process that it's noon. So what? I've missed nothing. It's quiet now, so I must've imagined the noise.

Then the knocking returns.

"Nellie? Are you home? Nellie?" Britta calls.

I reach for my phone wondering why she didn't call before

coming over, but it's dead. That happens when you don't plug it in.

"Hang on!" I holler as I pull myself out of bed. When I open the front door, I shade my eyes.

"Dang, girl. You look like—" Britta starts.

"Shuddup."

Instantly, all the heat I've kept bottled up since Jensen told me what she did rises to the surface. It's a struggle not to let it boil over. Maybe I should let it all out. I was nothing more than a target to her. But before I can say anything, Britta grabs my hand and pulls me toward the bathroom.

"Shower."

"No." I jerk out of her hold. All these years, I've let her run me around, but not now, not after what she's done. "What are you doing here?"

"When you didn't show up for graduation rehearsal at ten, I knew you needed an intervention."

"Exaggerate much?"

"Always. You can't miss this. This is it."

And on that one point, she's right. This *is* it. This is the week I graduate from high school, and the heat within me reduces to a simmer. I don't want to miss out on what comes next. Begrudgingly, I walk toward the shower, debating whether or not to confront her about the prank.

Once the water's running, Britta comes back into the bathroom.

"Anyway, Marbles wants to go to a movie, and I'm here to get you. He asked me who he should invite so you wouldn't feel like a third wheel, and I told him you spent all day yesterday with Jensen, and he said 'Cool' and that he'd text Jensen. And sure enough Jensen texted back that he'd be down if you're going, so I told Marbles you were in but then I had to bolt over here because you're not ready to go to a movie. So now we're going to a movie." She takes a breath then asks, "Did you and Jensen kiss?"

"Wow, Britta."

"Well?"

I turn the water off and stick out my hand, and she passes me my towel. I'm not going to talk to her about this. It's none of her business. Also, I don't want her to hear my voice. She'll know instantly that I'm super into Jensen and she'll assume we did kiss. Maybe Jensen told Marbles, too, and she's just trying to confirm. Regardless, she'll analyze our kiss with more thought than she's ever given any of our English lit assignments, and that's the last thing I need.

"Have you ever thought about working for the FBI?" I ask. "You would be good at interrogations."

"I'll look into it." Her tone grows sharper. "Did you and Jensen kiss or not? Because—"

"Because what?" I ask as I slide the curtain across. I pull my towel tighter across my body and position it to stay put so I have my hands free.

"Did you shave?"

"Britta." I roll my eyes. "Yes. I shaved. Now finish your sentence."

When she meets my gaze, there isn't a hint of color there. Her mood ring shades are failing me these days. Maybe it's because I haven't spent much time with her in over a week. I grab my bathrobe from the linen closet. I pull it on discreetly, because I'm a prude, I guess. Then I towel dry my hair.

"What were you going to say?" I am not going to fall for another senior prank. I'm not going to stand idly by. "You either tell me, or I'm not going to the movie."

"I was going to say, because Sterling's a better choice than Jensen."

I can't believe she said that.

"A better choice for what?" I ask.

"He's totally non-commitment."

"Britta." I frown as I comb my hair out. I almost suggest that Jensen is a player, too, but I don't. Because he doesn't want to be that guy. Not anymore. And I wonder if he never really was that guy but felt he had to be.

"We're three days away from graduation," Britta says.

"I know that."

"You want to start a relationship now? It's our last summer. Now's your chance to just have some fun. Jensen's not—"

"What? Not fun? Oh, come on, Britta. You've gotta do better than that. Jensen's practically Sterling's protégé." I can't ignore the fact. He might be trying to change, but he certainly knows how to have a good time. I pull out my makeup and decide to do my own before she takes over. I don't want her to touch me.

"Yeah, but he's not, like, as relaxed as Sterling."

"Says who? Just stop. I'm not interested in Sterling anymore." I start applying primer to my eyelids.

"You don't want Sterling?" she says to me. "Really? All those years of pining and doodling his name, and now that he's into you, you don't want to doodle *with* him?"

"You're gross."

"You've gone crazy."

"Yeah, well, that's what happens when your father dies," I snap. I can't take it anymore, but Britta's prickly too.

"Are you suggesting I don't know what it's like to not have a dad? Just because mine is in and out of my life doesn't mean I have a dad. I've been without one for years."

"Typical. You're going to make this about you?" I stop applying my eye shadow, and we lock gazes. There's venom in her gaze, and something more—something sinister. Has she always been this dark? I regret my words, but I won't apologize.

"Why did you even come to the funeral?" I say, taking this in a different direction. "You helped sabotage my first kiss."

Britta flinches, but I press on.

"Yeah, that's right. And you . . . You're self-centered and tacky. Giving me underwear as a gift? At some point, maybe you should stop thinking about yourself and be a real friend to me."

Another thought comes at me. It's bitter, but truthful.

"If my dad were here, he'd give it to me straight. He'd say, 'Nellie, if Britta were a boy, I'd want you to dump her ASAP. She doesn't have your best interests at heart.'"

Britta inhales sharply. The shadows spilling out of her can't handle this side of me.

"Fine. If that's what you want."

"It's not. That's the thing. I'd like us to be friends. I thought we were."

And just like that, another piece of me breaks, but I think I've said everything I needed to.

It's like she flips some switch when she bobs her head up and down and says, "Okay."

I think she finally understands me, but then she says, "Okay. It's Jensen."

The snark in her tone burns me up.

I return my attention to my makeup, sad that she can't see this friendship is falling apart. If it weren't for Jensen, I wouldn't go with her. When I glance back at her, I can tell she's plotting something. My chest tightens, but I try to be lighthearted when I speak.

"You can stop scheming now."

"I'm not—"

"Oh the lies you tell." I drag my words, giving them a deeper incantation. Normally, she'd laugh. This time, she doesn't.

I think about calling off the movie, but I want to see Jensen. I'm surprised she doesn't bail on me. Maybe she feels tied to me too. So we drive to the theater in silence, and fake that everything is fine as soon as we see the boys.

CHAPTER 18

Dress Rehearsal and a Movie

Jensen

Where's Nellie? We're starting graduation rehearsal, and she's not here. I peer around, watching every entrance to the gym, dread building in my gut. I can't believe she's not here.

As we all find our seats, a feeling of connectivity consumes the entire senior class. It's as if we all know this is it, and as much as we want out of here, we also don't want to leave. Because this gymnasium is home, and these people are family. I find myself talking to everyone who crosses my path as if they're the most important person in the world. Seniors I've never spent time with ask me about my plans, and we talk as if we've been friends for years. It's strange, but oddly comforting.

I spot the uber-wealthy Suni Ono talking to computer-geek Mike Stone. It makes me wonder if they're friends online.

Seconds later, I see Sterling engaged in a conversation with Jeigh Meredith. This makes twice now that he's taken notice of her. So weird. Sterling gives any hot girl the time of day, but when he spares me a glance, he just smiles as if this is awesome, which is how I know we're all under some sort of spell. That is, all of us except Nellie.

With 812 of us, it takes three and a half hours to call every-one's names and have us walk up to the stage and back to our seats, and it's annoying to sit through all of it. I swear Mrs. Winter spends more time yelling "Be quiet" than anything else.

On my left and my right are the same two people I've been stuck between since grade school. Emilie Nevarro and Nathan

Orchard, who have been dating since seventh grade, and I feel like a weird third wheel when we sit in alphabetical order. I worry they're going to hold hands across my lap.

Sterling's much better off. He's just over my left shoulder, and he's perfectly positioned between Whitney Laing and twins Rani and Alsa Linden. He's probably realizing for the first time that there's two of them. Whitney doesn't appear to be fighting for his attention, but her shoulder is practically glued to his. I'm trying to remember if she's ever signed up for a date with him when Marbles texts to ask if I want to catch a matinee with Britta and Nellie.

I tell him yes, and the minute we're released from rehearsal, I meet Marbles outside the gymnasium doors.

"Where's Britta?" I ask when she doesn't join us.

"She's gone to get Nellie. They'll meet us at the theater."

"Gotcha. Is Sterling coming?" I ask as we climb into Marbles's car.

"Not this time." He doesn't ask me about Nellie, because it's not like him to pry, and we end up complaining about how long it took to run through rehearsal. We beat the girls to the theater, and Marbles buys all four tickets, even though I offer to pay.

He just says, "Not this time," as if it's his new go-to phrase. He gives me two tickets and then taps his pair against his palm as we wait. As soon as we spot Britta and Nellie in the distance, he finally smiles.

"You really like her, huh?" I ask.

"She's okay," he says before walking toward the girls. I hang back, trying to decipher Marble's true feelings for Britta. Before I come to a conclusion, Nellie's gaze locks on mine, and I get the sensation that something's wrong. Then I note Britta's body language. Cold, hard, chin held high, two steps ahead of Nellie.

Something's up there, and it's not hard to guess now that Nellie knows the truth—at least the truth about the prank.

Nellie's wearing a lightweight, blue sweater that hangs off one shoulder. Her jeans are a shade darker than the sweater, and her earrings brush against her neck, but the only accessory she needs is a smile. It's missing, until her eyes meet mine. I swallow a lump in my throat and run a hand over the back of my head, unable to stop myself from grinning.

"Hey," she says.

"Hey back." Britta and Marbles hustle for popcorn, and we watch them for a second. They're holding hands. "You hungry?"

She nods and licks her shiny lips. "Sure."

I almost take her hand, but she grabs my arm, which is better, and holds on to me as we walk up to the ticket taker.

"Theater six," the attendant says, ripping our tickets in half.

"Thanks," we say in unison.

We get in line for popcorn, an older couple between us and Britta and Marbles. I whisper to Nellie, "Was your mom angry?"

When she turns, her face is so close to mine I could kiss her. I'd like to.

"I think so? I don't know what's up with her. She didn't yell at me. She just . . . gave up. It's like she wanted to fight, but then didn't. It was weird. There were two glasses of wine on the coffee table, though."

The line moves up, so we break apart. After Britta and Marbles get their snacks, they step aside, and about ten seconds later, they glance back at us. Britta gives us a look before she and Marbles walk off.

"What's up with her?" I ask.

"We got into a fight. Honestly, I was going to skip the movie until she said you were coming. I don't know—we're just not on the same page anymore."

"I'm really sorry."

"Thanks. It's not your fault."

We get a bucket of popcorn and drinks and Reese's candy, and when we get to theater six, there are only two other couples in the theater, neither of which are Marbles and Britta.

"Think they went to the bathroom?" Nellie asks as we take two seats toward the top.

"I'll text Marbles."

About ten seconds later, my phone buzzes. I show her Marbles's message.

> We changed our minds and went to
> a different show. Don't hate us.

"They probably want to make out," Nellie says. She doesn't meet my gaze. I wait for her to look at me, thinking that if she does, I'll kiss her, but she's too busy settling into her seat and balancing popcorn and candy.

She flashes me a quick smile, which is encouraging, and then the lights go down. The movie trailers begin, and I debate putting up the armrest but decide to leave it down for now.

Two seconds before the movie begins, Nellie leans in and whispers, "I'm glad it's just us."

"Me too."

The movie screen flickers blue, casting a glow over Nellie's skin.

Eventually, the movie captures my full attention, and Nellie and I are whisked away to a world that isn't ours. I always imagined I'd be hyperaware of the moment when Nellie's hand would find mine or vice versa in a dark movie theater, but it doesn't happen like that. We've spent several days holding on to each other, so it feels both natural and electric when we connect.

I'm pulled back to reality just long enough to look at her hand in mine. Her concentration remains steadfast on the screen. She's beautiful and brilliant. I'm lucky to know her, to be here with her, and I want to make every day with her count.

I want to remember this for a long time, and the only way I know how to trap a memory like this is to weave it into my writing.

From there, I'm fully engaged in the storytelling of the movie. During an intense scene, Nellie jumps and grabs my arm, which is funny. The ending is satisfying, but they do leave it open, hinting at a sequel.

Instead of rising to her feet, Nellie stays still. "Do you like to watch the credits? My dad used to try to spot interesting names."

"Then we better find one for him."

I had forgotten that detail about Sean, but I remember now— he'd watch the credits in search of character names. I wonder if Nellie knows that.

"Call out what you see," she says.

About four seconds later, she says, "Piquet Donaldson."

"Nice one." Then I spot one. "Ropen Hansen Markel."

"That is different. Oh, see it? Ahmiracle Rinaldi?"

"A miracle? Definitely interesting."

The names morph into locations and music credits. There's the producers thank you note, which lists off a bunch of companies and Twentieth Century Fox and such, and I wish I could freeze time and stay here with the epic soundtrack on repeat. But the credits keep rolling until all that's left are the corporate logos—Panoramic, Dolby, and DTS—followed by a message from the American Humane Society, assuring us that no animals were harmed in the making of the film. One last credit gets a little more screen time than the rest, DreamWorks Distribution, LLC, but then that's it. When I close my eyes, I can still see the final image. DreamWorks.

Man, wouldn't that be the dream?

I both fear and fantasize about Blood Rock being a movie. People are rarely satisfied with real actors after reading a book. What if I was unhappy with who they cast? I imagine a score composed by James Horner, Hans Zimmer, or John Williams. I dream of working with a screenwriter, of talking to the director, of visiting the set.

Which, of course, is ridiculous. But still. I want my own end credits. So, no, I haven't been overthinking it.

Under my breath, I say, "I don't want to leave," and when Nellie says, "Me either," I sink into my seat a little further, slightly defiant.

"I think Marbles wanted to sneak into another show," Nellie adds.

"I could do that."

"Me, too, but I should probably check in with my mom."

"I could do that."

Nellie elbows me, laughing. "You're going to check in with my mom?"

"I could try."

"Oh, this ought to be good." She hands me her phone and out of the corner of my eye, I see an employee come in to clear the room and make sure no one stays. Nellie sees him, too, and we feel pressured to leave, even though the attendant says nothing to us. This is proof that we're good citizens, and I'm not nearly the rebel Sterling is, I guess. I'm okay with that.

We do get up, though. Nellie leads the way, and I follow, while simultaneously texting a message to her mom. It's not hard to come up with something to say. The truth is usually best.

> I'm with Britta and Marbles and Jensen. We're going to see a movie. Is that okay?

I show it to Nellie. "Works for me," she says.

I hit send, but before I hand her phone back, I snap a dozen selfies, and then I pull Nellie into me. "Say cheese."

I take another one, and then another one, and then another, because she's not pulling away, and with each shot, we tweak our pose until it's just right. Until it says *we're together*.

"Okay, that's enough," Nellie says, holding out her hand, faking annoyance.

"Hang on."

Because I have to have copies. I'm using mad skills to send myself the photos while she tries to steal her phone back.

"What are you doing?" she asks, grasping.

"Nothing." I dodge her when she tries to tickle me. It's like when we bought the French bread, but this time, she's far more confident about tackling me.

CHAPTER 19

Graduation

Nellie

On the morning of graduation, I wake up to four text messages. Naturally, Britta wants to know what I'm wearing. I'm feeling snarky and tell her a cap and gown. She also says she'll be over at nine to get ready so I should hurry and shower.

Honestly, I can't believe she's coming over.

The only reason I can come up with is that Britta doesn't have other girlfriends. She's good at pulling people into her circle, but she's not close to anyone. I rethink my analysis about how she's like the sun. Maybe the reason no one is drawn closer is because they don't want to get burned.

But I'm not so good at repelling her, so I say nothing and let her come over.

We've got rehearsal from ten to noon, then the senior barbecue at two, and then we're going to her house to freshen up and change and be back at the school by six. Graduation starts at seven, and then the All-Nighter starts at ten and goes until six. Whew!

The other message is from my mom. She's been called into work but she's off at four and will pick up my grandparents and see me at the school. I text her back.

> Sounds good. Love ya.

I mean it, but it's also robotic. She doesn't respond. I pretend it doesn't matter.

The last message is the one I'm most excited about. It's from Jensen.

> I'm thinking of you. Can't wait to see you today.

I can't stop grinning as I stare at the photos he took of us. I wanted him to kiss me so bad at the theater, but it didn't happen. I'm not sure why, but I don't feel discouraged. This is stage one. The frosting phase. I feel warm just thinking about him.

The four of us were in two different cars yesterday. Without words, he and I both understood that we aren't ready for Marbles or Britta to know anything about anything. That's the number one reason why we didn't kiss. I think.

And on the ride home, Britta was a little more normal.

She even said she was sorry about snapping at me, and I apologized, but I'm not convinced either of us were sincere. But we acted like it.

Fake it till you make it can work on friendships, too, right?

I've got my hair done, and I'm in my bathrobe when Britta arrives. I hold on to the excitement of graduating.

"Maybe you got your beauty rest, but some of us were up half the night and need concealer," she says.

"You were up half the night?"

"Pre-grad celebrations."

"Britta?"

"What?" She smiles big but gives me nothing more. Apparently, she doesn't always tell me everything.

I let her do my makeup because it's relaxing and I can rest my tired eyes. When she's done, she starts on herself. She sets her makeup down and stares into the sink. The shift in her demeanor is noticeable.

"Hey, listen. There's something I need to tell you," she says.

I don't like the dark shadow that passes over her.

"It's my biological dad," she starts. She selects a purple eyeliner and picks up where she left off. "He's decided he wants back into my life, again."

"Again? Seriously?" He's done this to her about six times in the last six years. She's pretty good at not letting him get to her.

"TechCon offered him a job, and he moved back."

I note that she's using the past tense.

"Okay," I say. "When?"

"I don't know. I don't understand him."

"You think it's just another empty promise?" I've never seen or met Barry Tayvier; I just know he exists and that his child support checks don't.

She shrugs and starts stuffing her makeup into her cosmetic case and zips it up with too much force. "So, yeah, he's coming tonight. Good times."

"It'll be okay, B."

"Time equals love, and he spends all of his on women. His latest girlfriend is a real piece of work too. He even mentioned he might marry this one."

When she says nothing more, I try to cheer her up because that's what a good friend is supposed to do, right?

"Yikes. A stepmom? I'm sorry. Let's not think about that. What are you going to wear, for real?" Fun fact: Britta likes my clothes better than her own. This yellow shirt of hers is pretty awesome though. Maybe this time she'll stick with her own stuff.

"Not this. What are you going to wear?"

"My PixiePie grass-green top, my SensationX jeans, and my green Chucks—the ones I got in Oregon."

"Wanna trade outfits?" Britta asks as she walks ahead of me. I'm not surprised she wants to wear this outfit of mine. It's my favorite.

"No. I really want to wear what I've picked, B. You can have anything else."

I've put off wearing this for a month so it would feel new again, but her expressions are flickering off and on like a worn neon sign and I don't think she heard me.

She pulls her shirt off and tosses it to me, but I stand protectively over my green outfit.

"Not this time, Britta."

I hold her shirt out, insistent.

She narrows her eyes at me, and then takes back her yellow shirt. "Someone finally decided not to be a rug."

I don't respond to that jab. She turns and starts walking out without pulling her shirt on and yells at me, "Let's go, loser."

And just like that, I exhale a breath, proud of myself and yet completely disappointed in her, and that's how my last day of my senior year begins.

When we get to school, the energy is palpable. I scan the empty bleachers, recalling a variety of memories. Our mascot, a warrior, is intricately painted on the gym floor, but he's buried beneath the four hundred folding chairs, and something about this causes me to pause. There's a prick at the back of my throat, and again, I experience saudade. I want the status quo to stay the same because I'm already missing this place. I think of my Rainbow Dash key chain and correct my original assumption. She's not ready to fly the coop.

She'd rather spend another year here, where things are predictable, in the daily company of Jensen.

I spot the seat on the stage where I'll be sitting and as soon as I make my way up there, I'm greeted by a frenzied Mrs. Sharie.

"Oh, thank the staples! You're here."

"The staples?" I repeat, confused.

"I'm trying to keep it all together—get it?"

"Ah, yes." I force a laugh.

"You ready to do this?" Mrs. Sharie looks at my empty hands. "Where's your speech?"

Now I'm looking at my empty hands and questioning how I could've possibly forgotten—

"No matter," Mrs. Sharie says. "We can print you a new one. Unless you've got it memorized?"

I don't respond.

I started drafting the speech two weeks ago, but with the yearbook and my dad, I never finished it.

"Nellie, you do have a speech, don't you?"

"No. I mean, yes," I say, trying to soothe her. The fine lines around her eyes crinkle and deepen. I pull my phone from my pocket and wave it at her. "Yes, I have it."

She seems satisfied, while I, on the other hand, go into full panic mode. What am I going to do?

"Everyone, please find your seats." Mrs. Sharie coughs and adjusts the microphone. "Mr. Landon, do you mind?"

As she calls out Sterling, everyone's attention is drawn to him. I feel nothing at the mention of his name. He enjoys the scrutiny and rewards everyone with a toothy smile and pulls his shirt back on.

Mrs. Sharie launches into her practiced welcome, and then Jeigh leads the choir in a rendition of the school's alma mater. Time flies by as I struggle to edit my speech on my phone. Normally, I can type like mad, but my fingers are sweaty, and my internet connection is being fickle. When I hear my name through the microphone, I stop typing and look up at the hundreds of faces full of anticipation.

I swallow the knot in my throat, wishing I had a drink of water. I rise to my feet and look at Mrs. Sharie.

"Tonight," I whisper, "would it be okay if I brought a bottle of water with me?"

"Yes, of course."

With that, I approach the podium and adjust the microphone. I clear my throat, which makes me look unprepared. Never mind that I am. No one in the crowd would believe that for an instant.

I spot several faces that I care about, friends from StuCo and Honors English, Theo McNell who took me to Winterfest, Tomas and Shanna who randomly joined us for lunch. Britta. But when I see Jensen, I linger on him. He's practically beaming.

I take another moment to collect myself, and hope that everyone thinks it's for dramatic effect. Which works for me.

"I cannot in good conscience deliver my rousing speech and

spoil the surprise. In a few hours, when you hear it for the first and only time, I promise it will be worth it."

The students cheer like absolute fools, and Jensen claps as if I just delivered the best speech ever.

I promise it will be worth it? I feel stupid and inadequate.

The entire administration looks at me wearily, but nobody tells me to give my actual speech.

Mrs. Sharie follows my act with a big, awkward, "Nellie Samsin, your valedictorian!"

Then roll call begins. One by one, row by row, we start with Abigail Allen, who has been first on every class list since we were in kindergarten.

Andrew Anderson. Luann Awatha. Tomas Balderas.

Two seconds later, my phone vibrates again and again. Britta is bombing me.

> Rousing speech?

> It will be worth it?

There are a dozen emojis included with each comment, along with a gif of Hilary Duff laughing her head off. Then she sends one more message.

> Good luck with that.

Man, she and my mom make quite a team. Tears threaten to spill. Granted, maybe I'm implying tone to her texts and getting it all wrong.

I don't know.

I just have to keep going. I'm rereading the third paragraph of my "rousing" speech for the fifth time when Jensen texts me. He wants to know if I'm okay.

I tell him what's going on, and his response is the one Britta should have offered.

If anyone can draft and edit a rousing, presidential, epic, and life-altering speech in under an hour, it's you.

I'll search the web for some good one-liners you can add. Just tweak them to make them your own.

I look up and mouth the words, "Thank you."

Sure enough, he is quick to find me some inspiring material. When his name is called, I watch him shake hands with our principal. He's a shooting star that will never burn out, and I realize that I don't just like him. I need him. How did I manage to make it this far in my life without him?

He winks at me as he passes, and if it weren't for all the witnesses, I'd jump up and throw my arms around him and rise on my tippy-toes and bring my face close to his and tell him he's the best and that I looovvve him.

I love him?

I stop myself right there before those three words consume me. Meanwhile, Jensen walks across the platform and down the stairs with a recognizable swagger.

I don't just like Jensen. I almost whisper *fun fact* when I hear myself evaluate my feelings. I like Jensen, a lot. I love him as a friend, and I am so in love with the idea of us being together. However, when I try to tell myself that I do *not* love him, a shapeless misery rises in my heart. It's a different beast made of dark matter, and it will never leave me alone if I tell myself this lie.

"I do love him." I whisper it to myself, making sure no one hears, and the terrible blackness fades.

I love Jensen, I think again, allowing myself to consider it. *I love Jensen Nichols.*

But does he feel the same? The question weighs a million pounds.

When my name is called, I stand up and shake hands with the

administrators in line. *I love Jensen.* I pretend to pose for a picture and return to my seat. *I love Jensen.* My cheeks start to hurt because of my smile, and I'm not smiling because this rehearsal ceremony is making graduation real. I'm smiling because I love Jensen.

I'm stunned for several minutes, my speech all but forgotten as I process my feelings toward Jensen. I love Jensen, and I have for a very long time, but what was once friend-love is now something so much more. But is it real?

Or is it just because of the trauma and pressure of these last two weeks?

My phone vibrates again.

> Want some more help? You could share the doc with me.

I glance up at Jensen, and mouth "Yes" with a huge smile, though I know he has no idea why I'm grinning from ear to ear. In a matter of minutes, his avatar is present on my Google doc, which is now titled "My Rousing and Epic Speech for Graduation."

His first change is minor. The next is more substantial, and I watch him work instead of finishing the draft. He swaps one word for a stronger one. He moves sentences around, and after a couple of minutes, I remember myself. My job is to draft, and he cleans up my word vomit like he's a professional editor.

He highlights one section and leaves a comment.

> This part is really good, Nellie. I'm impressed.

And by the time Hero Yeager and Ruby Yeates cross the stage, I have a two-page document.

The choir sings again, and then on cue, we all pretend to move our tassels, and then of course there's yelling and such, and a huge exhale on Mrs. Sharie's part. She tries to remind us over the din to be early for tonight.

I don't know how yesterday's rehearsals went, but this one held a serious note to it, despite moments of laughter, someone tripping up the stairs, and my obscure "speech."

There's a lot of commotion as people leave, but Jensen makes his way to the stage and manages to extract me from the adults who are encircling me and offering their condolences. My hand slips into his, and he pulls me out a back door, headed in the opposite direction of everyone else.

"Where are we going?" I ask.

"Mr. Ming's room. You need to practice."

Mr. Ming is the debate teacher, and he has a podium, and I can picture myself standing behind it, reading the speech Jensen and I just wrote.

"Good idea."

Mr. Ming's classroom isn't locked, thankfully. Jensen sits in the middle row, third chair back.

I practice for a half an hour before I start to feel good about it. On my fourth run-through, Jensen doesn't interrupt me once, and when I finish, his silence weighs on me as if what just happened was spiritual. Somehow, we've managed it.

We don't make a sound until we're outside, the warmth of the sun inviting and perfect for a day like today.

"I'm starving," Jensen says.

I laugh, but the truth is, "So am I."

We take my car to the park, walk a quarter of a mile to the pavilion where the senior barbecue is being held, and arrive just in time to get in line and fill our plates. I scoop strawberry spinach salad onto my plate, and for the first time ever, it feels as if I'm no longer a quiet moon on the outskirts of orbit. There's a lot of hugging from students I barely know, and they say things to me I'm not expecting. Maybe it's because their hugs are really good-byes. The connectivity that binds us today is truly a cosmic miracle, and with each hug, I do the one thing Britta always harped about. I live in the moment. So when Nichole Brower says, "I'm sorry about your dad," I look her in the eye and say, "Thank you."

I say the things I should've said years ago.

"You're so fun, Nichole. I wish we had gotten to know each other better. And I love your bracelet."

"Thanks," she says. "I made it." She extends her wrist to me, and I admire her handiwork. It's a charm bracelet, and every item has something to do with *Blood Rock*.

"I like the sword."

"Me too," she says and then she's off, rejoining her friends. They all have charm bracelets and big smiles and bright futures.

When Jared Palenske says, "I'm sorry for your loss," I make sure to tell him that he's funny and really gave me a run for my money in AP government. He smiles at me before he leaves.

Sarah Smith says, "You're amazing, Nellie. I've been thinking about you a lot," and I tell her, "Thanks. I think you're pretty amazing, too. I hope your modeling job works out for you." She's been modeling for years, and this summer she's hoping to model full-time.

"Thanks, Nellie." Sarah says, before turning to join her friends.

I keep it up too. I make sure to compliment everyone who takes the time to talk to me, and I mean every word I say.

When Britta looks my way, I'm practically wearing a perma-grin and hear her voice. *Carpe diem.* But her expression doesn't match her words anymore.

And for a minute, it's like I don't even know her.

However, by the time I'm putting on my cap and gown, her expression keeps popping up like malware. But because I'm scheduled to be on stage, I don't get the chance to talk to her, and I can't text her because I've drained my phone's battery by writing a speech, sharing photos, and taking videos.

I have to preserve the remaining eleven percent I have left. When I spot my grandparents and mom coming through the main doors, I forget about Britta.

They're here.

It's not like I was worried they wouldn't come, but I do feel some relief when my grandpa spots me and gives me a thumbs-up.

Behind my mom is an attractive man wearing an orange ball cap and glasses, and for a second I think it's Marbles, but obviously it's not.

My mom takes her mother by the arm and guides her through the masses, Grandpa following behind them.

Everything's perfect.

Well, almost perfect.

The space next to my mom—the space where my dad should be—is a black hole that threatens to swallow me. A sting in my chest shoots up to my eyes, and my throat tightens. I squeeze my water bottle.

I hope she'll save a seat for him, as a sort of tribute. I want her to, but the ushers are squishing parents into the gym like Noah squished animals into his ark. Two by two they come, hand in hand, faces beaming.

Proud parents, left and right, arrive carrying candy and money leis and bouquets of roses and envelopes stuffed with gift cards and cash. I imagine someone will get luggage tonight while someone else will get a car.

And the flood in me rises.

I'm tormented when I think about what my gift might be. A portion of my father's life insurance? Because *life insurance is for the living, Nellie.* And my torment morphs to unimaginable devastation because my mom probably hasn't given a single thought to a graduation gift.

My knee is bouncing, my palms are clammy, and my stomach is tight. I almost run to the bathroom, but then I see Sumerli Nichols come in. She's alone and empty-handed, other than her purse. I calm down immediately and focus on her.

She's wearing a jade green dress and has her hair pulled into a French twist. She spots Jensen, and the delighted expression that dawns on her face is probably the exact same one she wore when he was born, and when he turned one, and two, and three, and every year and every day since. I try not to be jealous.

And then she looks at me. Her gaze is warm, confident, and

something else. Knowing? Maybe. She pumps her fist ever so slightly, and this gesture puts all my fears aside and anchors me. She's proud of me, and that courses through my veins like a drug.

And then I'm struck by another realization. Not everyone here is paired up. Of course there are single parents. There are grandmas without grandpas here tonight. Divorced couples sitting separately, perhaps. A lone best friend who previously graduated who came to be supportive. That man in the orange ball cap.

He's still trailing behind my mom.

Mom directs Grandma and Grandpa to sit next to Britta's mom and stepdad, and once they're settled, she takes her seat next to Grandpa. He's hard of hearing, but his sight is still good. He's looking right at me, too, so I wave again. But I'm waiting for Mom to put her purse in the seat next to her. To save it.

But she doesn't. She tucks her purse below her feet, and a woman in a business suit takes the seat that should be Dad's.

I inhale slowly and exhale equally slow.

It's okay. It's going to be okay.

My attention falls to the orange cap; it's an eyesore. He takes a seat directly behind Mom, and row by row, every seat fills up. Most people blend into the crowd, but those who stand out, really capture my attention.

Everyone here is living a complex life. Not just me.

Twenty-five minutes later, Mrs. Sharie stands up.

From that moment to the moment she says my name is a duplication of this morning, but this time we have an audience, and everything feels blurry.

I rise on weak legs. As I take my place in front of the mic, my heart begins to beat too fast. My fingers are shaking. All this time, I thought my heart was dead, but being with Jensen was like being on bypass—he kept my heart going somehow. But now, for the first time since Dad died, I can feel it pounding behind my rib cage, and it's super uncomfortable. And every word of my speech suddenly feels incoherent and unworthy of this moment.

I take another breath, look up at everyone, and see nothing at all. I blink, trying to get my eyes to focus. They don't. Not really.

"Years ago, it was my intention to become your valedictorian. It was a part of my *plan*." I'm rewarded with a light chuckle from the students. That's good. Because from here on out, I'll be improvising. "I promised you an epic speech, and I have it. Right here."

I hold up my phone and wave it, but then slowly set it down on the podium.

"The thing is—it's no longer the speech I'm supposed to give." I hear a baby cry, and someone coughs. I continue. "Thank you, Jensen, for helping me earlier today, and please forgive me for going off script." I look at him, long and steady. He nods at me, his eyes sparkling with curiosity. I force a small smile and go on, because in some ways, this is a last goodbye.

"As I sat here, I realized that what I want to say to all of you is what my dad would say to me . . . if he were here."

The crowd goes completely still. My mom looks at me as if she's finally coming out of her coma and remembering who I am.

I take a deep breath. My skin tingles, and the pounding inside of me is a drum, one that is mine alone. My nerves dissipate, and I come to a place that is all mine when I'm in front of an audience.

"The first thing he'd say is 'Congratulations. I knew you could do it.' And he'd be referring to my goal of being your valedictorian, of getting my associate's degree, and of being accepted into my first-choice college. He'd probably add something like, 'You've earned it.' And he'd mean it, but let's be honest—I didn't get here all on my own. So, thank you, to the faculty and staff here at Ataraxia High. You have given your all to us, day in and day out, and your place is secure among the stars."

There's applause, and someone shouts "Let's go, warriors!" I chuckle along with the crowd.

"The second thing my dad would say is 'Keep going. Don't you quit.' Someone here in this audience needs to know: You're of worth, and your life matters, and that anything you want is within reach. We are capable of amazing things. We were born to create, and sharing our ideas is a noble cause. We are the future, and whatever your ambition—don't you quit. You can do this.

"Because the truth is—we still have mountains to climb."

I feel a tear slide down my cheek. I think I'll spend the rest of my life trying to overcome the mountain before me, the one that exists now that my father doesn't.

"My dad always had a plan. He had a backup plan for his backup plan. But there were lots of times, God just said, 'Let's see how Sean Samsin handles this,' and then the worst would come raining down on him. And on those days, my dad would smile and say, 'Nellie, sometimes the best-laid plans are simply foundation stones.'

"So when you don't get that job, say to yourself: foundation stone.

"When you screw up at your first job, and let's face it, we probably will, just say: foundation stone.

"Or when your friends trick you into giving away your first kiss, or when the formatting for the yearbook is off, or when the very worst possible thing that could happen to you happens, and you don't get the chance to say goodbye . . . you say: foundation stone."

Tears are streaming down my cheeks now, and I wipe at them.

"And then you take every ounce of strength you have, and you pick up the stones. You take the good ones—and build."

I take one more breath, reining in myself, and then give my last words everything I can.

"So the thought I leave with you today is this: In your post-high school life, create your own world. Your greatest creation is yet to come!"

I step back from the podium, and the roar in my ears is a different kind of music. I'm sure they're mostly clapping because it's an obligation, but I don't care. I'm grateful I don't have to walk very far to sit down. Finally, I'm able to meet the eyes of those who love me. My mom is smiling and clapping alongside her parents, and for a second, I forget that things are intense between us. Grandpa's clapping his hands above his head, and Grandma's clap is like a toy monkey crashing its cymbals but it's adorable. Sterling's smiling, and he looks genuinely proud of me, although I suspect he's still hoping I'm interested in "taking lessons."

Britta's golf clapping.

I focus on the one face that means the most to me right now. Jensen and I smile at each other until the crowd dies down, until the emcee speaks, until "Pomp and Circumstance" begins playing.

He nods at me and then, to my surprise, shapes his hands into a heart.

I love Jensen. And maybe . . . *maybe* he loves me too.

Abigail Allen stands and leads her row forward, up the stairs, and toward the line of administrators. Her hand is shaking when she accepts her diploma. Then, like we practiced, we graduate.

There are shouts from the crowd. The occasional "We love you, Julie!" or "We love you, Rett!" and the endless clapping gives me a headache.

Jerome Chandler, our six-foot-six point guard, approaches Mr. Lockwood, who was also the boys' basketball varsity coach, and they perform an elaborate hand shake before hugging. Jerome takes his diploma, turns to the students, and in a deep, booming voice calls, "Warriors!" I think he's the one who yelled it during my speech, actually.

When Callie Hansen shakes hands with the principal, some guy on the left-hand side of the gym stands up with a dozen red roses and yells, "Marry me, Callie!"

She turns to look at him, and I can't see her face, but she yells back, "Okay!" and then she moves along, and the names continue. I spend a few minutes contemplating if it was a joke or for real. I honestly don't know.

When it's my turn, I join the line where I belong alphabetically, and I receive my diploma case. I shake hands with the line of administrators. I hear them say "Congratulations" and "Your dad has every reason to be proud of you."

Mrs. Sharie starts crying when I come to her, and this time,

I console her. We hug, and she holds on to me for an extra five seconds.

"You're absolutely incredible, Nellie. I wish you all the best."

When I pause for my photo, Mom is clapping again, and my grandpa is shaking both his fists in the air. My smile widens, and I feel invincible, and time stands still. I worked so hard to get to this moment.

The man in the orange cap leans forward. He places a hand on my mother's shoulder and squeezes. He's congratulating my mom—a kind gesture anyone might offer to their seat-neighbor—but when my mom reaches up and takes his hand, my whole body stiffens. The zing in my veins poisons me because there is no mistaking what I'm seeing. It lasts only a moment, but then I really see him. It's him. Mr. Home-Wrecker. The ball cap and glasses were enough to mask him.

My turn in the spotlight is up, and by the time I sit down, I'm utterly heartsick. An anxiousness I've never known grows in my belly.

Britta approaches the stand, and the man's attention falls to her.

And then the whole world tips on its side.

Because the man sitting behind my mom, holding her hand, drinking my dad's wine, driving the Camry, coming to my house, and kissing my mother is Barry Tayvier.

Britta crosses the stage, and her pointed expression grazes over me, and if I thought I was raw before, I was wrong. She's known this whole time about her father and my mother, and she's smug about it.

She basically told me about it this morning.

His latest girlfriend is a real piece of work too. He even mentioned he might marry this one.

Britta turns her back to me.

Worst of all, my mom claps harder for Britta than she did for me.

CHAPTER 20

Senior All-Nighter, Part 1

Jensen

It takes forever to get through every student, but when it's finally over and we've moved our tassels, we're free. We're finally free.

My mom weaves her way through the crowd, and her arms wrap around me as she places a kiss to my forehead.

"Now you can tell the world who you really are," she says.

"I have to turn in a manuscript first. Remember?"

"Still." She holds me by the shoulders, looking at me as if she doesn't want to forget this moment, and I can see the tears building in her eyes, so I pull her into another hug. Without meaning to, I think about Nellie's lecture on the health benefits of hugs, and I hold on to my mother longer, which makes me think about all the times *she* snuggled *me* after we fled from my father.

"Who are you going to the All-Nighter with?" Mom asks as she scans the crowd.

"Everybody. Who are you looking for?"

"The Samsins, the Landons, anybody really. I feel like there are dozens of parents I should be congratulating or something. I don't know. This is my first graduation. I'm not sure what I'm supposed to do."

"So, wait, you *didn't* graduate?" I bump my shoulder against hers.

"You know what I mean. Oh, there are the Samsins."

She leaves me behind, and I try not to laugh, but I can't help it. I trail after her, and when I join them, I don't make eye contact with Angela. I do with her parents, who I recognize from the funeral, but then all my focus is on Nellie. Her grandma hands her a drawstring bag.

"Here's your stuff, Nellie, dear."

"Thanks for bringing it, Grandma."

"Hey," I say quietly to Nellie, as my mother says hello to everyone. "You killed it."

"Thanks," Nellie whispers back.

"What did Nellie do?" Grandpa asks.

"He said I killed it, Grandpa. It means I did a good job."

"Well, of course you did a good job."

Nellie locks her arm in his instead of mine, which somehow makes me like her all the more. "Thanks, Grandpa."

"Angela," my mom says, "congratulations. Nellie is a gem."

"Yes, well, Nellie's worked hard. School is everything to her. And now, college."

"UNLV," Grandma adds. "And then grad school." She reaches across her husband and pats Nellie on the hand.

"That's the plan, Grandma."

"It's been the plan for years," Angela says. "I mean, you have a ten-point chart to get there."

"It's a five-year plan, Mom, but close."

"Nellie, I just wanted to let you know how proud of you I am," my mom says. She reaches into her purse and pulls out an oversized, mint-green envelope and presses it into Nellie's hands. "It's not much, but I have truly enjoyed getting to know you. You've turned into such a lovely young lady, and it's been fun to have you around lately."

"I'm sure it has been," Angela says.

My mother holds Angela's gaze, completely unscathed.

"It has. In fact, Nellie's spirit is the best characteristic Sean passed on to her. A part of him will always be with us because of her."

"Oh, that's so sweet of you, Sumerli," Nellie says, throwing her arms around my mother's neck. Their embrace is full of warmth, and I can tell from Angela's expression that she's ice. I wonder if my mom had every intention of showing Angela up. I kind of hope so.

"I'm really sorry for your loss," I say, directing my comment to Nellie's grandparents.

"Thank you, young man," Grandpa says.

"Excuse me a moment?" Nellie says, detaching from my mom. She steps away, and I watch where she goes, and when it's to hug Jeigh, I suspect she didn't suddenly need to see Jeigh as much as she needed to escape.

"Were you able to get into my husband's computer, Jensen?" Angela shifts her weight from one foot to the other, and I'm so glad she didn't ask this in front of Nellie. That would've been a problem.

"You've got Sean's computer?" my mom asks. Shoot. I should've told her.

"Yeah. You know I'm good with computers, Mom. Just trying to unlock some files for Mrs. Samsin."

"Yes, my husband dreamed of publishing a novel, but he never really put his work out there. Jensen's offered to help. I understand you have a relative at Ogma Publishing?"

"Oh, yes. Of course," Mom says. She side-eyes me, understanding. "I'm sure Sean's work is worth submitting."

"What are we submitting?" Nellie asks, rejoining us.

"Nothing," I say.

"We should get going," Angela says. "It's getting late. Nellie, are you going to the party with Britta?"

The shadow that crosses Nellie's face surprises me. "No, Mom. I'm going with Jensen."

"I'm happy to take her."

Angela offers me a closed-lip smile, but really?

Nellie turns to hug her grandparents, and I can see her hesitation as she hugs her mom.

It takes another half hour before Nellie and I have said all of our goodbyes. The Landons thank me for trying to keep Sterling in line, at which Nellie blurts a laugh, and then we all join in.

When Britta and her parents join us, Nellie walks away. I'm introduced to Britta's biological dad, Barry, but excuse myself to join Nellie.

Mr. Kaempher stops us, and when Britta joins us, Nellie stiffens. He has nice things to say to each of us, and his praise is overexaggerated but appreciated. When Mr. K comments on my photos, it's Britta who chimes in.

"You always caught my best side, Jensen." She leans into me, running her hand over my arm.

"You know you don't have a bad side, Britta," I say, playing to her ego as I simultaneously remove her hand from my arm.

"Except that's not completely true, is it?" Nellie says. It's not like her to throw out a zinger, but dang. She barely turns to Mr. Kaempher when she says, "Thanks for all you've done for us, Mr. K," and then walks away.

"Hey," I say, rushing after Nellie. "You wanna wait up a second?"

"Sorry."

"It's okay. We don't have to be friends with Britta tonight."

"Thanks."

We jump in line to return our rented gowns. I glance over my shoulder to see that Britta's been joined by Marbles, Sterling, and a couple other friends, so she'll be fine. When my phone pings with the specific tone I set for my assistant, I open her email.

> It's the big day! Very excited for you to graduate! If you have the pages done by next Friday, June 15, than I can work on the big announcement. I would also like to set up an interview with Mikey Michael's. I've dropped him a line, and he's very interested.
>
> Until then.
>
> Becca

I appreciate the note, although the thought of talking to a national news anchor is a bit overwhelming. Mikey is a decent **news** reporter, but I am not newsworthy.

I close out her email and turn to Nellie. "You want to talk?"

"We're not going to make it."

"To the party? We'll be fine." I check the time. We've got twenty minutes. "Seriously, you can talk to me."

"I know. It's just my mom. And Britta. And I miss my dad. I don't want to think about any of it."

"I get that."

When it's our turn, we hand in our gowns, and our names are crossed off the list. We keep our caps and tassels.

Nellie looks so good in the outfit she has on, and I can't wait to dance with her tonight. I'm pleased when she lets her attention linger on my outfit as well because I know she's seeing what my weight-lifting class has done for me. I specifically picked this shirt because of the way it fits.

With a shy smile, she pulls her bag over her shoulders. "Come on. We have a party to go to."

"I heard that last year Dave's older brother snuck in some weed and didn't get caught," I say to spark some conversation.

"I've heard that rumor too." Again, she hands me her keys, and I drive her car. "What did you think of Barry?"

"He was fine. Why?"

I check the time and press the gas pedal down. Why is she asking about Britta's dad?

"Nellie, what's going on?" I ask as we park.

"Nothing, come on. We're barely going to make it!" She fakes her enthusiasm, grabs her drawstring bag, and starts toward the door. "Jensen, hurry!"

"I'm on your six, girl!" Because she's right. We've got four minutes to spare.

She laughs, but I can tell it's not real. When we get to the entrance, we hand our tickets to the chaperone, and we're in, but there's a large group behind us. Graduation went longer than we all thought it would.

I catch Nellie by the elbow, pull her into an alcove, and take a breath. I stare into her eyes, wanting more than what she's giving me, and from the look on her face, she knows it.

"What aren't you telling me?" I let the weight of my words hang between us until she drops her gaze. "Please? I hate to see you hurting."

She sighs, and the tension in her body finally gives. "I will, but does it have to be now? Can't we just—can we just go and have a good time?"

"Okay. But you'll tell me?"

"I promise."

"Okay." But it's not really okay. I'm kind of annoyed.

By the time we make our rounds, we're pleased with our options. They've got Vegas-style card games, a mechanical bull, a caricature artist, a photo booth, food and drinks, *Family Feud*, a jumbo Twister game, finger painting (which is the only thing that seems weird, but oddly appealing), darts, a homemade version of *Jeopardy*, and a dance floor.

The booths are closed until eleven, and for now, the party hosts are focused on feeding us, which is great. But I am totally captivated by the Jeopardy game. The categories are just written on pieces of paper—topics like "Sports" and "Movies," but to my surprise, one is titled "*Blood Rock*."

Good gravy.

We haven't had anything to eat since the barbecue. The music is great, and the dance floor is filling up.

When the DJ plays a slow song, I take Nellie by the hand and pull her toward the floor.

Her chin rests against my shoulder, and as our friends finish eating, they join us. Sterling smirks at me, as if he wants to be in my shoes. Britta rolls her eyes. Marbles makes kissy lips and scrunches his nose. I see them, but I couldn't care less.

With them are Jerome, Shalee, Jeigh, Mike, Shanna, and the twins—people that I won't see much after tonight. Sterling's quick to put himself between the twins.

It's an odd combination of people, but I don't try to puzzle

out why the rich girl and the computer geek are suddenly together, or why Marbles is eyeing Jeigh, or why Shalee has come
out of her shell and is tagging along.

They all join us on the dance floor, and when the music
changes to something fast, Nellie shrugs off her dark mood. She
screams with delight, and everyone follows suit. We are on fire,
dancing and showing off.

When Sterling comes our way, she doesn't shy away from
him, and I feel a rush of jealousy. But that's dumb. I know she's
with me.

Everyone is best friends with everyone, and we're having a
blast. The first hour flies by, and after a few rounds of cards and
a game of Twister, another hour has passed, and I'm really loving
where things are headed.

Thank you, Twister.

There's a dance-off between Tandy Merick, captain of the
dance team, and Sterling, and several others. Awesome. Nellie
pushes me forward, and like a fool, I join in with Sterling and
Marbles.

Six songs later, I'm overheated, and Tandy is officially the winner of the impromptu competition. She's never been part of our
circle, but she is now, and there's no denying the girl's got moves.

I'm ready to sit down for a while, and so is Nellie. We turn
our backs to the crowd as the song finishes and are walking away
when Britta hollers out something that causes everyone to freeze.

CHAPTER 21

Senior All-Nighter, Part 2

Nellie

"Look, guys! Nellie Samsin's finally learned to loosen up! Wooooh!"

At the sound of Britta's voice, I jerk. My fingers are laced with Jensen's, and we, along with everyone else, all stare at Britta.

"What did you just say?" I ask, daring her to say it again to my face.

The next song starts, but those closest to us don't move a muscle.

Britta takes several steps forward and comes toe to toe with me. "You're pathetic. You and your stupid *plan* are pathetic."

I flinch as she sways forward, and I smell the alcohol on her.

Marbles tugs on Britta's arm. "Hey, leave her alone."

I've known Britta to take a few drinks here and there. But drunk or not, why is she suddenly attacking me? I've done nothing.

"Why would you say that?" I ask, my head pounding in rhythm with the music.

"Because it's true," Britta says. "You're so stupid."

And because I'm nervous, I laugh. Which Britta hates. Her eyes narrow.

"Britta," Marbles tries again, tugging on her arm. "That's enough."

"Let go of me." She jerks out of his hold, and that's when I erupt. The boiling heat of what's happened overwhelms me. From the kissing prank to her superior attitude to her backhanded compliments—all of it.

"Oh, I'm sorry," I say. "I didn't realize my goals were interfering with your life. Say it all now, Britta, because this is it for us. What else is on your mind?"

"Well, let me think about it."

"Can you even do that?"

Her lip curls, her eyes darken, and it's like black smoke swirls within her, darkening her soul by the second as she becomes otherworldly. But my walls are up, and I refuse to let her hurt me. Not tonight. I've been through enough these last two weeks, so before she has an answer, I spit out what comes next.

"I lied this morning. I don't want to be friends any more."

"Good, because I'm sick of how you think you're smarter than me."

"I *am* smarter than you!"

"Well, for someone so smart, you're pretty stupid. Couldn't math out that Angela Samsin plus Barry Tayvier equals who cares if your dad is dead. Your mom's probably glad he's dead."

Anger rushes through my veins, straight into my hands. In the span of a second, my right hand whips across her face. This is the second time I've slapped someone. The sweat along my hairline and neck is far worse than when I struck Sterling. The sting in my hand, twice as painful.

"I wish *you* were dead!" I snap.

I hear the audible gasp of those around us, a first for me, and I hate that this meanness in me is so close to the surface.

Inside, I crumble to pieces. I did do the math. It took me longer to get to the answer, but I did figure it out. I know without looking that Jensen's on my heels, and I hate that he just saw that. I don't feel like I'm crying, but tears fall over my cheeks anyway.

"Stop following me," I say, but he doesn't listen.

"Nellie, stop."

"No. Stop following me."

"No."

I'm totally out of control. I don't know why he's still with me. Isn't he tired of seeing me like this?

When we're far enough away from the fray, he catches me by the elbow, and instead of jerking out of his hold, I spin around and fall into his embrace—the one that shields me from everything, the one that makes me forget.

I collapse into him, soaking his shirt with my sobs. I don't know how much more heartache I can take. Eventually, we find a bench to sit on. I lean my head against his shoulder, heavy and spent.

When he speaks, he uses my language. "Did you know when a star is born, it means a nebula has to collapse? So don't fight it. It's okay to crumble, because this isn't the end. This is your beginning."

I sob even harder. "It hurts."

"According to a recent poll, most babies report that being born is incredibly difficult."

I give a soft, quiet laugh, one that doesn't quite sink into my soul, because the truth is I'm sad. I'm just sad, sad, sad.

When I finally find my real voice, I whisper, "I hate how she always corrects me, how she talks down to me, as if I don't know what I'm doing. I hate that she doesn't actually like me. I'm never good enough. And worst of all, she doesn't love me for me."

"Are you talking about your mom? Or Britta?"

His question stretches out before me.

"I don't know," I finally say, burying my face in my hands.

"It's going to be okay."

I can't see Jensen's face, but I want to believe him. I know I haven't been a great friend to Britta these last few weeks, but I was doing my best.

Jensen soothes me by tracing the lines in my palm, but the sting from slapping Britta remains.

A darker side of me is glad I hit her. If I were in one of my beloved stories, this is the kind of stuff that would make me the villain. I don't want to be proud of it, but I am, and for now, I don't chase the feeling away.

I'm staring at our shoes when a lanky shadow falls over us.

"Marbles," Jensen says. He stands up and offers me a hand, and the three of us glance back to the party. I don't see Britta.

"Hey, Nellie," Marbles starts. "Is it true? Is your mom with her dad?"

"Yeah." It hurts to say it.

"Oh. I'm sorry about that. Still, it's no excuse for her to treat you like that. And . . . I'm sorry I was a part of the whole kissing thing."

He wraps everything into one apology, and while it's not okay, I appreciate that he's trying. "The kiss is history. Don't worry about it."

"Also, I reported her for drinking, so she broke up with me and swore at Sterling, which was kind of funny. She's been sent home."

"I can't believe you did that," I say.

"After you turned away, she about attacked you, but to every-one's surprise, Jeigh stepped in, so then I jumped in, and there was a bit of a fight, but we got it sorted out. Besides, I didn't really want to spend tonight with her anyway."

"Kind of bummed I missed that," Jensen says. He and Marbles share a laugh.

"Yeah. Good times. Well, I'm going to go play some craps with Jeigh, and then I'm out. In twenty-four hours, I'm on a plane to DC, so in case I don't see you two for a while, take care."

"Wait. DC?" I ask.

"I got an internship at the White House."

"What?" Jensen and I say in unison.

"Yeah," Marbles says with a smile. He winks at me, and then he's gone.

"Was that a joke?" I ask.

"I don't think so."

We stand there, bewildered, and our spirits a little higher. I'm sad that Britta's night has come to this, but I'm also elated to know that Jeigh would stand up for me. And it's clear who Marbles really likes.

"You want to get out of here?" Jensen asks.

"As long as we don't think about how much money we wasted on our tickets, then sure."

"Agreed."

We walk over to the doors and meet up with Mrs. Johannson. She gives us the speech about not being able to come back, but I sense she'd let us back in if we wanted to return.

"I hate to see you go, Nellie."

"Yeah, I'm sorry. I'm just not feeling well."

"Do you want us to call your mom?"

"Nah," Jensen says. "I've got her."

Mrs. Johannson nods at Jensen, hugs me, and then we're out.

Once we're in my car with Jensen at the wheel, I slump back and pull the seat belt across my body. Nothing's going according to plan, so maybe I should just let go of everything.

"Let's go to your apartment," I say.

"I don't think that's a good idea."

"Why?"

"Because."

His simple answer isn't enough. "I need more than that, and I need it now. I can't take it anymore. How do you have an apartment? How do you have that car? Why can't we go to your place?"

"It's complicated, Nellie. I'm not sure we should open that can of worms tonight."

"Why not?"

"Because you've had a bad night, and I'm not ready to talk about it, okay?"

"You're not ready, or you don't want to?"

"That's not fair, Nellie."

His voice is deep and low, and I realize we've never really fought. I don't want to tear Jensen's world to pieces, but I'm rocking my world, splitting the ground between us. Earthquake and aftershocks. I don't mean to, but the heat in me coils and prepares to go off again.

He's got both hands on the steering wheel, his gaze fixed on the road, his brows knit in concentration. His lips form a hard line. The worst part about it is that he's still beautiful. A menacing, bad-boy kind of pretty.

The air is thick between us, full of tension.

"If you take me to your apartment," I say, "we can have our own party. Just don't take me home." I slide my hand over and place it on his thigh.

He doesn't look at me, but he does glance down at my hand. "Don't," he says.

He brakes for a red light, and I feel the muscles of his thigh tighten.

"Jensen."

He swallows, and then puts my hand back in my lap. He takes a hard right, pulls into our neighborhood, and then parks in my driveway. I flush cold, and something inside of me cracks into a million little pieces.

"The last thing I want is—" he starts, and I hold my breath, afraid he's going to say *you*. I can practically count how many times he inhales and exhales. "The last thing I want is for you to behave like Britta."

I hear his words, and they make sense, but the fire inside of me burns those words black.

"But maybe she's right." I unbuckle my seat belt and lean over the armrest and bring my face close to him, wanting him to look at me. I've never been so bold, but all this time, Britta's been rubbing off on me too.

Jensen turns and meets my gaze, and there is a fire in his eyes that gleams gold and hot. I press my mouth to his, hungry and desperate and afraid of losing him, and he kisses me back, earnest and hard. There is so much drive and angst in our kiss. But it only lasts for a second, before he pulls away from me.

"Nellie . . . we need a little breather."

"A break?" I sink back, dejected and broken and completely disheartened.

"A breather."

"That's the same thing. You're breaking up with me? Because I want to kiss you?"

"That's not what I said."

"So you don't want to kiss me?"

"I just did, didn't I? You're trying to prove something. You're not in your right mind."

He doesn't know that his words confirm a fear of mine, but they do. I feel like I'm going crazy.

He goes on. "You want to forget everything that's happened, even if it's just for a minute. But I can't be your stronghold when your kiss becomes a weapon."

"That's not what I was doing." I know it's a lie the minute I say it. That's exactly what I was doing. *What's wrong with me?*

His hands fall into his lap, and I feel his energy seeping out of him.

I've ruined the night. I've ruined everything. I've been dealing with broken glass since the yearbook drama, and now I've cut us.

"This isn't like you," he finally says, looking out his window. "You're a different kind of drunk right now, and—"

"Whatever." I pull on the door handle and get out. Britta was the one drinking, not me.

I'm a few steps away from my front door, and I want him to come after me. Instead, the headlights cut through the darkness and he's gone. Gone in my car, and I don't have to look back to know which way he went. He headed out of the neighborhood, and not to his house. So, he wants to go this apartment, just not with me? The idea hurts all the more.

Inside, my house is empty. The only light on is the one above the kitchen sink, and my mom's bed is made.

I can't help but assume she's with Barry. Barry, the stupid, non-child-support-paying home-wrecker of homes.

Maybe my dad figured it out. Maybe that's what caused his death.

I fall into my own bed, alone and trembling, but under the pressure of it all, a part of me hardens. The earthquake is over, and the ground snaps shut.

Things that were soft and sweet, slowly burn red-hot like heavy iron in a kiln, and the hammering behind my eyes begins to flatten me out, and when I get into the shower the next morning, all the heat leaves me, until I'm cold and unbendable.

I turn the water off, and in the silence that follows, I say, "I'm moving out." I believe my father hears me.

I listen with all my heart for him to whisper back that I'm making a mistake, but I don't hear him, and that's all the sign I need. I was going to leave for college at the end of the summer. So what's a few weeks?

I need to find a place to stay because I can't stay here another night.

After a long time of staring into space, I realize Jensen and I aren't made of glass. I wasn't myself last night, but I have to try to repair the damage I've caused.

When I text him, I have plenty to say.

> I'm really, really sorry about last night. I hate myself. You were right, and I was wrong, and I have no idea if you can forgive me. I was out of my mind crazy and maybe I still am. I don't know. But I'm sorry. I can't stop thinking about what you said. If we need to take a breather, I understand.

He doesn't feel about me the way I feel about him. Tears are streaming down my cheeks again, and I think it's my body's goal to die by dehydration.

> But before we do, I really want to apologize in person. Please, can I come see you?

After I hit send, I'm a bundle of nerves as I wait for a response. I distract myself by pulling out my five-year plan, and instead of wadding it up into a ball and throwing it away, I draw a single line through all of the remaining points and write in big, all-capped letters: MOVE OUT.

It feels right.

I go to the garage and find some boxes, then get out my luggage and begin packing up my shirts and pants. I can't really think about anything other than Jensen. I worry he's blocked me.

When my phone buzzes, I startle. My breathing grows ragged as I reach for my phone. My heart is pounding in my ears, my fingers trembling, as I click to see who's messaged me back.

One unread message from Jensen Nichols. I click on it, sweat building.

> I'm sorry too. I want to see you as
> well. Can you come to my apartment?

At this, my world resets. It's as if Jensen is the axis on which I spin right now. And after I tell him yes, I'm even more determined to find a place to stay. If he can live on his own, so can I.

I check my bank account, knowing it's more sapling than great oak, but a six-month lease would let me put down some temporary roots. For the first time since before the funeral, I'm grateful my dad had prepared me for life after high school, and instead of missing him, I feel empowered.

–CHAPTER 22–

Where to Go

Jensen

I drive away from Nellie's house, mentally repeating what I just said. *I can't be your stronghold when your kiss becomes a weapon.* I used a line straight from *Blood Rock*, but she didn't even notice.

And what did I mean, a breather? I don't know what I was thinking, other than I panicked, and then it was too late to take it back.

And then it hits me. I'm in Nellie's car. I turn around, returning to her house. But I don't want her to think I'm coming back for her, so I kill the lights and engine and roll to stop alongside the curb.

I want to slam the door shut, but I can't. I'm soundless as I leave her car and walk home.

Then I take my mom's car. I shoot her a text explaining why I am taking her vehicle, apologize, and then I send her some money so she can take a Lyft to work. I'll have to swap cars with her at some point, but I can't think about that right now.

It's well into the night as I drive to Clay's facility, and when I walk in, the nurse at the desk is surprised to see me.

"I know it's not visiting hours," I say. "But can I just sit with him?" I must look desperate, because she buzzes me in after finding me in the system and checking my ID. I fumble to put my driver's license away as I walk toward Clay's room.

He's asleep, and the soft sounds of his room are a constant reminder that I'm living and hurting. Things he's not—not really.

But I need to be here. Doing so always grounds me. I'm his big brother, and it's important to me to show that to Clay as best as I can. Which is why I tell Clay everything. All the things that are great, things that are embarrassing, things that hurt. I confide in him, in hopes that if he were able to carry on a conversation with me, we'd share all our secrets with each other. At least, I think that's something brothers should do. Its hard, but I believe Clay knows more than he can convey. I just wish he could tell me what to do.

I pull up a chair and take his hand. His face is so much like mine I can barely take it, so I close my eyes and rest my head on his bed.

Clay needs a haircut, and in the next few years, he'll probably need to start shaving. Not that he'll be able to do that. We'll have to do it for him.

I let my mind circle around that thought, repeating "he needs a haircut" until I place those words in another world.

Hagon needs a haircut, too, but he's getting used to its length. He pulls it back and secures it with a leather strip and turns to Sokha. In a hushed whisper, Sokha repeats the plan—not that he needs reminding. It's more for clarification. They can't afford to fail.

"I got the one on the left," she says.

"But he's bigger than the one on the right."

Sokha's devious smile is the one she saves for a nasty fight, and that's the image I settle on, the one that takes me into the dark. Is it any surprise that Sokha plans everything and Hagon helps execute it? Not to me.

Somewhere around five, I wake as a nurse doing her rounds comes into Clay's room.

"I'm sorry," she whispers. "You're not supposed to be here."

"I know." I stand up and walk over to the window as she takes his vitals. He's so used to it, he doesn't even stir. I stare at the mountains for a long minute.

"Clay's got a bedsore I need to see to," she says, breaking the silence. "I'll be right back."

After she's gone, I return to Clay and wake him. His eyes brighten at seeing me, which makes me smile.

"You snore," I start. "Though, you know that, Mr. Grizzly Bear. Listen, your nurse is coming back to take care of you, but before she does, I wanted to tell you that I graduated high school last night. It was a long meeting and you didn't miss much. But you know what it means, right? I can finally spend my time writing."

Clay nods, something he does when he's happy. Or sad. Or unable to control his neck.

"When I come to see you next, I'll hopefully be done writing about Sokha and Hagon retrieving the Blood Rock, and if I am, I'll read you the pages."

Clay bobs his head again, but then his eyes glaze over as if he no longer sees me. In moments like these, I tell myself that he's picturing my story. I like to think he's of sound mind in there, because it's too depressing to think otherwise.

"Clay?"

It takes a moment, but I call him back to me, and when his eyes are on mine, I tell him something I've never told him before.

"I like this girl. Nellie. You'd like her too. She's smart, and she's so beautiful, man. Well, anyway, I was a butthead to her last night, and I need to go apologize. So I'll have to come back later, okay? I love you, buddy."

He barely seems to register that I'm leaving.

As I walk away, my back aches and my mouth is dry. I drive to my apartment and crash for a few more hours. I'll apologize when I'm human again.

I wake to the sound of my neighbor vacuuming. I grumble and pull myself out of bed. After a long shower, I plug in my dead phone, and as soon as the battery hits one percent, it pings with a very long message from Nellie that starts with

I'm really, really sorry about last night.

On some level, I'm glad she's the one to apologize first. I

know it's stupid, but I feel like I deserved that. I tell her to come over, despite my uncertainty. There's a tugging at my mind that says I need to get to work, but procrastination is king, and I'm the happy jester who doesn't realize I'm to supposed to rule the kingdom.

Shortly after sprint-cleaning, I shower, throw on some clothes and cologne, and fix myself breakfast. While I eat, I respond to Rebecca.

> Thanks. Graduation is officially behind me, but man, I'm exhausted. I've got some plans today, but then I'm all yours. I'm not sure I'm ready to announce—not sure I'll ever be ready—but we did agree to do it after graduation. Let's just wait until I've turned in the manuscript.

I hit send and turn my attention to Sokha and Hagon for just a moment. I mentally review the scene I thought up last night, check the word count of the manuscript, my plot map, and stare at some images I've collected for inspiration. A familiar excitement builds in my gut, and I want to write, which is a good sign.

I close my laptop at the same time there's a knock on my door.

I find Nellie on my front step and offer her a soft hello.

"Hey," she says, rubbing the back of her neck.

She's wearing a hoodie, yoga pants, running shoes, and a weak smile. She walks in with trepidation and spins to look at me as soon as I've shut the door.

"I'm really sorry. I was—I was a mess. You were right. I was trying to prove a point, and I'm—I'm really sorry, Jensen. I can't stop replaying what I said. I just hate myself. I don't want to fight with you. You're the only one in my life right now I trust."

I should say something back, but I don't have the words. They're all stuck in my computer. So instead, I reach for her hand

and pull her to me and hug her for a long, long time. She fits like a glove against me, her chin resting on my shoulder and mine on hers. I love how she smells and how her fingertips brush the back of my neck.

"I'm sorry too," I finally say into her hair. "I was a total butt-head jerk-face."

She pulls back to meet my gaze, and I think she's about to make fun of my word choice, so I kiss her, because I don't want to hear her say that I wasn't those things. I was worse than that.

She's like summer, the way she kisses back. Almost lazy but definitely bright, and this kiss isn't like our first kiss or the one last night.

This one says *sorry* and *I love you*, even though I don't know if she actually loves me. I don't know if I love her. But I do care about her. Far more than I want to admit to anyone. Even to Clay.

When we break apart, it isn't easy. There's no authoritative figure telling us to cut it out, no school bell that's about to ring, no onlookers.

Which is why I don't let go of her.

"I can't be the only person you trust," I say.

"You are. It feels like everyone's keeping secrets, and I just can't take anymore."

The voice in my head screams. I'm toast.

"When did you return my car?"

I lie. Man, I am the worst. "Late. Very late."

We move over to the couch and sit down. She folds her legs under her, but her hands find mine, and we sit together as if it's something we've been doing for years. Years ago, we did sit to-gether like this. We weren't holding hands, but our shoulders would touch as we'd watch cartoons.

I'm dying on the inside. I don't know how to tell her the truth and keep this relationship alive.

She's going to hate me when she finds out.

"So, this morning, I packed up my whole room." There's a hint of pride in her voice, and it catches my attention entirely.

"What?"

"Yeah. I'm moving out."

"I thought you were staying through the summer." If she says she's headed to UNLV now, this *is* over. And I don't want it to be over.

"I am. Actually, I was hoping you could help me find a place. I can't live at home. I just . . . can't."

My overactive brain says, *Invite her to live with you,* and though I work to drown out that voice, the words slip out.

"You can stay with me."

She cracks a big smile, and then looks at my bookshelf. "That's really nice of you. Seriously. And it would be so easy to say yes. But we're not there. And I think deep down, you know that too."

There's a long pause between us, and I guess I do feel a little differently. I've known her for almost my whole life. "Is that the only reason?"

"No. I also feel like I need do this. I don't need anyone. If that makes sense. I mean, I need you. I want you . . . I mean . . ."

"It's okay, Nellie. I get it." I nod, attracted to both her honesty and her vulnerability. "Being on your own—adulting. It's a big step."

"An important one."

"Is there an algorithm we could use to confirm you've come to the right conclusion?"

"Ha ha. You're funny." She elbows me, and her seriousness lightens. A closed-lip smile lights her face.

"Okay, but just so you know, my offer stands," I say. I would give up all my writing to ensure she has a roof over her head.

"And I appreciate the offer, I do."

"You have all your stuff in your car?"

"Well, not the furniture." She give a small laugh. "But everything I'd want or need. That's what took so long."

"Okay." I shift things around in my mind, trying to sort out what to say next. "I don't know if you can move into a place in a matter of hours. Usually they have to run a credit check, and you'll probably need a cosigner, and you don't have a job—do you?"

"See, this is why I need you."

"It's nice to be needed. Actually, I hate to ask but . . ." My mind is racing with options. "How much money do you have?"

"Four thousand, eight hundred, and seventy-six dollars."

"That's—that's actually not bad."

"I've been saving. And I can get a job."

"Are you sure you want to throw your money toward rent? I hate to see you spend money when you can live at home for free."

I officially sound like my mother.

"You sound like my dad." Nellie huffs, leaning into the couch.

"I'll take that as a compliment."

Months ago, Mom made a valid argument that I didn't need to move. She's gone eight hours a day, but I didn't want to be the guy who stayed at home. You graduate, you move out, you move on. You start your life.

"You know what I mean," she says.

"Yes, I do, and look, I don't want to fight." The worry I feel matches the worry I see in her eyes. "I just want what's best for you. And if you want to move out, I get it."

Because I do. I don't need her to spell out her reasons—any of them.

"I think if you pay cash up front," I say, "we can make it work. But, you're not going to be here for six months, are you?"

This is the question I really don't want the answer to. I don't want to hear about her moving away, but it has to be addressed.

"Honestly, I don't know."

"You don't know what? If you're going to UNLV?"

"Yeah. I don't know." She rises to her feet and begins pacing. I watch her rub her neck, pull on her shirt, tug at her hair, and talk with her hands. "It's just that . . . I can't even imagine moving to Nevada without my dad driving me and carrying boxes into my apartment and kissing me goodbye on the forehead. I'm never going to have that, and I know it's dumb, but I want that. That's how I'm supposed to start college. I know that's not a good reason not to go, but my point is, I'm feeling—unsure. And I can't stand to even think about my mom right now, and you . . . You're here, and I don't want to leave."

"I can't be the reason you stay." I hate to say it, but it's the truth.

She stops pacing, drops her hands. She takes a long hard look around my apartment before meeting my gaze.

"You're not holding me back. You're holding me up."

I let the weight of her words envelop me. They work their way through my mind and hitch a ride to my heart. She's been holding me up, too, she just doesn't know it. And that's when I realize why I don't want her to leave. Without her, I'll feel the full impact of Sean's death. She's the last bit of him that I have.

"Okay, then we find you an apartment." Because if she's determined to stay, who am I to suggest otherwise? "Let's see if there's one here in my building."

She returns to the couch and exhales like she's been holding her breath.

I call down to the manager's apartment and put the phone on speaker.

"Coventry Apartments, this is Tanis speaking. May I help you?"

"Hi, Tanis. It's Jensen Nichols in apartment 227."

"Oh, hello, Jensen. What can I help you with?"

"Everything's good here. I'm actually wondering if you have an apartment for rent. It's for a friend."

Nellie glances at me and crosses her fingers, a goofy smile spreading across her face.

"I have a couple of options. We have a three-bedroom apartment on the first floor, a studio on the second floor, and a two-bedroom on the fifth floor. Obviously, the security deposits and rent amount varies for each. What is your friend looking for exactly?"

"Studio?" I suggest.

Nellie nods in reassurance.

"The studio has a security deposit of four hundred," Tanis says. "And because it's furnished, the rent is eight seventy-five a month."

Nellie has her phone out and is doing the math.

"And lease options?" I ask.

"Three, six, and twelve months, though the three-month is as expensive as the six-month. If your friend signs for a year, I can do the first month free and knock off twenty-five dollars per month."

When Nellie holds up three fingers to indicate which lease she wants, my whole body tenses. This is getting real.

She shows me the numbers. The total is just under four grand. She'll have nothing for food.

"If she pays cash up front for the three-month lease, what kind of discount can you give her?"

Nellie tips her head at me as if she's never seen me before.

"Let's see." There's some clicking of keys and then, "I could do eight twenty-five a month."

"Is that the best you can do?" I pressure Tanis, sounding just like my mom. Nellie's eyes grow bigger, and I fight off a smile.

There are several beats of silence. We hear Tanis breathe and shift in her seat, and then with a soft hum, she says, "I could take fifty off her security deposit, but only if she has a spotless credit check."

I can't imagine Nellie has a tarnished record anywhere.

"Okay," I say, looking at Nellie for instructions on what to do next. She isn't sure, and it's only now that I consider we should have looked at other apartments—other less expensive, further-away apartments.

"Okay, thanks. Give us twenty minutes, and if it's a go, we'll come to your office."

"That sounds great, Jensen. And the finder's fee of one hundred dollars comes off your rent next month. Talk to you soon, I hope."

The line goes quiet, and I hang up the phone.

"Finder's fee?" Nellie asks.

"This month's special," I answer, my tone falling flat. "But trust me, I didn't even think about that when I suggested you live here at Coventry."

CHAPTER 23

No More Secrets

Nellie

"It's not like you set up the promotion. Really, you're fine. You're more than fine."

"You think I'm hot, Samsin?"

"You wish!" I slug him in the shoulder, laughing, but he catches me by the wrist, and for a few minutes, we wrestle each other. I give it everything I've got, because I want to win, but so does he. When he pins me, I'm on my back, and my head is in the corner of the couch.

"Mercy," I call. "Mercy!"

"Do you think I'm hot?"

"Yes, you're hot. Of course you're hot. You're so hot the sun is jealous!"

He doesn't loosen his hold, but something in his eyes changes. As if he's seeing an alternate world and not me.

He stands up and says, "Just a minute." When he disappears into his bedroom, I feel a little rejected.

"I remembered something," he says when he comes back. "I had to make a note of it, so I didn't forget."

"What?" I'd love to know.

"It's nothing. Really."

"That's a lie."

"Maybe a small one. But it's nothing I want to talk about just yet."

I tip my head, trying not to be annoyed that he's keeping

secrets. This time I'm cautious as I pry. "*Just yet?* As in, you'll tell me—sometime soon?"

"Maybe," he says. He walks past me to the kitchen and fills a glass with water. "You thirsty?"

He fills me one even though I don't answer, and we sit at the bar, shoulder to shoulder. I'm filled with questions, but he's keeping his mouth busy by drinking. When he sets his cup down, he brings up finding an apartment for me.

"We should find something for less," he says.

"Why do you live here, if it's expensive?" I counter.

"It's furnished, and I don't want roommates."

"Do you think I should do the roommate thing?"

"You could. It's up to you." He looks at me like I'm rushing into something, and I know I am, but I don't care. I want to rush. I want to rush this, and I want to rush things with him, because it makes me feel alive and it chases away the pain that's taken up residency inside of me.

"I'm not sure I want to live with strangers right now." Maybe in the fall. Three months of my own place with space to breathe feels perfect. "I can always make more money. I'll deliver pizzas if I have to."

"Like I said. It's your decision."

"Let's go look at the studio," I say with confidence, and Jensen nods.

I feel comfortable as we meet with Tanis. I feel excited as she unlocks the door and lets us in.

Instantly, I love it. It's quaint, clean, and has a little personality with its aqua wall, hardwood floors, and an arched window. It's weird that the bed is so prominent, but it's a studio, so where else would it go? You'd think they'd provide a screen or something. To our right is a kitchenette with a brick backsplash and mugs hanging from small hooks under the cabinet.

Tanis gives us a quick tour, which feels silly since it's basically one room, and she points out that there's air-conditioning and that cable and utilities are included. All things I didn't even consider when I made this hairbrained decision.

The king-size bed has a brand-new mattress cover still in its case, and Tanis explains that the mattress protectors are provided by the complex. They're mandatory, and it will be up to me to provide bedding. Other than the bed and the full-sized couch, everything else is minimal—the table, the washer and dryer, the fridge. But the chrome faucets shine, the windowsills are spotless, and it doesn't smell bad.

Tanis lets me open drawers and cupboards as I explore the space, and it's more than enough. This is awesome. A little overwhelming, but awesome.

"What do you think, Jensen?" I ask.

"I think it's really nice. Spendy, but nice."

He's very concerned about the money, but I'm not surprised knowing he hasn't grown up with it, fancy car and furnished apartment aside. So maybe . . .

Oh my gosh. Has he been lying to us all? Is he actually wealthy? Why would he lie about that?

Something is not adding up, but I don't know what it is. Maybe that's what he wants to tell me but isn't sure how to explain it.

I seriously do not know. But what I do know is that I adore this place. It feels like a fresh start.

"I'll take it."

We end up in Tanis's office, and it takes over two hours to get everything ironed out. While Tanis runs a background check on me, Jensen and I go to the bank for a money order. I feel sick as my balance shrinks, but when all is said and done, I have a key to a studio apartment, and I feel great. Independent.

It takes us a more than an hour to bring in my stuff. I'm sweating and starving and exhausted when we plop down on my couch—my couch!—and take a break.

"I can't believe you did this," he says. "But then again, Nellie Samsin is able to do anything she sets her mind to."

"Oh, yeah, right."

"No, I'm serious. Look at you. You don't need a plan for everything."

I let the silence build as I consider how far I've come in such a short amount of time. I'm proud of myself. Glancing at him, it's obvious he's proud of my recent accomplishments, too, so when I say, "Thanks," I really mean it. Then I ask, "What do you say we get cleaned up and go out? I'm hungry."

"Are you asking me on a date, Samsin?"

"Jensen," I whisper, begging him not to tease me.

"You know, Marbles used to tease me about you. Told me I was too dumb for you."

"You're not dumb."

"Debatable, but we can wait for the jury to decide."

We chuckle, and I envision Marbles with a clean-cut hairstyle and a suit, and I can't believe he didn't tell anyone he was going to DC. I shake my head, unable to quite picture him going by his real name—Martin.

"Anyway," Jensen continues, "Marbles stopped teasing me, eventually."

"Why?"

"Wouldn't you like to know."

The room fills with expectancy on my part. Lately, I feel like Jensen isn't telling me everything, and I want more. I'm silently begging he'll open up, and this time, my wish is granted.

"He said it wasn't funny anymore because I didn't just like you. He said I was in love with you. When he called your name in the cafeteria as the winner of the vote? That was the moment I realized he was right."

My lips part as he tells me this. I can't believe what I'm hearing. "Are you saying—"

"That I love you? Yeah. I love you. Fun fact—I've loved you since the day you made me a mud pie with dandelion heads. I just didn't know it until recently."

I'm in shock, unprepared to reciprocate. I know how I feel,

but I just sorted that emotion out yesterday. I have to say something. Anything.

Anything will do, Nellie Samsin. Just say it.

"Thank you?" *Oh, lovely.* "No, wait. That's not what I mean. I mean, that is the sweetest, nicest thing anyone's ever said to me, but—" I throw my arms around him and hug him tight, and once I'm not looking at his face, I whisper. "I love you too."

"Really?"

"Yes."

He squeezes me, and then he stands up, pulling me with him. "Let's go get something eat, yeah?"

"Kind of abrupt change in subject, don't you think?" I say.

He shrugs his shoulders and backs up and blows me a kiss. "You can handle it," he says as he takes off back to his apartment to get ready for our date.

I'm reeling, however, barely able to function. I can barely concentrate as I try to get ready. I mean, he just said the three most important words and then was like, "Let's go eat."

Ugh. Boys! But then I giggle. *Fun fact. I love you.* He's such a nerd! But he's my nerd.

I shower and shave my legs, and I do my makeup the way I like it, and I blow-dry my hair as quickly as I can. I'm completely dressed, and he hasn't come back to get me, though we never established a plan for that. But who cares! I don't need a plan!

Since he's not that far away—Holy crap! He's not that far away!—I pull on my shoes and grab my things and go to his place.

I knock on his door for the second time today. It's getting late, and my stomach is starting to hurt—I'm that hungry.

When he opens the door, he's pulling on a shirt and his hair poofs out. He flashes me a toothy grin, but I'm still frozen because I saw more skin than I'm used to. He is so hot.

"Sorry," he says, walking back to his room. "I'm almost ready. Just got distracted."

"Doing what?" I call. The TV is on, but the volume is turned way down. On the kitchen table, he's got his laptop open, and when I walk over to take a closer look, it looks like he's—writing?

When he comes back, he comes right to my side, shuts the computer, and then his face falls, as if he realizes his mistake. He shouldn't have closed the laptop.

Because there on the surface is a very specific decal: a moon surrounded by the words "I NEED MY SPACE."

"That's my dad's," I say, knowing I bought that sticker for him for Father's Day last year.

CHAPTER 24

Here We Are

Jensen

"I can explain."

Nellie scoops up the laptop and pulls it to her chest. "Why do you have this?"

"I'm sorry," I say, lowering my hands. Nellie looks like she might attack. "I wanted to tell you, but it never felt like the right time. Your mom asked me at the funeral if I could help her get into it."

"Why would she ask you that?"

"Because I said I was good with computers."

"Why would you say that?"

"I barely remember how it came up. You went to the bathroom, and I felt awkward standing there. Your mom asked me how I was doing, and all I remember saying is that 'I'm good with computers.' Which I am."

The lie just rolls out, and the expression on Nellie's face holds me prisoner. I'm cornered, trapped. I shouldn't have lied. I should've told her the truth.

Your dad's my mentor. I've been writing. Books, actually. You may have heard of them.

But no. I lie because the truth sounds so unrealistic, so stupid, so inconceivable. The truth is not going to set me free. She made it clear she can't take anymore lies. So if I tell the truth now, I'm done for. This is so messed up, and I'm the one who messed it up.

"I'm sorry, Nellie. You can take it now. I got into it."

"You did?"

At this, her hard expression softens. She tips the computer away from her, looking at it.

"Yeah, I did. That's why I wasn't ready."

Another lie.

She softens some more, and then slowly, very slowly puts the laptop back down on the kitchen table. She runs her fingers over it, and I notice how she tries really hard not to tear up.

"That's good," she says. "I'm sorry I snapped again. I don't know what's wrong with me."

"There's nothing wrong with you. I should've told you I had it, but every minute we've been together has been a minute I haven't thought about the laptop—not until today."

Look at me! I'm a professional liar. A gambler, an actor, a politician.

"I'm sorry," I say again.

"Me too. That's really nice of you, but do me a favor?"

"Anything."

"Don't do my mother any more favors, ever again."

"You got it."

As we lock my apartment door, she turns on me. "Okay, that's it. Out with it."

"With what?" I am extra jumpy, convinced she'll see right through me at any moment.

"The car. The apartment. Explain. I can't have any more secrets between us."

"Ah." Inwardly, I tell myself to chill out. I keep my tone light as I deflect. "Well, you can't know everything."

"Why not?"

"Because, even the most open-book people I know don't tell each other *everything*. It's not normal."

"That's probably true." We step out into the evening air, and it's refreshing. Maybe we've been cooped up too long, because it feels good to be outside.

"Okay, test number one," I say as I take her hand.

"A test? No, I want answers."

"I know, but first you gotta pass three tests if you want to be my girlfriend." I'm stalling, but I think she'll take the bait.

"Oh, do I now?"

"Unless you don't want the position. In which case, I'll fill it with—"

"Video games."

"I was going to say 'someone else,' but whatever. Do you want the job or not?"

"Are there benefits?"

"I believe you've had a taste of them." At this, I wiggle my eyebrows and jerk my chin upward.

"Oh my gosh. What am I going to do with you?"

I can think of lots of things, but I stay the course and distract her from my car and the apartment. Her car is right here, so she drives, and I thank the stars she doesn't press me—for now.

I know it'll come back to haunt me, but for now, we're okay.

"Where do you want to eat?" I ask.

"That's the test?"

I say nothing. Because, yes, it is. Sean once told me a woman usually knows what she wants to eat, and I believe him.

"Somewhere they have soup."

"You pass."

"That's good. I've been a high school graduate for exactly one day, and I've already passed my first real-life test."

"Test number two," I say, chuckling at her comment.

She turns her blinker on, merges onto the freeway, and wherever we're headed is up to her. Apparently, there will be soup.

"Go on," she says.

"You're a witness to a real-life Robin Hood. He steals money from a bank but gives it to an orphanage. Do you turn him in, knowing there's a good chance the authorities will take the money back, leaving a lot of kids in need, or say nothing?"

"Real-life Robin Hood, huh?"

"Yeah."

"That's how you got all your money? You stole it?"

"What? No. Of course not. And besides who said I have a lot of money?" Shoot. I didn't see this one coming. I was too busy concocting a moral dilemma for her to unravel.

"No one said," Nellie says.

"I don't steal." I lie, but I'm not a thief. "Come on. What do you do?"

"I say nothing."

"But you're a witness."

"Yeah, but he did a good thing, helping those kids out."

"He did a bad thing, stealing the money."

"To help kids in need."

"So you care about kids?"

"Of course I do." She side-eyes me. "But I have no plans on having any, anytime soon."

"I wasn't asking. Wow. That was an Olympic-sized jump in thought."

"I'm gold-medal material, what can I say?" She pulls into the parking lot of Super Salads and kills the engine. "Did I pass the test?"

"Yes."

"On what grounds?"

"You sound like a lawyer. Okay, test number three."

She takes in a big breath, shakes her head at me, and then gets out of the car. We decide to hold off on my third question until we're seated and have our meals.

She dips her bread into her chicken noodle soup, and while she eats, I present my final question.

"You're in love with the Blood Rock series."

"That's not a question."

"I know, hang on. You're in love with the Blood Rock books, but the author announces that they won't be finishing the series. Ever. How do you feel?"

"Ever? Why?"

"No one knows."

"Well, that's rude. I mean, if Jen Dimes were to go blind or lose both her hands, she could still hire someone to type for her."

"That's a little gruesome, but also not the point. How do you feel?"

"I'd be angry."

"But it's just a book."

"Yeah, but promises have been made. The world is at risk. And I want my happily ever after."

"But it's not real."

"It's real to me."

My breath catches, and I try to cover with a cough. I definitely wasn't expecting that, but her answer is so raw it breathes a different sort of life into me. Her comment is going to stay with me for a long time.

"Well done, young one. You pass," I say, struggling to keep my tone light.

"Fabulous."

"Okay, so, Nellie Samsin, do you want to go out with me?"

She stops chewing. Then she visibly swallows. She bobs her head up and down, before she says, "Yes. But we're already out, so you're going to have to reword your sentence."

She has a point, and I can do better. Go big or go home, I suppose.

I slide our dishes over and reach for her. She slips her hand into mine. I take a conspiratorial look around and then lean in. "You make me happy. I love being around you, and I love you. You're smart and funny, and so pretty. So I'm wondering . . . if you'd like to wear my pin."

She laughs so loud that several people turn to look at us. She lowers her voice, and I swear I see stars in her eyes. "Jensen, the 1950s called. They want their jargon back."

"You like old stuff."

"Not that old!"

"Fine, I'll return the jargon—after you answer me."

Funny thing. I researched pins. I was curious. Writers research all sorts of weird things. Hagon wears a sort of Celtic sash and uses a pin to hold it in place, and giving that pin away, I thought, could be significant. I used the idea at the end of the first book, and Sokha is seen wearing Hagon's family pin.

"Jensen, you're crazy. And kind. And smart—and I know you try to hide it from me so you can ask me for help. And yes, if you had a pin, I'd wear it."

"Cool. So it's just you and me? Girlfriend, no space?"

"Yes. Boyfriend, no space."

We both smile and then pull our meals back in front of us.

Her foot finds mine as we eat, and I like thinking about her as my official girlfriend. I hope she feels excited about calling me her boyfriend.

Somewhere between bites, Nellie's mood shifts.

"I know what I need to do."

"What's that?" I move my salad around, poking at it with my fork. I've eaten most of it, and what's left of the lettuce isn't appealing. I should've ordered a sandwich.

"I should get my dad's books published for him."

I stop stirring and meet her gaze. She's completely serious as she looks to me for comment. I stall by clearing my throat and taking a drink. She can't publish Sean's books. I'm going to do that. I *need* to do that. What does she know about publishing anyway? I set my fork down and look to the door.

"I don't know, Nellie. That seems like a lot of work."

"You don't think I can do it?" she asks.

"That's not what I said."

"I know that's not what you said, but I'm not afraid of how much work it'll be."

"I know that. It's just . . . maybe he's not that good of a writer?" As soon as I say that Nellie's expression darkens, and she leans back in her seat, arms folded. I scramble to fix it. "I doubt that, though. He's probably really good. I'm sorry. I guess I just think it's a romantic idea. And there's going to be some harsh realities that come with it. It's not like you can just slap something up on Amazon, and boom, be done."

Except.

I should tell her right now—tell her that I'm the exception—but it really doesn't feel like the right time. I can't tell her my life is going exceptionally well because of her dad. It's the dire opposite of her own life, and it feels . . . wrong.

"How would you know?" she says. "And besides, it wouldn't be about making money or going viral. It would be about putting his work out there."

I've felt like a fraud for a while now, but this feels worse. I swear all we do is apologize to each other lately—and it's my fault. If I were to just tell her . . .

That's it. I've got to do it. No more secrets. Isn't that what she asked for?

"You're right. I think if you want to do it, you should." I have no right to his stories. "You shouldn't let anyone stop you from doing something for your father, including me. Especially if it's to honor his memory."

I have to clear my throat again, and when I look away, I have two seconds to paint a smile on my face—one that's convincing. I'm about to say "I need to tell you something" when she stands.

"Come on," Nellie says, gathering our trays. Her phone begins to ping rapidly with notifications. "It's late, and we're both exhausted."

The chill in her tone robs me of my courage. What was I thinking? Telling her on the heels of her idea, here in this little café, that I'm the creator of *Blood Rock*? I'm an idiot.

Instead, Nellie drives us back to the complex, and I sit there like a stone, and her phone continues to ping. She's driving so she doesn't look at it, and I don't ask who is bugging her because I can guess. Instead, I allow myself to wallow, to say goodbye to Sean and his work. When we get back to the apartment, she'll take the laptop and that will be the end of that.

But when she pulls into a spot, she doesn't turn the engine off.

"I'll talk to you later," she says. She doesn't get out of the car.
"You're not coming in?" I ask.

"No. I've gotta go home."

She offers nothing more, so I climb out and shut the door and watch her drive away. She stops at a red light, and then my phone pings at me.

> I'm sorry. It's my mom. She's freaking out. So I've gotta go talk to her. Thanks again for helping me today. You're the best. ♥UrGF

I feel bruised as I return to my place, but her text helps. Also, now I have a window of time, a small chance to do something about Sean's work. I stare at his computer, knowing she will come back for it, and I decide the only thing I can really do at this point is to save copies of Sean's stories before she starts changing them.

After I transfer everything to an external hard drive, I crawl into bed, with a single dark thought circling overhead. I should have copied the files and then deleted them so she'd have nothing to edit.

I'm not saying I'm superior to her in any way. Heaven knows, she's so much smarter than I am, but I do know more about story-telling than she does. At least, that's what I tell myself. The truth is I'm probably the most insecure egotist I know.

You are, Hagon whispers, brushing his hair away from his face, *but get up and write anyway.*

Yeah, we're stranded here because of you. Let's get moving already. Sokha twirls her ruby-studded knife in one hand and then throws it into the moss-covered earth with an exaggerated sigh. She plucks it from the ground and throws again and again, stuck on repeat.

I'm still wide awake at two, so I throw the covers back, grumbling as I pull on sweatpants and sit down at my desk. Hagon is calm, but Sokha will not shut up—which is unlike Nellie. But whatever. Once I give in, the words flow.

CHAPTER 25

Face Time with Mom

Nellie

My mom is freaking out. I'm sure she immediately noticed the telescope wasn't in the living room. Then, she probably poked her head in my room and found everything else gone. I ignored three of her calls during dinner, and now the texts are coming through.

I read through her messages at every red light, bracing myself.

> I'm not sure what's going on, but you're freaking me out. You've clearly packed up your things . . . and what? Moved out? To where?

> This is unacceptable, and when you don't answer my phone calls, there are consequences. When I called Britta, she said that you hit her last night at the party and have been using her as a scapegoat.

> Nellie! What is going on with you?

> You have some explaining to do. So every time you said you were with Britta, you weren't? I don't know why you felt you needed to lie to me.

I expect you to be home before
curfew tonight.

You're not the only one who's in
pain. I'm sorry I'm not as good at
communicating as your dad was, but
he wasn't as perfect as you think.

"You're such a hypocrite!" I'm tempted to throw my phone
out the window. I can't afford another one though, and not re-
plying means running the risk of her canceling my phone plan.

I'm sick to my stomach at the thought of confronting her, but
I have to. I'll let her say her piece and then I'll counter, just like
any good lawyer would.

My rebuttal builds in my mind, line upon line. From her constantly being absent, to her lack of affection, to her affair with my
former best friend's dad, to my plan of moving out anyway. I even
prepare a closing line. Maybe I should be a lawyer instead.

I arrive just before ten. I back into the driveway, leaving the
keys in the ignition, certain I'll be too shaky to insert them when
I walk out. Because I *am* walking out.

An eerie silence hangs over my whole house. Probably because it's lost its purpose. I shut the door and turn to face her.
She's sitting in her wingback chair with a bottle of wine on the
end table next to her half-full glass. Since when does she have a
drink every night? It used to only be a Sunday thing.

I say nothing as I sit on the couch opposite her, and I stare at
the bottle instead of meeting her icy expression.

She says nothing either.

I'm too impatient for the silent treatment so I'm the first to
speak. "So. I'm here."

"You want to tell me what you've been up to?"

"Sure. Where do you want me to start?"

"How would I know? Maybe with the day you started lying?"

My mother's questions reflect my own. What I want to say is, "You tell me!" but instead, I start with the night Dad died.

"The yearbook had some issues, and Jensen and I were assigned to fix it. It was the same day Dad died. You weren't here, and when Dad didn't show up, I got worried. I think you know what happened from there, for the most part.

"Since that day, you haven't been here. But Jensen was around, and so, yes, I told you I was with Britta because I knew you wouldn't want me to be with him."

"That's not true."

I rise to my feet to pace. This is what I've had bottled up, what needs to be said so that I'm not snapping at Jensen. "You pretend to care, but somewhere along the line, your concern ended when it came to me—except for now. Now that Dad's gone, you suddenly care who I'm with, where I'm at, what I'm doing."

"You think I don't care?" Mom cuts in. "You stopped caring about school and turned to Jensen."

"So what? Not only do I have my associates now, I graduated with four-point-two GPA and honors. My teachers love me. I could've set the trash cans on fire, and I would've still been the valedictorian. I didn't have do *anything* at that point except breathe. And that's all Dad would've asked of me. But the minute I didn't do what you expected, it's like I became a juvenile delinquent."

"That's vastly inaccurate, Nellie."

"Is it?"

"Yes. It is."

I cross my arms and stare at her, and because I don't know what else she wants, I have to ask. Which makes me so mad. She's the adult.

"What do you want from me?" I chirp. I hate that all I want is for her to love me. Instead, she looks at me like I'm an inconvenience.

"At this point, Nellie, I don't know. You clearly don't want to be here."

"Why would I?"

"Because this is your home. But you've made up your mind, haven't you? No matter what I say, you've convinced yourself that I don't care. You couldn't be more wrong, and for that I'm sorry. Sorry that I've been so broken up on the inside that I'm barely functioning."

Her voice cracks, as if it's hard for her to say this, but I don't believe her.

"But you're not broken up, are you? Or are we going to pretend that you're not seeing Barry Tayvier?"

She flinches and I press.

"That's right," I say. I can't seem to stop. I'm not sure I want to. I need to get this off my chest. "Maybe you thought I wouldn't recognize him. And at first, I didn't. But I'm not stupid. I'm not as blind or as deaf as Grandma and Grandpa."

"That's enough—"

"No. You want to know when I started lying? Why don't you answer your own question? Have you ever considered that maybe Dad knew? That maybe *you* broke him and that's what triggered his aneurysm?"

"That's enough!" she screams as she stands up. Her neck has turned red, a sign that she's physically and emotionally so hot she might break. But she doesn't deny it. She doesn't say, "That's not true, Nellie! I was faithful to your dad until the day he died." No, she doesn't say that.

On some level, I know I've done it. I've unveiled the truth.

I hold her gaze and see the bitterness in her eyes, but I will not back down. She can hit me, if she wants. I give her plenty of time. If she does, I'll know where I get it from.

But when she doesn't do anything, I finally give my closing argument.

"I've rented a studio apartment."

"What?"

"I was always going to move out. It was part of the five-year plan." I mock myself. That plan did me a lot of good and helped me become the girl I am now. But none of this was part of the plan, and now I'm Major Tom, floating off into space unknown. "I'm not far, and unless you plan to cut me off completely, I'll have my phone. I know you're mad at me. But I'm mad too. And grieving," I add, thinking of Jensen and how understanding he's been of me. "And until I figure out how to forgive you, I can't stay here."

With that, I turn to leave. She says nothing. She does nothing. I move slowly, giving her every chance to call for me. But nothing.

I ignore all the residual emotions that come up and rely on instinct to drive back to my apartment. I end up on the couch, in my clothes, with mascara streaks down my cheeks. I cling to a blanket because I have no sheets, and the last thing I look at wrecks me. It's no longer a tool that'll bring me joy, even though it was from my dad. Now it's just a witness to everything that's happened at home.

Stupid, dusty telescope.

CHAPTER 26

The Big Announcement

Jensen

I'm not the fastest writer, but for whatever reason, tonight the words are coming nonstop. It's six thirty in the morning, and I haven't slept all night, and my eyes are screaming at me, but I can't quit now. I keep the eye drops close by and the snacks and drinks flowing, because I've tapped into a vein of pure gold, and I have to keep mining.

So when I come to a point in the story where I can breathe, I do. I save my work, and then instead of shutting down my computer, I leave it up in case the rush comes back.

I crash for the next six hours, oblivious to the world. When I wake around one in the afternoon, I find several messages from Nellie, minutes apart.

> Sorry about last night.

> Yes, I made it back to my apartment, and I had the worst night ever because we didn't buy sheets and the couch sucked.

> I was hoping you might want to go shopping with me.

> Yes, I'm asking you out, Nichols.

They're hours old now, and I quickly reply.

> Sorry. I'm just seeing these. I slept until one. I'm up now.

I wonder when she's going to start job hunting, but if I know her at all, she'll take a few days to sort it out. She'll make a list of where she'd like to work, weigh out the pros and cons.

Then I fall back to sleep. Total accident. I don't even remember closing my eyes. So naturally, when I wake up to more messages from her, I feel terrible.

> Jensen, are you okay?

> Did you accidentally mute your phone?

> I got some sheets and some groceries, so never mind about coming shopping with me.

I roll onto my back and call her. She picks on the first ring.

"There you are!" she says. "Is everything okay?"

"Yes. I think everything just caught up to me, and I crashed. My phone was on silent too."

I glance at the clock, realizing it's nearly three.

"What time did you go to bed?" she asks.

"I don't know." Small lie. "Sorry I didn't reply or go shopping with you. How'd it go?"

For the next fifteen minutes, I get a play-by-play of how her morning went, and I'm chuckling when she complains about how tiny the washing machine is. She surprises me when she says she called one of Sean's colleagues about a job. Just when I think I know her . . .

"It's a miracle I remembered him," she says. "But he offered me a job at the funeral. Somehow my brain hung on to that sliver of information. So I called him today, and he hired me on the spot. I start on Monday, and he said he'll pay me nineteen dollars an hour."

"That's really awesome, Nellie."

"I think he feels like it's something he can do for me, because of my dad."

"Whatever his reason, I'm happy for you. He's smart to hire you."

There's a short lull in the conversation, and her next question catches me off guard.

"Do you think I could come over and snag my dad's laptop? I've got a few days, and I'd like to get started on his books."

A few days. As if that's enough time to read through his work, let alone run it through edits. It takes an unearthly amount of strength to say yes.

I meet her at the door and let her in before she knocks. I know I look a mess, and I probably smell since I haven't showered or shaved or brushed my teeth. At that thought, I take a step back from her.

"You okay?" she asks as she scoops up the laptop.

"Seriously, I'm just hammered."

"That's so weird. I hope you're not coming down with something."

"Watch, it's probably mono."

"We haven't done enough kissing for that."

"I agree we haven't done enough kissing."

She blushes, which is adorable.

"So about tonight," I start. "You want to go out?"

"That would be great. I was thinking we could swing by the library. I'd like to check out some books on publishing."

I try really hard not to groan.

"We could do that, or we could go for a run. Without my weight-lifting class, I'm going to have to start working out on my own." I suppose I could join a gym.

"We could do that," she says as she scrunches her nose. "Okay, call me?"

"I will. Let's say six?"

"Perfect." With Sean's computer in her arms and an uncertain expression on her face, she leaves, shutting the door behind her.

Ever since the All-Nighter, we haven't been on the same page. It's like we're in two different books. I'd like to change that. Tonight. I'll tell her.

All this has sparked some ideas for Sokha and Hagon though, and I've been using that. Something tells me if this whole thing with Nellie goes south, it will be pure book fodder. I mean, I don't want to break up with Nellie, and I know Sokha and Hagon need to end up together, because if I don't give the readers a happily ever after, I'll have mobs of women wanting to kill me. Nellie included.

I appreciate that Sean taught me about the promises authors make without knowing it. But still, it's so much harder to deliver than one might think.

Because real life isn't full of happily ever afters.

If Clay's life was a book, the first five pages would've been filled with feedings, sleeping, and diaper changes, and one angry, verbally abusive man.

But the mother would be a beautiful, strong creature. She's got her faults, but she's learned from them. She's practically perfect now. I smile at that thought and send my mom a quick message to tell her I love her.

Clearly, a reader would fawn over the handsome three-year-old boy who likes his baby brother and keeps handing him baseballs. Readers would adore the fact that he's already practicing throwing a football into the tire swing.

The inciting incident wouldn't be hard to spot.

It wouldn't be easy to read either. I'm not sure I could capture the true emotions of that day because I don't even remember it. Just like I don't remember handing Clay baseballs. I just know what I've been told and what I've seen in pictures.

Regardless, from there, Clay's story would be filled with adversity and conflict. There'd be no money, poor living conditions, times where he'd be cared for by that same handsome boy, now the ripe age of nine. The happiest scenes in the story would revolve around books and footballs.

Sure things would improve.

But there's no happily ever after for Clay. There's only page after page of life without living.

I sit back down to my manuscript, and when I quit, I've got another five thousand words, for a total of eleven thousand words for the day.

A ten-thousand-word day is pretty epic in the writing world, and I'm feeling proud of myself.

I set an alarm on my phone and flop onto my bed, mentally exhausted. I close my eyes, plotting out the rest of the story. I know how it goes, but since I haven't written it down, I'm not exactly sure.

I try to feel out the story, sensing it the same way I know Nellie's in this building, but it feels like it's just out of reach.

I wake up twenty minutes before my alarm rings. I'm wide awake as I step into the shower, because I need to tell Nellie I'm Jen Dimes. She needs to know now. I stand under the running water for nearly fifteen minutes, mapping out what to say and how to say it, and how to prove I am Jen Dimes.

I'm afraid she'll laugh at me.

I'm in the middle of getting dressed when my phone starts blowing up. My notification for Rebecca goes off, but it's a text, not an email. Odd. I get seven more text messages, and my phone shows I've missed a phone call from my mom.

She probably sent the seven texts, too, so I relax. But she only sent one message. The rest are from other people. I start with her message, surprised at what she has to say.

Why didn't you tell me you were announcing today? Mom.

So we're live! Rebecca.

I think the news station messed up. Marbles.

What a joke! Shalee.

Dude, it can't be true. Sterling. *Where are you anyway?*

Jen Dimes? Yeah, right. Britta.

No way. Jeigh.

My stomach is in knots. I open Rebecca's email. I thought I'd made it clear we weren't going to announce anything until *after* I turned in book three!

There's a press release, including a photo of me next to the name "Jen Dimes."

JEN DIMES FINALLY REVEALS HER IDENTITY— AND IT'S NOT WHAT YOU THINK.

I read the article attached one line at a time.

> When Jensen Nichols wanted to buy an Xbox, he decided it was time to take his writing to another level. With the help of a mentor, the then-sixteen-year-old student self-published the first book of the Blood Rock series, which quickly earned him enough money for the gaming system. By the time he was seventeen, he released *Shadow Stone*, the second installment in the series. The third book is well underway, and fans couldn't be more excited. Nichols lives in Valley View, Utah, with his mom and brother. He enjoys football, spending time with his friends, photography, and sketching.
>
> Apprehensive about revealing his true identity while in high school, he selected a clever pen name: Jen Dimes is Jensen Nichols.

I double- and triple-check the image, as if I don't recognize myself. But it's me alright. At least it's a photo I like. I can't believe this is happening.

"I don't understand." *How could Rebecca do this to me?*

I scroll back to the email message I sent her yesterday when I was feeling completely confused and betrayed. As I reread, shock sets in.

My email back to her is riddled with typos, incorrect spacing, poor punctuation, and one major word replacement—thank you, autocorrect.

> Thanks. Gratuation is officially behind me, but man, I'm exxhausted. I've got some plans today but then I'm all yours,I'm not sure I'm ready to announce—not sure I'll ever be ready— but we did agreee to do it after graduation Let's just do this until I've turned in the manuscript.

I thought I wrote "let's just wait." I swear I wrote that. *Let's just do this?*

No wonder Rebecca went live.

This is my fault. I was sleep-deprived, edgy, and a bit out of my mind.

My social media notifications are climbing into the hundreds, while two more texts come through, a couple of emails, and then the phone rings again. It's my mom.

"There's been a mistake," I say.

"Really? You're not Jen Dimes?" she deadpans.

"That's not funny." I explain the email, but she's laughing. Instead of being worried, she's laughing.

"Oh, honey! That's funny."

"Stop laughing."

"You were going to tell the world anyway. So what if it happened sooner than you thought? You can plan all you want, but sometimes, life just gets in the way. God has a funny sense of humor, and this time, the joke's on you. Just roll with it."

"I'll never get the manuscript finished now." My phone dings as someone else tries to call me, but I ignore it.

"Sure you will." My mother's confidence in me astounds me sometimes. "You'll spend the next few days, maybe weeks, sorting this out, but then you'll shut the doors, turn off the Wi-Fi, and work."

"You make it sound so easy." My other line rings again.

"Listen," Mom says. "You're not a rock star. You're not a movie star. You're an author. This will blow over. I'll bet you a smoothie that in a week, you'll miss the attention."

Man, I hope she's right.

Whoever is on the other line gives up, and after another minute of talking with my mom, we say goodbye.

"I love you, Jensen."

"I love you too."

When I look to see who was calling, my heart gives a heavy thud and my breath catches, because I'm too late. Nellie was calling.

CHAPTER 27

Jen Is Really Jensen

Nellie

I can't believe it. I turn the volume up on the television and sit down on the edge of my couch as the six o'clock evening news announces the true identity of Jen Dimes. Marbles texted and said to turn on the television, and later tonight I'll probably question why it was him to tell me to turn on the news.

Elaine Haycraft, the news reporter, is announcing that my childhood friend, my calculus study partner, my *boyfriend* . . . is Jen Dimes.

I don't believe it.

Elaine's hands are empty, and she folds them on top of her desk as she sits next to her coanchor. Her smile indicates she's a fan.

I pick up my phone and dial Jensen, almost without seeing the keypad. My eyes and ears are glued to the screen. The line rings and rings and rings until it goes to Jensen's voicemail, and I hang up. He hasn't been answering me at all today.

Elaine goes on about how incredible it is that Utah has produced *yet another best-selling author.* She lists off a few other names, but I struggle to process.

It's got to be a mistake. Maybe a scam? Did someone make it up? Oh, man, what if it was Sterling?

Since I'm already hardened steel, you'd think I wouldn't bend, but this story is twisting everything. I so desperately want it to be a big joke, a huge misunderstanding, because the thought that Jensen's been carrying around a secret of this size—without telling me—it's just too much.

It's too unbelievable and so far-fetched, I don't even feel angry. I feel skeptical, and I keep laughing.

I mean the pen name and Jensen's real name make for a funny pairing but come on. There's just no way. The more I think on it, the more I suspect this has to be one final prank—Sterling's magnum opus. But . . . how? Elaine would have done her homework and confirmed the story, right?

So . . . it's real.

This isn't a joke.

I've read stories where the heroine is the last one to figure out a hidden truth about the man of her dreams. The best, worst-kept secret in the world. I'm not saying that I'm some Lois Lane or that Jensen's the man of my dreams, because I can't be *that* girl. He's not *that* guy.

I can't quite picture him sitting at his computer writing—until I do.

I think about our librarian teasing him. I think about his stacked bookshelf and the book he handed to me to read, telling me it was better than *Blood Rock*, and the tone that he used when he said all that, and then suddenly, I can see it.

I can picture Jensen with his laptop, and he's writing. Just like my dad.

Oh my gosh.

I recall the melancholy and heartache Jensen displayed the night we found my father. I always thought it was shock, but now, as I recall those vivid memories, the secret Jensen's been harboring becomes even more layered. At the funeral, his eyes are filled with tears.

I call into question everything that's been going on—most prominently, I question why Jensen's spent so much time with me.

"All of us here at KKTV3 were stunned when we received the news," Elaine says. "And Mr. Nichols's assistant, Rebecca Brown at Brown Bear Editing Etc., has announced that with the last installment of the Blood Rock series the first two books will also go to print. They are in the process of booking a tour, but dates haven't been released. We are now joined by Lucy McIntyre."

The screen splits to show Lucy standing outside of a Barnes and Noble bookstore. A woman stands beside her, and the two of them are flanked by a crowd of men, women, teens, and children.

"Elaine, I'm here at the Sugarhouse Barnes and Noble bookstore with Missy Shanks. Missy, tell us what you think about Jen Dimes being an eighteen-year-old young man from Valley View."

"I think it's a bit of a show. I'm a fan of the books, but why the secrecy?"

"That's a great question, and we here at KKTV3 hope to find out."

"Wow," I say out loud. "Judgy much?"

"Thank you, Lucy," Elaine says, a beat too late as they wait for the audio to get through. "Jensen surely has a sense of humor, considering his pen name. We've all had a good chuckle at that. Now, let's join Tim Carter."

The screen changes again, and we're looking at yet another news anchor standing on campus at Ataraxia High. It's weird to see my school's front doors on television.

My phone is buzzing with all sorts of notifications, and a part of me wants to storm over to Jensen's apartment, but I cannot move. I have to know what Tim's going to say.

"Elaine, I'm here at Ataraxia High. Campus is quiet since yesterday was graduation, but here in these halls, Jensen Nichols was a straight-A student, a star athlete, and the school's photographer. I can understand why Mr. Nichols would choose to publish under a pen name," Tim continues. "High school can be quite the battlefield. Still, for a kid who can't buy beer, his grasp of fictional corruption and intrigue is impressive."

"I couldn't agree more, Tim," Elaine says, again a beat too late due to the connection. "Not to mention how well he depicts love and angst in his work."

Yeah, Elaine's a fan.

A heavy knock on my door pulls my attention away, though

I keep my eyes on the television as I walk to the door, but then check myself and peer through the peephole. What if KKTV3 has come to talk to me? I'm not sure how I'd feel about that.

But it's not them.

It's Jensen.

He's got a hand on the back of his neck, one in his pocket, and he keeps checking over his shoulder. And instead of being upset, I pull my door open and usher him as if it's my job to hide him.

"Oh my gosh!" I say as I pull his arm. For good measure, I throw the dead bolt. "Jensen, is it true?"

He holds my gaze, and it takes him two heartbeats to say, "Yes."

"They're saying you're Jen Dimes." I want to be very clear here.

He looks at the TV. "Can we turn that off?"

I grab the remote, then freeze. They're showing Jensen's yearbook photo. How did they get that? Did someone give the news station a yearbook? What is happening?

It's hard to turn the TV off, but I respect Jensen's request.

"My assistant released the news today because I accidentally agreed to it. There was a typo in my email, and Rebecca took it as a green light to release my identity. I wanted to tell you first, but now it's everywhere. It's a nightmare."

He walks over to the window and stares out, and for a brief moment, I see my friend's anguish. His shoulders, usually strong and square, drop, and I hear him let out a shaky breath. When he spins around to face me, however, I'm not sure I'm looking at my Jensen anymore. Suddenly, he belongs to everyone.

"I was going to tell you tonight." He comes back to me and takes a good look at me. "You should sit down. You look a little pale."

He guides me to the couch, and we sit down.

"You were going to tell me tonight?" Oh good gravity, am I a freaking parrot?

I can feel the pressure in my chest expanding. There's a stale, metallic taste in my mouth, and my whole body feels heavy and dense.

"Yes, Nellie. I'm Jen Dimes. I'm the author of the Blood Rock series."

Pale or not, I stand back up and walk away from him. "I need a minute. I need to think."

"I didn't mean to lie to you."

"I believe you," I say without thinking. "Please, just give me a second." There's nowhere to go where I can be alone except the bathroom. I'm not usually claustrophobic, but I can't breathe. The room is so small, and I need fresh air.

Unthinkingly, I grab my apartment keys.

"Nellie, please. Please don't leave."

The desperation in his eyes slays me. How many times have I begged him to stay? I say nothing as I put the keys back. I press my thumbs into my temples, and then rub my eyebrows, trying to ground myself into reality.

I take three deep breaths, determined to process what this means, for me, for him, for us.

"Ask me anything," he says, calmer than I feel.

I swallow and nod, and then turn away, unable to meet his gaze. His eyes are full of concern and fear, the kind that presses into me and reminds me that he's vulnerable too. But I have to run through this on my own first before I ask anything more of him.

I start with cons. My mental spreadsheet begins to form.

He didn't tell me the truth. And he could've.

Instantly, though, I realize the problem. When in the last ten days has he had a good window to tell me? I've been an emotional wreck and volatile and stressed with finals and a funeral and faking my way through graduation. How do you have that conversation when someone is struggling through the loss of their father? *Oh, I know your dad just passed away, but I need to tell you the biggest thing about me that no one knows.* You don't. You don't do that.

Next. What does this mean for me?

For me, it means my boyfriend is a famous, best-selling author.

Suddenly, I know why he's not going to college. All the times he could've bragged that he was Jen Dimes but didn't.

Jensen's watching me, studying each new expression as it dawns on my face. For him, it means his secret is out. One he's kept for . . .

"How long have you been writing?" I cock my head, looking for clues that aren't there.

"Since I was thirteen. I've improved, if you're wondering."

My voice and mind reconnect, and I am flooded with things I want to know. "I'm sure you have. Now what?"

"That's a good question. A lot of things, I guess. I need to finish book three, for starters. But offhand, I'm mostly concerned about you. I'm hoping this isn't a deal-breaker. Because you said . . ."

"Oh. Yeah." I look away, unable to fully register the pinch in his expression. *No more secrets.*

I pace for a second, unsure. I did say that. What was I thinking?

"Well," I say, looking up from the floor, "I was thinking like no more awful secrets. This isn't really terrible news. Can I ask— how are you feeling? About the news breaking?"

"Panicked. Freaked. It feels like an out-of-body experience, like it's not real." He looks out the window and then back to me. "Worried."

That's when it hits me—in the wake of the news, he came to me.

"I wish you would have told me sooner."

"Me too. I should've just come clean right away." He rubs a hand over his face but doesn't look up. "It's why I couldn't explain the apartment, or the car, when you asked. And I wanted to tell you, honest. I almost did, several times, but I just felt so stupid. And scared."

"Jensen Nichols—afraid of me?"

When he looks up, he's sober. "You're more intimidating than you realize."

Rarely have I ever thought of myself as unapproachable. I walk back to the couch and plop down next to him.

"This is unbelievable," I say.

"Totally. And it explains why I'm not sure about college."

"Because your future is already on track."

"Yeah."

"Maybe your future is bright enough it'll shed some light on mine."

He's kind enough to laugh at this. My laugh is darker, because he's the shining star, and I am definitely moondust in comparison.

"I am going to have to deal with publicity and thousands of fangirls?" I ask next.

"If you decide to remain my girlfriend, yeah. I want you in my life."

I don't know how he manages to be so raw, but I appreciate it more than he knows. I slip my hand into his, not wanting my clunky words to ruin the moment. Unfortunately, we're so quiet that we can hear that my neighbor is watching the news too. When we hear the reporter say Jensen's name, we glance up and look at the wall separating us from the next apartment.

It's absolutely bizarre.

"That's weird," he whispers, and when we lock eyes, my countless feelings distill down to one. I still love Jensen. And he wants me. And something about that causes me to look at this with a fresh perspective.

My friend has been living another life, one he's kept private for reasons I may never fully understand. And the more I let the reality of this truth blossom, the more I realize how protective of his image he's been. With friends like Sterling and Marbles, no wonder he used a pen name. I can't fault him for that.

"Nellie. There's more—more that you should know."

I tense, not wanting there to be any more.

"Obviously, my mom knew the whole time, but . . . so did your father. He knew. He knew because he'd been helping me."

Time stops, and the buzz in my ears consumes any outside noise. I'm surprised and also not surprised at all. I'm quiet for long enough that Jensen begs, "Nellie, say something."

"Of course he did," I say, no sarcasm in my tone.

I recall something very specific now—something Jensen said about the Blood Rock books while we were fixing the yearbook. "Oh my gosh. You devil."

"What?"

"You made me think you hated the books—when we were fixing the yearbook."

"Oh, yeah, about that . . ."

I start laughing, and he does, too, softly, as if he's afraid to show his feelings.

When I look at him next, it's through a new lens. He's still Jensen. He's still my friend. But he's larger than life now. He's Jen Dimes. *He's Jen Dimes.*

"How did my dad end up helping you?"

"We connected at a conference. Once he knew I was interested in writing, he just adopted me—all over again. He offered to help with editing and stuff, but the truth is . . . It wasn't just about the writing. He was the father I never had."

He recounts things I know about my dad, like how he'd stay late at work to write, how he'd go to writing conferences, or take phone calls to help friends with their story ideas, but when Jensen tells me that *he* was the one who stayed late at my dad's office after hours working on plot holes, that *he* was at those same conferences with my dad, and that *he* was on the other end of the line of those phone calls, my expression changes from understanding to wide-eyed surprise. When Jensen finishes, he looks embarrassed and guilty.

"All this time we've been together," I say, "was it because he died?" There is no anger in my voice because I'm not upset. He *has* missed my father. I've seen it. But I have to know if the only reason he's spent time with me was out of pity.

"Yes. And no. I wasn't lying when I said I loved you. I spent years keeping that secret from your father—you have no idea the effort that required. But I had to, because at that time in my life, I needed him. I couldn't risk his help over my feelings for you."

I frequently have nothing intelligent to say when I'm with Jensen. He's just so much better with the words. Like, way better. I let out a soft "Huh."

"You say and do things that remind me of him all the time," Jensen says, a bit of pride in his voice before it turns soft. "And sometimes it stings to be reminded that he's gone, but for the most part, it makes me happy. A part of him lives on in you. And I'm at a place in my life where I need you more than I need him, I think. I mean, I miss him, and I'm nervous I can't do this writing thing without him, but I think, maybe God knows that, and everything will pan out."

"Well, I don't know about God in all this, but I suspect you're right."

I lace my fingers with his, and I'm surprised when he says, "Can you forgive me? I know you've been hit left and right lately with . . . stuff."

I study our linked hands and his furrowed brow and the set of his lips, and then I know exactly what to say. "Okay, test number one."

"Test number one?" A faint smile breaks across his face.

"I figure you gotta pass three tests if you want to be forgiven."

"I suppose that's reasonable." We both know how it's going to end, but it's my turn to run the show.

"Unless you don't want to be forgiven. In which case, I'll have to—"

"Play video games?"

"I was going to say find myself another boyfriend, but whatever."

We both laugh, and then he takes the challenge. "Okay."

I take a deep breath. "Explain the apartment and the car."

"Isn't it obvious?"

"Just tell me."

"It's not that complicated. I can afford them. But since I want to be totally transparent with you, I'm planning on using the money from book three to pay off my mom's mortgage. I don't say this to brag. I'm just saying it so you know. It's important to me to take care of her."

Well, if that isn't the best. I move on, because this is my game, and it's my turn to be in charge.

"What about my dad's computer?"

Jensen shifts his weight and looks away before meeting my gaze again. I squeeze his hand, but I doubt it lends him much comfort. "I asked your mom if I could have it—but only to pull his stories off it."

"Because you want to publish them." Sometimes I can puzzle things out immediately. Now that I know what I know, this makes perfect sense.

He nods. "It would mean a lot to me. Because if it weren't for him, I'd be nothing."

"That's not true."

"It is."

He seems hesitant, so I give him plenty of time to find the words. It's hard to sit still, to be patient, but I'm afraid if I make any sudden movements it'll spook him.

"Your dad connected me with a friend of his—Dennis. Do you know him?"

"I don't think so."

"He did all the artwork for the cover."

"That's not a big deal."

"I'm not done. We had no idea that Blood Rock would do what it's done. You have to believe me. All I wanted was an Xbox. When the money really started rolling in, I paid your father. He'd done so much for me—reading and editing and then formatting the manuscript into an ebook and then an audio book. He helped me put the story online. I wanted to pay him for his time and effort. And then I paid Dennis, who promised to never tell a soul that he did the cover art, to help protect your dad."

"Wow."

"Yeah. The thing is, your dad couldn't explain the extra

money to your mom. So he deposited it into a bank account and didn't tell her."

"Even my dad had secrets." I try to smile at this, because again, Jensen's not telling me bad news, but still. I wonder if my mother knows about the money. Is that why she said he wasn't so perfect? No way to know unless I ask her.

"Yeah. I know he used some of it to buy you a car, but I have no idea what's left. I can guarantee you, though, that no one knows about that money, except me and my mom, Dennis, and now you."

I'm floored to hear this, of course. I can't imagine what my face says, but Jensen's is full of worry again. I try to erase his concerns by rubbing my hand over his.

"How much are we talking?" I ask.

"Twenty thousand."

I stand up and look around like I'm lost. I feel lost. I glance at him a couple of times, just to make sure he's still there and that this is real.

"You're telling me that my dad had a secret bank account with thousands of dollars in it?"

Jensen nods, his lips quirked into a pucker.

"Is there anyone out there who doesn't have a secret?"

"Probably not," he says.

"I don't have secrets."

He laughs at me. "Yes, you do."

"No, I don't." Our conversation swerves like a race car, around one bend and onto another track.

Jensen laughs even harder. "You liked Sterling, and it was the worst-kept secret of all time."

I purse my lips and shake my head, but he's right. I wasn't so good at keeping that secret.

"Well, I don't like him anymore." I plop back down on the couch, and Jensen pulls my legs over his lap.

"I've gathered as much, but I gotta tell you, I'm really glad to hear it."

My laugh feels like a weight lifting. There is so much good in this scenario, despite everything else. My thoughts are scattering like dandelion seeds in the wind. I'm stunned and unable to hold all the little bits of information that make up this beautiful puzzle.

"I have a car—because of you."

"Yeah."

"And he had it painted red."

"*Blood* red."

We both think about what that means, and I smile. This is impossible and amazing and completely maddening.

I almost can't pick up the game I started, too overcome with emotion, but the third question is taking shape, and it's going to be glorious to ask.

"Is there anything else? Any more big reveals?" I figure he didn't call me out on some of my other questions, so I'm going to pretend I haven't overextended the game.

"None that I'm aware of."

"Okay, are you ready for another question?"

"I'm ready."

"*Blood Rock* is made into a movie, and you're even more famous than you are right now. Your ego is as big as your fan base. You're invited to all the parties, and there are girls who would do anything to be by your side, but we're still together. Your publicist wants you to put on a smile and be present, but I'd rather hang out at home in our sweats, away from the paparazzi. What do you do?"

"That's easy. I'm an author, who has written these books quietly, in my sweats, at home, for years. I might be tempted by the publicity and the women, and I won't argue with you on the ego part. We both know I've got one. So if the party is *Blood Rock* related, we go. Sorry. If it's a fundraiser for Shaken Baby Syndrome? You know I'm going to that. So, how about this: Come with me to the parties, and I promise to make sure we get plenty of quiet time at home."

I sigh softly because he is so perfectly awesome.

"Fair enough. Last question. Tell me how it ends. What happens to Sokha and Hagon?"

"You want spoilers? It'll ruin it."

"No, it won't."

He pulls me closer and whispers into my ear like we're in fourth grade, except we're not. My grip on his arm tightens as he starts to speak, and I swear I don't breathe. I can't believe he's telling me. He doesn't give me much, just enough to satisfy my curiosity, and when he asks me to promise him to never repeat it, I say, "I promise."

I press a kiss to his cheekbone and whisper, "You are more than forgiven. Also, I love you."

And that's the truth. When the news first broke, I was worried about all the wrong things, but there has been nothing hot inside of me that could be labeled as anger. All I feel is cool waters running over shiny metallic surfaces. Jensen loved my dad. Maybe as much as I do, and perhaps that binds us together more powerfully than any math equation or yearbook dilemma, but he also loves me for me.

"Maybe we could publish my dad's books together," I suggest. "You and me. We do have a little experience working on projects together."

Softly, he runs his fingers through my hair and bites his lip before he says, "I'd really like that."

"Nellie Samsin coauthoring with Jen Dimes."

He laughs, and he doesn't rearrange our names so his is first. I don't see a celebrity. I see my friend who is secretly a word nerd. With every passing second, small details and memories start to pop up.

"I can't believe you made me think you hated the *Blood Rock* books!" I mock him with those words.

"Sorry?" he says, though he's not sorry at all. He tickles me, and we get a little physical, but then settle into each other as if we can't get close enough.

"And your quiz," I say. "Was that because you're not going to finish the book?"

"No, that was because you keep taking up all my writing

time and I was starting to think I'm never going to get this book finished. I still think that."

He laughs again, and it's contagious.

"You're blaming me?"

"Of course I am." He runs his fingers over my knee, and it tickles, so I grab his hand and force him to stop, but it doesn't work. He just reaches up and touches my hair, his fingers trailing through it's length. The feel of his hands in my hair sends a shiver through my whole body, but when he runs his thumb over my lower lip, I nearly lose my mind.

"Why write when I can be with you?" he says, staring at my mouth.

"Seriously, if I have to choose between you or the book, it'll be the book—"

"No, it won't."

There's a fire in his eyes, and the heat transfers to my skin until my entire body feels warm, and his kiss is full of things he doesn't say, but so is mine.

At some point, I push him back, struck by another thought.

"Fact. I always wanted someone to kiss me the way Hagon kisses Sokha, but now I think I *am* kissing Hagon."

"Fact," he mimics. "This is book research."

I laugh as he grabs the back of my neck and pulls me closer. He smiles and asks if I'm hungry.

"We could order a pizza," I say. I draw lines over the veins in his arm, mesmerized that he's here and he's real and he's my favorite author. Then another thought pops into my mind. "Can you prove that you're Jen Dimes?"

"I thought you might ask."

He retrieves his phone and opens up his email, and I see an address that matches the one on his website: jendimes@gmail .com.

"Good gravity," I breathe as I snatch his phone and click on the link. He has over nine hundred emails. More than half are new today.

"I know, right? Like how obsessive can they be?"

He uses my phone to order pizza while I scroll and scroll through his messages, skimming the subject lines, completely fascinated.

> Jensen Nichols is a fraud.
> Jensen, Marry Me.
> I'm your biggest fan.
> I love that you're a man.
> Why would you lie about your identity?
> When will book 3 be out?
> Can I get your autograph?

The messages vary from supportive to psychotic.

As soon as Jensen finishes ordering us dinner, I show him a certain email. He hums and clicks on it.

> You're the worst friend.

I basically said that to Britta the other night, and a pang of guilt sweeps through me, but I refuse to let it in. I'm not ready to talk to her or mend that relationship. Instead, Jensen and I read the email together.

> You stole my story idea. We were on the bus coming home from that stupid science fair, and I shared my idea about two friends who are bound to a blood rock. I'm suing. Expect to hear from my lawyer.
> Darren Thames

"Oh my heck, Jensen. What are you going to do?" On some level, I'm glad it's not from Britta.

"Nothing." He closes the email, but not before we see another dozen messages pour in. When he clicks out of the email app, I see that every app used for communication has a notification.

"You need to hire an IT guy, in case someone threatens to kill you or something."

"I'm not worried. I'm a kid. Nobody cares about a kid."

"Clearly Darren Thames cares."

"I don't even remember him."

"He remembers you."

"Yes, but everyone remembers me *now*. I'm sure it won't be long before my dad comes around."

I flinch because Jensen is far too relaxed about the possibility of his dad showing up. "Jensen. Doesn't that worry you?"

"Today? No. Tomorrow, maybe. The guy's a jerk, but he doesn't know where I am, and we haven't heard from him in a long time. So, it's whatever."

I'm going to get a headache at this rate. Since dinner won't be here for a while, I get up and grab some ibuprofen. I don't even ask if Jensen wants some; I just offer it to him along with a water bottle. He takes three pills and chases them with a swig of water.

"Fun fact," I say.

"Oh, I love these. Go on."

"Ibuprofen on an empty stomach is bad for the liver."

"Interesting." He raises his water bottle. "Here's to our livers."

"Fun fact: Toasting with water is bad luck." I click my plastic bottle against his.

I sit back on the couch with him, finding that place in his arms where I seem to fit perfectly. I feel the tension ease out of him; maybe, like Sokha, I have some magic in me.

He closes his eyes, and I ask, "What do you need?"

"Just stay with me."

This is my apartment, and if it were anyone else, that would be an odd request, but it's not. "I'm not going anywhere."

Once the pizza arrives, we turn the television back on, only to catch another report of Jen Dimes. The reports are surreal and incredible, and we laugh at the things that are funny and at the intense fans the reporters find to interview. And when the news ends on a good note, we have no problem rolling into *The Tonight Show with Jimmy Fallon*.

CHAPTER 28

Undecided

Jensen

Years ago, I went for a ride in a go-cart. I was afraid to take the corners too fast, scared I'd flip over and crash into the straw bales. By the time I was older and more experienced, I realized the carts were made for speed and that they didn't go nearly as fast as I thought, and I gained the confidence to press the pedal to the floor.

That's how I feel about everything in my life right now. I'm ready to speed things up. But also I want to take some things nice and slow.

Rebecca calls me the next day to check on me, and we discuss how to handle the staggering number of emails. The PR team puts together some more material, which I approve, and they start scheduling the interviews. I'll have a week before they start.

I'll need to find a balance between Nellie and writing and the publicity, but Rebecca assures me it'll become more normal and probably will peter out at some point. Still, all I want to do is hang out with Nellie.

Naturally, my closest friends are freaked out, and as much as I want to address their questions individually, it's too much. I send one massive group text to confirm that what they're hearing, for the most part, is true.

After a couple days of writing and hanging out with Nellie, and one night where we set up her telescope to check out the moon, she finally has the courage to call her mom. She has me stay right beside her as she checks in. The conversation is stilted, awkward at best. They barely discuss anything of importance, with the exception of me.

The call lasts seven minutes, and when Nellie hangs up, she exhales hard. We share a look, but nothing more.

The next phone call we make together is to the bank. It's not too difficult to access Sean's account once we discover that he listed Nellie's name on the paperwork.

"It's like he knew," she says when we get off the phone.

Later that afternoon, I'm sitting next to her when she logs into her UNLV account. It shows that she's a physics major, how much she's been awarded in scholarships, and when she's eligible to register.

"College was always the plan," she says, "but I don't know that I'm ready to go."

She leans against me, and I lean into her. We stare at the screen for a while because what that page really means is *change*. It means she'd have to move. I'm not ready to talk about moving to Vegas with her nor do I want to volunteer to do so, but I also don't want her to give up on her dream, on her plan, and while it pains me to think about it, I cannot ask her to stay here.

Thankfully, she says nothing about it. We have a little time on our hands before anything must be decided, and I think she knows that as well as I do.

Everything is coming at me at a million miles per hour, but not her. Nellie has always been a constant in my life, even when she withdrew from me like an eclipse, even when I hid behind the blinding light of Sterling and Marbles. It took a while for us to gravitate back to each other, but now that we're aligned, I don't want to tempt the universe. I'd rather just let the sun and moon rise and fall on us, like it does everyone else. And her plans and my plans don't need to be fixed constellations right now. Whatever we decide is already written in the stars. At least, that's my belief.

Nellie leans forward and clicks on her declared major. She changes it from physics to undecided. And we sit there for a long time, staring at the screen.

Undecided.

"You sure?" I ask.

"Yes. My plan is that there is no plan until it comes to me. Then, I'll have a new plan. But for now, I'll just take it one day at a time."

"I like it."

Then, because I'm me and I've taken one too many lessons from Sterling's book, I start to nibble on her ear. I'd rather make out than make decisions. I run a hand up her arm and pull gently on her so she turns away from the computer screen. I don't tell her she's not in charge of the universe, though I suspect if she wanted to be, she'd find a way.

Instead, I lean into this. Today, she's here with me. Today, there aren't deadlines.

Today, it's just us, and we're in a good place, somewhere beyond friendship and light-years away from fear. If I had to place us on a map, we'd be our own galaxy.

Epilogue

MeganLovesHagon257

I will never forget when Sean Samsin approached me one afternoon about doing some cover art for a kid who was writing a book about a blood rock. We sat in my office while Sean told me the basics.

"The premise is good, but that's a terrible title," I'd said.

"It is," Sean agreed with a laugh.

Then he told me about Jensen as a person, and now that Sean is gone, I can recall that conversation with more clarity.

"He comes from humble circumstances, and all he wants is to make enough money to buy an Xbox."

"An Xbox?"

Sean nodded. "I thought it might help him out if he had a good cover. Don't spend too much time on it."

"You know me," I'd said. As the head of the graphic design department, I barely had time to work on my own projects, but when it came to requests like this, I tended to overdo it. And in this case, I knew right off the bat that I'd end up doing just that. There was something in Sean's expression, a sort of longing, and I couldn't refuse my friend. Now that he's gone, I'm so glad that I didn't.

"I do know you," he'd said. "You won't quit until it's some of your best work."

"Is his writing any good?"

Sean walked away with a chuckle and said the manuscript was in my inbox.

I read it in three days.

Sean was always really good at spotting talent. I should've known he wouldn't have asked me to do the work for "some kid" if the story hadn't been impressive.

Still. I had no idea I would be captivated by the young man's work. I sketched with pure abandonment for the first time in a long while, because it was just for fun, for some kid, for the sake of an Xbox. The result of that creative freedom ended up being the cover art for *Blood Rock*.

I have never divulged that information, not even to my daughter, Megan.

It was a pleasure to do *Shadow Stone*, as well. And I never expected "Jen Dimes" to give me a cent, let alone ten grand. I wondered why a young man would choose a name like that, but now that the news has broken, I get it. Very clever, that Jensen Nichols.

When I received the check and the letter, Jensen wrote,

> I cannot thank you enough for taking the time to share your talent in order to enhance mine. I look forward to passing book three over to you, and I can't wait to see what you envision for *Starlit Mountain*.
> We'll be in touch.

Pretty cool kid, if you ask me, though I stand by what I said. Terrible titles.

I'd like to meet him in real life. I'd like to talk about his work and our mutual friend.

When my fifteen-year-old daughter learned about Jen Dimes's true identity, she spent the day staring at Jensen's picture and reading every online article she could find. His fans were falling in love with him left and right, including my kid. Unfortunately for her, and many others, it appears Jensen is already taken. Looks like he and Nellie are pretty serious.

In my free time, I work on the cover art for *Starlit Mountain*, and it brings me pure joy—a sort of enlightenment that has reinvented my love for what I do.

I don't think I'll tell Megan that I'm a part of the process. I don't want her to badger me to death for insider information. And I definitely won't be telling anyone that I've started another drawing—one of Jensen and Nellie together.

They seem entirely suited for each other, and the artist in me notices the details. The way he stands protectively beside her when they're caught on camera at the mall. The way she studies his face as if she's seeing it for the first time while he answers one quick question for the news reporter. I'm inspired by their young love, and I wonder what Sean would say.

I like to think he would appreciate my work. It's a far cry from what I usually draw, and I can't explain why I feel compelled to draw the young lovers, but I do not dictate what I draw. My best work happens when I allow the art to flow through me, and I follow my muse wherever she leads, whenever she shows up.

When the news reports the history of Jensen and Nellie's relationship, thanks to their talkative friends, I think it's both captivating and unfortunate. According to Martin Woodall, who is standing on the stairs of the Capitol in DC, Jensen Nichols had a thing for Nellie Samsin since the day Jensen picked up a camera and pointed it at her. That's when he saw her as more than just the girl next door. Martin laughs, points a finger at the camera, and says, "You win this one, Jensen."

I'm not sure what to make of it, but when Jeigh Meredith, another mutual friend, reports that Nellie and Jensen were destined to be together, I smile to myself.

And so when the painting is complete, I pay a premium price to have it hand-delivered to Jensen's home address, something I only have because he mailed me a check and I hung on to the envelope. I can only hope I've captured them just right, and that the look in their eyes resonates with them, because the eyes are the hardest.

After that, I work on a piece to put up on FanFavorite .com. This art is completely different from the style of the cover art or the portrait of the lovers, but it keeps coming to me in my dreams. I created an account as a way to continue drawing the world Jensen created, disguising myself because I thought my art would be better received and gather more attention as MeganLovesHagon257 verses DennisDares2Draw.

Maybe it was silly to create a different avatar, but it's done now, and MeganLovesHagon257 is padding my retirement fund, so I'm not about to change it. Perhaps someday, I'll tell the world the truth. I don't know. Some secrets we keep for ourselves because they harm no one at all.

Acknowledgments

I started writing in 2011, and just like Stephen King said, it was because I read a book and thought, "I can do better." Was that egotistical? Absolutely. But that's how I got my start. Many thanks to **Kambria Reeves**, whom I love, and who reignited my love for stories because of her obsession for *The Hunger Games*. Thanks to **Dana Gallant**, whose love and support I will never forget. You listened to my first story idea and said, "It'll all come down to execution." Boy, were you right, and my goodness, how those words have stayed with me. They actually apply to everything!

I am an extrovert and love trying new things. So I've tried a lot of hobbies, but none of them, especially this writing thing, would've survived a day without **Kyle Larsen**, whom I love, love, LOVE. Thanks for supporting me despite all my crazy ideas, for buying us dirt, and for living the dream with me, every single day. Including the goats. And the bees. You're my everything. If every husband were just like you, this whole world would be made right. They'd all love soccer too much and fall asleep the second their head hit the pillow, but really are those even flaws? Your green flag is supporting me even when you think I'm nuts. Remember when I said I wanted a dot-com for no good reason? Thanks for picking out the website and giving me a nickname that every writer friend of mine uses around me. **Seriously**. Thank you.

And a special thank you to our four beautiful children, who are our entire world:

Catelyn, you are the first person I ever loved instantly and my personal ray of sunshine. You've got everything going for you, and you can do anything! Thanks for making me a mom. **Landon**, you're the first boy who owned my heart without ever doing anything, and I love listening to you. You're a hobbyist at heart, like me. Embrace it but work hard so you can play hard. **Jocelyn**, you are the first child I felt confident having, and you are a priceless gem that can never be replaced. Keep your chin up, know your worth, and never quit trying! **Brooklyn**, you're the one I thought we'd have first, but you surprised us and arrived last. So keep surprising me and never dim your light. You are gold and going places. ALL FOUR OF YOU NEED TO READ MORE. Now, GO CLEAN YOUR ROOMS.

I'd like to thank my parents, **Lynn and Cindy Pack**, who taught me more than I can write down and who have loved me always. To **Kelly and Mac Larsen**, who have helped in all the ways. You mean the world to us, to me, and are a huge reason I've been able to do this.

Thanks to immediate and extended family members. You are the best! I'm lucky to have such a large family that is supportive! I love you, and I like you. Thanks to my awesome sister, **Janelle**, and pretty dope brothers, **Chad, Blake**, and **Blaine**, and your supportive families who cheer me on! Thanks to the best cousins, aunts, uncles, and even a few second cousins once removed a gal could ask for. I feel loved and supported when you ask about my writing and life.

To everyone tied to Snake River Writers, Storymakers, and ANWA—if we met there, thank you for being a part of my journey. You've taught me so much and cheered for me and encouraged me, and my writing life is rich because of you wonderful storytellers.

To my soccer and cheer families—thanks for listening to my stories through all the games and competitions. You people are priceless.

To all the darling, vibrant, and extraordinary teens who inspire my writing; Thanks for being YOU! I love you for real. _____, you're amazing! Go do all the great things! And then come tell me all about it so I can write about it!

To my weird, ridiculously beautiful, talented, dedicated, and amazing friends: Gena Hamilton, Kallie Oler, Aimee Baker, Valerie Andrus, Autumn Parker, Kerri Hansen, Charlie Pulsipher, James Duckett, Daniel Noyes, Frank Cole, Melissa Gamble, Shelly Brown, Rachel Larsen, Dennis Gaunt, Wendy Swore . . . To everyone at Table 17—Rett Anderson, Steve Carroll, Jason Akinaka, Jared Palenske, and Dennis Gaunt (again!) And to my ever-planning/scheming partner, Nicki Stanton—THANK YOU! You all have been through thick and thin with me, from retreats, rejection letters, and one seriously broken hip. DEEP DEBT. I owe you all at least one trip to the Bahamas or something.

To my Shadow Mountain peeps, I hope to make you proud. I know this book would be nothing without you wonderful people.

I am grateful to my loyal friend and very patient and talented editor Lisa Mangum, who came into my life though divine intervention, who fell in love with Sterling, and who took me to meet Jensen and Jared. (#SUPERNATURALFOREVER.) I'm glad you're the boss of me. Thank you for pulling me back into this, and I hope in the end, you have no regrets. You've got the skill to take me out at the knees and then hand me stilts to lift me higher.

I give all my love, and my couch, to The Quad Squad: Serene Heiner, Megan Clements, and Jeigh Meredith. You are the wind beneath my wings and the reason I get out of bed on Wednesdays. Heaven and Hell both know I'm nothing in the writing department without you three. NOTHING! My jokes would fall flat, my Dr Peppers would lose their savor (flavor?), and

I would never be able to find the right wordz (and then edit it out anyway) without your endless support. You are the best friends a gal could ask for at 3 a.m., and why we don't take vacations together—just the four of us—is beyond me. Oh yeah. It's because of our kids and our budgets. Thank you for letting me weave you into every book I write. I plan to do that for forever.

Okay. I missed someone—I just know it. Remind me to put you in book two, I guess.

Seriously,

Gina